Cha

The old lady walked slo\

almost feeling her way along the bay windows which jutted out

onto the pavement in this street of terraced houses. In her long

white nightdress she appeared ghostly in the dim light cast by the

street lamps, especially as the slight mist which had fallen as

dark came to the town was enveloping the lights and reducing

their power. The sky was equally hazy, although dark, and no

light came from the moon or stars to lighten the scene.

The policeman noticed the old woman as he rounded the

corner from the main road where the street lights were brighter

and, at first, could have taken her for a ghost, before he mentally

shook himself and realised she was an old lady of flesh and

blood. Feeling rather foolish over his initial reaction to her, he

strode along the street towards her to find out why she was

outside on such a cold night and so late, wearing only bed clothes

and with nothing on her feet.

"Where are you off to at this time of night?" he asked, his voice louder than he had intended, with the vestiges of his original fear still in his mind. But the old lady ignored him and continued feeling her way along the street, muttering under her breath and with the same sense of purpose he had noticed the minute he had turned the corner into Queen Street. It was as though she couldn't see or hear him.

"Hang on; I said 'Where are you going?' " he repeated and then he took hold of her arm to halt her because she still wasn't acknowledging him. She stood still, arrested by his hand, but she still didn't look at him, staring into the distance and muttering louder than before. He could distinguish the name 'Simon' in her mutterings now and he grabbed this straw.

"Are you looking for someone?" he asked. "Someone called Simon? Tell me who he is and I'll help you find him. What's *your* name? Is Simon a relative of yours?"

The old lady still didn't answer him, but remained halted by his hand, muttering under her breath and lifting her feet as though she thought she was still walking. The constable felt helpless and inadequate in the face of her non-verbal rebellion and could almost hear the duty sergeant sneering at his lack of success with a helpless old lady. He decided action was better than words and pulled gently on her arm to turn her round so that they were facing the right way to walk to the police station on Middlesbrough Road. He had a moment's fear that she would refuse to move for him, but she turned as he wished and made no demur when he slipped off his regulation cape and draped it around her shoulders to keep her warm. He could do nothing about her bare feet, but he had at least tried to do his best for her. He continued to talk to her as they moved slowly along, hoping that she would perhaps respond if he asked the right question or said the right word.

"Where do you live, love? Is it near here or have you walked a long way tonight? Will there be anyone at home who could be worrying about you? Do you think they might be out looking for you now and we might bump into them? They'll be relieved to see you, I would think, if they've spent time looking for you. Are you going to tell me your name, now that we are friends and you're wearing my cape?"

She didn't answer any of his questions. She still muttered under her breath and over and over again he caught the name 'Simon' but he got no response when he asked who Simon was. He was relieved to see the Police Station in the distance when they turned off Albion Street into Middlesbrough Road, even though he was dreading what sarcastic comments the sergeant would make when he entered the station accompanied by a half-naked old lady.

His dread was unfounded because he could hear raised voices as he and the old lady pushed their way through the outer office door. Opening the inner door revealed the source of the noise. A couple were at the sergeant's desk and the woman of the pair was pounding on the desk with her fist to add emphasis to the points she was trying to put across. It was the first time the constable had ever seen the sergeant lost for words and a jaundiced eye might have noticed that the sergeant looked almost frightened.

"My mother is very well looked after, I'll have you know. It's just that she occasionally forgets who she is and where she is. It's not the first time that she's opened the door and let herself out, but she's always done it in daylight before and people who know her have brought her back. Why aren't you getting off your fat backside and going to look for her, instead of making insinuations about decent, hard-working people?"

The sergeant couldn't look the woman in the face, but raising his eyes to avoid her had let him see the constable and his companion as they stood just inside the door.

"I think this must be your mother now, with one of my constables." he shouted above the woman's continued verbal attack. The woman stopped shouting immediately and whirled round to face the newly-entered pair. One glance at her face almost made him feel sorry for the sergeant, and that was a first.

"Mam!" The woman cried, rushing to take the old lady from the policeman's arm. "Where have you been? Why did you go out in the middle of the night with no coat or anything on your feet? Oh what's happened to you?"

"Meet Mr and Mrs Wilson, Constable Wood. You seem to have rescued Mrs Wilson's mother for us. Where did you find her?" the sergeant asked, giving Constable Wood one of his famous stern glances. Wood knew that he had to be correct, concise and professional in his reply, otherwise the sergeant would be giving him the worst duties over the next few weeks.

"Found the lady wandering along Queen Street, sir, the section nearest to Normanby Road. She was unable to answer any questions, so I wrapped her up in my cape and brought her straight here, hoping her relatives would have contacted you or that you would know who she was. She was talking about Simon, sir, about the only thing that I could understand of what she said. Is Simon a relative of yours, madam?" he asked, turning to Mrs Wilson who was emptying a coat and shoes out of a bag she was carrying.

"Never heard of him." Mrs Wilson snapped, dropping the constable's cape onto the nearest chair and wrapping her mother in her own coat. She forced the old lady onto the chair on top of the constable's cape and crouched down to push shoes onto her mother's feet. Standing up, she grabbed her mother's hand and began dragging her towards the door. With a curt 'thank you' which was aimed at Wood she exited, leaving her husband to follow. He gave the two policemen a rueful smile and then followed his wife out of the police station.

"Phew!" Sergeant Adams grunted. "Thank God you came in when you did, Wood. I was beginning to think I was going to have the delightful Mrs Wilson here for the rest of my shift. Not a pleasant thought!"

Wood screwed up his courage to ask the question which had been bothering him since he had entered the station.

"Do you know the Wilsons, Sir? Cos I thought that poor old lady didn't seem to recognise her own daughter."

"Oh Mrs Wilson is her daughter, don't you worry. That 'poor old lady' is Abia Lymer and Mrs Wilson was Abia Lymer as well, before she married Jack Wilson, although what possessed him to take Bia on is beyond my understanding. Still, there's no accounting for taste, is there? But I'm glad you brought her back when you did, cos five minutes of Bia Wilson in a temper is enough for me."

"What's wrong with Mrs Lymer?" Wood asked.

"Oh she goes gaga now and then. It's her age, I suppose and possibly it's a defence mechanism from living with Bia Wilson. I might try it, next time I have to deal with her! The old lady's gone missing a few times now, but it has always been during the day before. People have found her all over the town, but she seems to usually make her way towards the docks. Strangely enough, the Wilsons live on Queen Street, near where you found Mrs Lymer. They have the corner shop where Queen Street crosses King Street so Mrs Lymer was perhaps trying to get home this time. Don't worry about her, lad, Bia takes good care of her mother, it's just well-hidden under that sharp front she has. Go and get yourself a hot drink in the canteen and then you can write the report up. You needn't go back out tonight."

Wood was taken aback. It was the first time the sergeant had been pleasant to him since he had moved to the area, so he moved hastily before the sergeant had time to change his mind and revert to his normal character. Once Wood had left the front office, Sergeant Allen sat back down behind the desk and considered the events of the last hour. He would keep an eye out for Mrs Lymer's name coming up in the duty log again; it wouldn't do any harm to check and it could do a lot of harm if he didn't.

Back in Queen Street, the little cream van pulled up outside the corner shop and disgorged its occupants onto the pavement. Jack opened the side door of the house with his Yale key and they all trooped inside. Bia took her mother straight up the stairs and into old Mrs Lymer's bedroom. She bustled about, getting Mrs Lymer tucked up in bed and cuddling the hot water bottle to alleviate the cold she must be feeling.

"I'll go and get you a hot drink now and then you can go back to sleep. Let's hope you haven't caught cold going outside in your nightie at this time of the year. I don't know what I'm going to do with you, Mam; I really don't, wandering around the town in your nightie. What would me Dad have said, eh? He'd have said I wasn't looking after you properly. That's what he would have said and me doing my best for you. I just don't know what else I can do. Mind you, it amazes me that you can walk when you go on these night-time jaunts of yours, but ordinarily, you can't take even one step when you are in your right mind. It would save my legs if I didn't have to gallop up and down those stairs, bringing your meals and everything. Still, I suppose it could be worse. You might be wetting the bed all the time, like Mrs Outhwaite's husband. I wouldn't like to be doing the clearing-up after him."

She turned to leave the room, but stopped when her mother spoke directly to her for the first time.   "I don't know who you are, pet, but you really look after me well. Thank you."

"That's ok. You don't have to thank me." Was all Bia managed to say in reply.

Back downstairs in the kitchen, Bia was grateful that Jack had thought to fill the kettle and set it to boil while she had been upstairs with her mother.

"Is she ok?" he asked.

"I think so. We won't be able to tell if the cold has done her any harm, not yet for a while anyway, but she still doesn't know who she is. She's just told me she doesn't know who I am but that I look after her well. She should have said that to David Allen when he was accusing me of negligence at the station."

"Don't get in a flap, Bia. He wasn't accusing you of negligence. He knows as well as the rest of the town that you've looked after your mother since Sam died and that she keeps losing her memory as well. Ten years ago, she would have been asking him if he enjoyed going to the Grammar School, she was always interested in how he was doing. Tonight, she didn't know who he was and he knew that. Stop worriting and get this tea down you and then you get back to bed. It's going to be a busy day tomorrow."

"I'm not going to the funeral tomorrow, not after this with Mam tonight." Bia answered immediately. "I can't leave her when she's got the wanderlust on her; she might end up at the police station again."

"I've thought about that and I reckon our Vickie can look after her Nana while we're at the funeral tomorrow." Jack had his answer ready because he'd been prepared for this. "You know the lass enjoys being with her and it'll keep her out of the way of young Keith while he's working in the shop. Otherwise, she would be spending all day standing in the shop and making eyes at him, stopping him from serving customers."

"Well, we needn't worry about that. Keith will be going back to university after Christmas and she'll have a whole term to forget him in. I'll take this drink up for Mam and then I'm going straight back to bed. Don't be long down here, Jack."

"I won't." Jack answered. "I'm just going to check that the shop is okay and I'm going to put the latch down on the Yale lock on the side door. If your mother tries to get out that way again tonight she'll not be able to open it. Good night, pet."

Bia made her way upstairs and put Nana Lymer's cup of tea on the bedside table. It was wasted effort, because the old lady was now sound asleep and it seemed unlikely that she would wake again that night. Bia sighed heavily, wondering just how much longer she would be able to care for her mother. She couldn't do a day's work in the shop and then spend the night traipsing the streets looking for her, she was no spring chicken herself. At least she had Victoria, who would carry meals up to her Nana and she did seem to enjoy sitting with her Nana and talking to her, when the old lady was lucid. There was no point in worrying about it; that didn't help anybody, she just had to get on with it and hope that a miracle happened and Nana became easier to care for, although there was only one way that it would get easier and Bia didn't want to contemplate that.

The next morning, Victoria was already up and dressed when Bia went downstairs to the kitchen and had even filled the kettle and was making herself toast.

"It's a good job that you are up early, young lady. I need you to sit with your nana so that she doesn't wander again today." Bia said. "Your Dad and I are going to Aunt Jessie's funeral and we can't leave her when she's this muddled in her wits. You will have to sit with her to make sure she doesn't try and get out again. We had a hell of a night last night with her. She got out about two o'clock in the morning and we searched for her for ages, but we had to go to the police station in the end. Luckily, a young constable had found her and he brought her to the station while we were there, so no harm done, but she was only wearing her nightie and she could end up with double pneumonia. You can watch her for me today?"

"Course I will, Mam. I enjoy talking to Nana, she makes me laugh."

"Well, she might not make you laugh today. She didn't know who she was last night and the policeman who found her could only get one word out of her and that was 'Simon'.

"Who's Simon?" Victoria asked. "I've never heard of a Simon before."

"Neither have I." Her mother answered, "But that was the only bit of sense that the constable could get out of her last night. He seemed to think she was looking for this Simon, whoever he is. I think it's just another example of your Nana living in another world. One thing's for sure; she certainly wasn't on this planet last night."

"I'll take her breakfast up and see what sort of a day she's having today."

"Yes, you do that. That will mean that we can at least go to the funeral. Don't take any nonsense from her while we're out." Bia watched her daughter carry the breakfast tray out of the kitchen and along the hall to the stairs. She was praying that her mother would be aware of her surroundings this morning, so that Vicky would be able to care for her while they were out at this funeral, but she wasn't confident that it would be so.

Vicky entered the bedroom and found her Nana Lymer sitting up in bed, wearing a pretty pink bed jacket, with her hair nicely brushed and a big smile in place on her face.

"It's my favourite granddaughter and bringing me breakfast in bed, I see. What have I done to deserve this special treatment?" Nana said, as Vicky opened the door.

"Mam and Dad are going to Aunt Jessie's funeral today and Mam's asked me to sit with you, so that she knows you're safe while she's out." Vicky answered.

"Does that mean I've done something to make her think I'm not safe, then? You'd better tell me, it'll come better from you than your mother, if she's in one of her 'martyr moods'."

"You went out again last night, in your nightie and with nothing on your feet." Vicky said. "Don't you remember anything about it? That's why Mam's worried about you today and why I'm sitting with you, to make sure you don't do it again. Evidently, a policeman found you and took you to the police station and Mam and Dad brought you home from there. Can't you remember any of it?"

Nana Lymer's face was creased with worry.

"I'm getting worse, aren't I?" she said. "This is happening more and more often and I can't remember any of it. What can I do to stop it? If I carry on like this then your mother won't be able to look after me and I'll have to go into a home and I don't want to do that. How can I stop it?"

Vicky took hold of Nana's hand, distraught that she was causing her so much distress and wishing that she could do something to alleviate it. An idea formed in her mind and, although she was reluctant to force her Nana into doing something which could distress her further, it seemed as though a way out of this was possible. She gently stroked the frail hand she was holding, took a deep breath to steady herself and said,

"The policeman who found you last night said you kept on saying the name 'Simon'. He was under the impression that this Simon was important to you, but he couldn't get you to tell him who Simon was. Do you know someone called Simon? Do you think you could have been looking for him?"

The hand she was holding had jerked as Victoria spoke the name 'Simon' and Nana Lymer had dropped her gaze to the counterpane which her other hand was kneading as though it was a lump of dough.

"You *do* know the name." Victoria said, gently. "Who is he and why would you be searching for him in the middle of the night? If you talk about it, it may help you."

Nana Lymer was silent for so long that Victoria was worried that she had retreated back into the half-world that she sometimes inhabited, the times when she wasn't living in the real world. She was regretting mentioning Simon now, because Nana Lymer was frowning and there were tears forming in her eyes.

"He was important to you, this Simon, wasn't he?" Victoria said, lowering her head so that she could look into Nana's eyes. "I don't want to upset you, but don't you agree that it might help if you talked about him? I won't tell anyone else, if you don't want me to, I promise."

Nana was silent for a couple of minutes, but then she raised her head and looked Victoria straight in the eye.

"It's not a nice story, what happened to Simon, and it goes back a long time. I thought I'd got over it years and years ago, but obviously I haven't, otherwise I wouldn't be wandering the streets looking for him now, when, in my right mind, I know I'll never see him again. But I don't know if you are strong enough or old enough to hear a story the like of this."

"I'm fifteen, Nana; I'll be sixteen next month. I'm not a child and if it helps you it would be worth it wouldn't it?"

"Yes, I suppose you're right, but I don't want you to tell anyone else what I'm going to tell you." Nana said. "And, I'm only telling you so that I can lay this ghost to rest and make it easier for your mother to care for me. Promise me you won't tell a soul what I tell you? Please, Victoria, this is very important to me."

"I promise, Nana. I'll never tell another living soul. Cross my heart and hope to die." Victoria was very concerned over just how agitated her Nana was getting. Whatever the story was, it was troubling her deeply and it probably would do her a great deal of good to get it out in the open.

"Don't use that phrase lightly, Victoria. We none of us know when we're likely to die and there's no point putting a jinx on yourself." Nana was very stern, which was highly unusual for her.

"I promise I won't breathe a word of what you tell me, Nana." Victoria agreed. "Is that good enough?"

"Your word is good enough for me." Nana hesitated, composing her mind and deciding where exactly she should start with the terrible tale with which she was about to burden her granddaughter. "Your Granddad Sam was my second husband," she began, realising that she had to start right back at the beginning of the whole episode. "My first husband was a man called William Drinkwater whom I married in 1910, a long, long time ago. He was three years younger than me, but I thought he was the best of the bunch I had to choose from and I was twenty five years old. I didn't want to wait for marriage for any longer, because I was desperate to have a child and I was worried that, if I didn't get married soon, I might get too old to have one. Looking back on it now, I can see how silly that was but, at the time, I thought my time was running out. It was a stupid thing to do, to marry someone just because he was the best of the bunch, but that's what I did."

"So you didn't love him, Nana? Not at all?"

"No, child." Nana smiled at her granddaughter. "No, I didn't love him, but I know that he loved me, in his own way,

21

and I thought that would be enough. He had a decent job in the iron works and he wasn't a drinker, so I knew he wouldn't squander his wages in a public house or become a wife-beater like some of them did. So I agreed to marry him and we had a very quiet and very cheap wedding in May 1910. After the wedding, we moved in with his parents and his two sisters, because we couldn't afford to rent a house of our own, but by the summer of 1912, four months before our baby was due, we moved into a house on Albion Street and I thought we were set for life. I had a husband, a house and a baby on the way, what more could I wish for?"

"Were you happy? Isn't that important?" Victoria wanted to know.

"I thought I was at the time." Her grandmother continued. "I had everything that I had wished for from being a young girl. What more could I possibly want? Then, just before my baby was born, I realised that I had achieved what I had been aiming for and that it wasn't enough. William was a pleasant, hard-working young man, but he was beginning to bore me. I organised everything in our lives and he went along with everything I said or did. I was in charge of the family finances because William gave me his pay-packet, unopened, the day he received it. There weren't many who did that in those days. I had chosen the house we were living in because I was the one who had discovered it was up for rent, I was the one who had viewed it and put a deposit on it; I was the one who had chosen the furniture, whether second-hand or new and I was the one who was carrying the child I had craved for. William didn't seem to be doing anything; we didn't even have conversations anymore. But there was nothing I could do about it. I had made my bed and I had to lie in it. What else could I do?"

"Couldn't you have left him, or got divorced?" Victoria asked. "Then you could have lived on your own and you might have met a man who didn't bore you."

Nana Lymer smiled sadly at her granddaughter's innocence.

"I had no reason to divorce him." She said. "He wasn't a philanderer or a drunk. I and my unborn child weren't in any danger from him and, anyway, divorce wasn't an option in those days. I just had to get on with it and hope that he could acquire a character and a personality change somewhere along the line. And, of course, he was the breadwinner. In those days men went out to work and most women stayed at home and cooked and washed and cleaned for their family. If a girl had a job, like being a teacher for example, she would have to give it up when she got married."

"I didn't realise that life was like that then." Victoria was amazed at the distance society had travelled in just over fifty years. She had ambitions to become a teacher and thought she probably wouldn't have got married if it had meant that she would have had to have stopped teaching.

"It was the War that changed everything, not the war that finished nearly thirty years ago, but the Great War, the War to end all wars as they called it when it began. But I'm getting ahead of myself. I was talking about 1912, when I was a young wife with a baby on the way and everything to live for. None of us knew then that the whole world was going to change for ever."

"Nana, was the baby Simon? Was that who you were looking for last night? And if it was, what happened to him? Have I got an Uncle Simon somewhere?" Victoria asked.

"You're moving the story on too quickly, pet, but yes, my baby was a boy and I named him Simon." Nana said. "He was born on October 8th 1912. Of course, once he was born, I was too busy to worry about being bored because babies take such a lot of caring for and he was the most adorable baby I had ever laid eyes on. His hair was blond with a wave in it and his eyes were huge and the blue of the sky on a summer day. I loved him so much it hurt. He was the be-all and end-all of my life and I'm afraid I ignored his father because I was so tied up in the adoration of my child. I think I even forgot about William *being* his father, although I continued to keep the house clean and put food on the table, organise our finances and make decisions about trivial matters and always, always I cared for my child."

"Did William notice what you were doing? Was he jealous of the baby?" Victoria asked.

"Oh yes, he noticed, more than I could have given him credit for, if the truth be known. William didn't say anything to me, that wasn't his way, but he became even quieter when we were together, until I stopped telling him what Simon and I had done every day. I didn't consult him on anything, I just went my own sweet way and he became more and more withdrawn from me. He was always good with Simon, though, and played with him and talked to him when I was busy cooking or when I went out shopping. I should have seen what was happening, but I didn't because I was so wrapped-up in being a mother, I forgot about being a wife."

"Then one day, when Simon was about a year old, I went to the butcher's to buy some pork for our tea." Nana continued. "Simon liked to eat pork and I even remembered that William liked pork crackling, so I would go to the best pork butcher in the town, Dennison's on Normanby Road. I'd left Simon at home with his father because William was on night shift that night and

I only expected to be about ten minutes. There was no one else in the shop when I got there and Dennison's eyes lit up when he saw me. He had the false impression that I thought he was attractive in some way, but he couldn't have been further from the truth. He looked like one of the pigs that he sold; fat and greasy and smarmy. He chose that day to ask me to kiss him and when I refused, he said some terrible things to me while he was serving me and I was furious with him. I probably over-reacted, but I found him so repulsive that I was almost physically sick at the thought of him touching me. I grabbed my meat, threw the money at him and ran out of the shop, sobbing because I was so angry. When I got home, William wanted to know what had upset me so, stupidly, I told him.

"On his way to work that night, William called in at the shop and threatened to call the police if Dennison ever came near me again. Dennison wasn't happy with that because he'd been in trouble with the police the year before for fighting in one of the public houses. If he'd been caught again, he could have gone down for both things and that made him hate William so much."

"But why didn't William just thump him for trying it on." Victoria asked. "Why threaten to go to the police about it?"

Nana smiled. "Cos William wasn't a big man and Dennison was built like a barn door – as broad as he was high. William was a physical coward and I think that made the pig butcher so angry with him. He could have dealt with a man threatening to hit him, but not one who threatened the police. William didn't tell me what he had done, but a busybody who lived in one of the houses near the shop made a point of telling me a couple of days later. Of course, I told William it was a stupid thing to have done and I warned him that Dennison would get his own back on William, but he didn't believe me. He thought he'd acted like a man and that I was belittling him by arguing. Anyway, it didn't matter what I said to William, it was too late, the damage had been done."

"Why?" Victoria asked. "Perhaps Dennison would have thought twice about it if he thought the police might arrest him."

Nana Lymer sighed. "That wasn't the way his mind worked." She said. "He was a bully and had frightened people all his life with his size and his aggression. He could cope with the threat of physical violence because his size and manner normally frightened others off, but he couldn't cope with a threat hanging over him which wouldn't be alleviated by aggression. He despised William from that day onwards. Things might have turned out very differently if William hadn't acted as he did, but we'll never know what would have happened. The damage was done and all three of us paid for that one deed, in different ways."

"What ways, Nana? What happened after that?" Victoria asked, desperate to hear the rest of the tale, but fully aware that Nana Lymer was looking very tired now.

"Take these breakfast pots away, pet and would you get me another cup of tea?" Nana asked. "This story-telling is thirsty work, you know!"

"I'll go and make your tea and then I think you should have a rest, Nana." Victoria said. "I can wait a while for the rest of the story, until you've had a little sleep, anyway."

"You're a good girl, Victoria. I'll just rest for a while and then we'll go on with the tale. I reckon it's doing me good to get it out of my system and I want to get it finished before I die."

"You won't be doing that for a long time, Nana. I won't let you!"

Nana Lymer smiled at her granddaughter's retreating back, fully aware of just how long it was going to take to get through all that had happened to her during the Great War. But she did feel a lot more settled in her mind now that she was facing what had happened rather than trying to shove it to the back of her mind and pretend it had happened to someone else.

Nana Lymer slept after her cup of tea and Victoria's parents were home from the funeral and back working in the shop before she awoke, hungry for her lunch and keen to get on with the tale. When Bia brought her lunch to her, she asked her if Victoria wanted to sit with her again, nervous that the girl might not be interested in what had happened to her Grandmother over fifty years before. She needn't to have worried, however, because Victoria was as keen to hear the story as Nana was to tell it and she arrived at 1.30pm, armed with another cup of tea and eager to move on.

After she had reassured herself that her Nana was rested enough to carry on with the tale, Victoria made herself comfortable on the little chair next to Nana's bed and turned enquiring eyes on her grandmother. Nana Lymer screwed up her face in concentration and then began.

"It was just before Christmas 1913, when William threatened the pig butcher with the police. I remember it particularly because I didn't set foot in his shop ever again, so we had poorer quality meat for our Christmas dinner that year. I swore I would find a better butcher, even if I had to walk to Normanby or Eston to find one, so that we would have a decent dinner for Christmas 1914, but that was a promise I wasn't able to carry out. The Great War intervened and life changed so dramatically, the quality of meat wasn't high on anyone's list of priorities."

"William and I settled into a new phase of our relationship. I concentrated on Simon, talking to him, playing with him and showing him what wonders our world has to offer, while still keeping house dutifully for William. He played with Simon and took him for long walks,

but William and I rarely spoke to each other. Simon was too young to understand that there was a huge gulf between his parents, but I worried about what would happen when he *was* old enough to understand. What would I tell him? How would I explain the strained atmosphere in our home? Would he compare his home life with a child who had two loving parents?"

"But then that Grand Duke somebody or other got himself shot in some foreign city and suddenly we were at war and it was so different from any other war which Britain had fought in before. It wasn't happening thousands of miles away in a foreign country which nobody had ever heard of, it was happening just across the English Channel and people said that was only about twenty miles away. That made it so much closer and so much more frightening. I can't explain properly, but people worried that the Hun might invade England and we hadn't been invaded for centuries. Simon was just under two years of age and had no idea what was happening, but he could sense the tension that everyone in Britain was feeling at the time and he was often fractious and bad tempered."

"At first, when war was declared, our lives didn't really change, but then men in uniform began appearing on the streets and newspapers and advertising hoardings began asking for volunteers for the army, and so many men went off to war. I was sickened by the jingoism and I couldn't help but wonder how many of those young men were going to come home again. The way the papers had it, our heroes were just going to land in France and the Low Countries and the Hun were going to give up and run home and so our lads would soon come back. But fighting meant men being wounded or killed, whole families being deprived of their loved ones and it wasn't long before we saw some of the results of that fighting."

"I don't recall when the first wave of the wounded landed back in Blighty or how long that was from when war had been declared, but it happened pretty quickly. I remember being glad that William wouldn't have to go. He was a married man with a child and at first, they were only asking for single men and it was still volunteers they were asking for, but, as time passed and the war wasn't won quickly (as the media had told us it would be), there began to be talk of introducing conscription. I was worried, but I told myself he was married, he was in a job that produced iron and steel for the war effort and he was older than so many of the ones who were volunteering. I was trying to convince myself that he wouldn't be called up and that, somehow, we would get through it together. Then, one night, he came home late from work and dropped his bombshell on me. He had volunteered!"

"Volunteered? But why? He didn't have to go, did he?" Victoria was taken aback by this revelation.

"No, he didn't have to go to war, but he wanted to." Nana Lymer continued. "He wouldn't explain to me why he had done what he did; he wouldn't talk about it at all. We had lost the knack of communicating with each other the year before and even this didn't bring it back to us. It didn't matter how much I pleaded with him not to go, how much I begged him not to and, in the end, threatened him. He was determined he was going to go and 'do his bit' for King and country and I just had to accept it. I railed against it, asking him what were Simon and I supposed to do while he was away, what were we supposed to live on? How were we going to pay the rent and buy food? Did he want us to die, starving on the streets? He said he would send his army pay home and that we would manage without him.

After all, hadn't I managed everything about our lives for years? Why would this be any different?"

"He was very bitter then, Nana. He thought you wouldn't miss *him* at all." Victoria said, showing an understanding far beyond her age.

"Oh yes, he was a bitter man, there was no denying that and he was also a very stubborn man. I've noticed that trait in other people who are basically weak. They acquiesce to everything for years and then dig their heels in over one point, even when they know that they are wrong, and they won't let go of it. William was like that over this enlisting. He made the most important decision of our married lives without me and that decision changed the course of all our lives. Every terrible thing that happened after he enlisted happened because he decided he was going to go to war and he wouldn't listen to me."

Nana paused while she drank some of her tea, giving Victoria the chance to say something, but Victoria was silent. She was trying to imagine how helpless Nana must have felt when William announced his decision and she couldn't change his mind. How did Nana survive those four years until William came back at the end of the war? Then she realised that she didn't know if William *did* come back. Had he died on a battlefield somewhere and Nana had married Granddad Sam? Had Sam accepted Simon as his own and, if so, what had happened to Simon? Victoria realised there was a lot more still to be told.

Nana finished her tea and took a deep breath to begin again.

"So he left Simon and I and went and enlisted in the Yorkshire Battalion, along with the other thousands of husbands, brothers and sons enlisting in other battalions, across the whole country. There were thousands of women, children and old men who lined the streets of the town and waved and cheered and sang the National Anthem as their menfolk marched past in their cobbled-together uniforms, some of them carrying weapons, but most without, cheering as they marched away to war. I wasn't there. I wasn't going to be part of the frenzy which was whipping up patriotism to such an extent that children were trying to enlist. Boys, some as young as twelve, were flocking to the Enlisting Stations, swearing that they were old enough to fight for King and country and, sometimes, they were accepted and the lies ignored. Some of those young boys fought on the battlefields of France and Belgium and died before they reached the age they had claimed to be when they enlisted."

"They marched off to war, my husband among them, all declaring they would teach the Hun a lesson or two and still be home in time for Christmas. I didn't believe a word of it. I knew the war wouldn't end that quickly. I didn't waste my time thinking about it, because I had a child to support and I wasn't going to sit at home waiting for William's non-existent Army pay to arrive. For goodness sake, there was a war on, was it likely that the army in the field would get paid regularly like they did at home? It was a different world and so I had started making plans as soon as I realised that William was going to leave us and I wasted no time in setting those plans in motion."

"But what did you do with Simon?" Victoria asked. "You couldn't go out to work and leave him, he wasn't old enough. Did your mother look after him?"

Nana smiled at Victoria's concern for the child.

"No, I had no intentions of leaving Simon with a babysitter. He was my child and I loved him to distraction and I wasn't going to miss any of his childhood by farming him out to various relatives while I went out to work. My plan was to keep Simon and me together."

"First of all, I went to see Mr Vine in his office on Station Road. He was a local solicitor, but he was also my landlord and I needed his permission before I could put my plans into action. I knew he had a soft spot for me, from when I had seen him when I first rented the house and I intended using his liking for me to get my own way."

"The day William marched off to war I presented myself at Mr Vine's office, wearing my best black skirt and a hand-embroidered white blouse. I hoped I looked business-like, because that was the impression I wanted to give him."

'I need to ask you a favour, Mr Vine.' I said when his secretary showed me into his inner sanctum.

'Anything I can do, dear lady,' he said as he pulled a chair up to his desk for me. 'I understand your husband has enlisted?'

"He made it sound like a question, although I knew he was well-aware of the names and numbers of those who had gone in that first wave of volunteers. He was an extremely patriotic man and it was that patriotism that I wanted to milk to get my own way in that meeting. I pretended to be as enthusiastic about his enlisting as William was, because I knew this would sway Mr Vine to look on my plans favourably and I was prepared to use any lever I could."

'He has, Mr Vine.' I murmured, looking suitably downcast. 'He's gone to do his duty for King and Country, as all decent men should.'

"He dipped his head as though he was in the presence of the King himself and then looked me in the eye."

'So, how can I help you, dear lady? We must look after the families of our brave boys until they return home, victorious.'

'William has promised to send his Army pay home to Simon and I when he gets paid in France, but I am worried that in the turmoil of war, that money won't get through to us. I've promised William that while he is in France doing his duty, I will support him in every way that I can, taking the worry of mine and Simon's welfare off his shoulders.'

"I could see this approach was working on Mr Vine and I didn't care how many lies I had to tell to get my own way. Simon and I were going to survive this war, whatever happened to William and if I had to lie my way to Hades in order to carry out my plans, the end result was well worth it. I had Mr Vine on the end of my fishing line and I reeled him in as adroitly as I could."

'I would like to open a little shop, so that I can support my child and myself without William having to worry about us and I would like your permission to use the parlour of my house as the shop premises. I know that you kindly rent us the house to live in,' I added hastily as Mr Vine drew back a little at my direct demand. 'But there's space in the parlour to put up a few shelves to carry the stock and Simon and I can live in the kitchen. With William away fighting at the Front, we don't really need a best room.'

Mr Vine's face changed again at my mention of the Front, as I had known it would. I pressed home this advantage quickly, before he had chance to think about it anymore.

'Of course, I would pay extra rent, Mr Vine. After all, I can't expect to pay domestic rent on business premises. I wouldn't expect you to have to help support a soldier's family if I can do it myself.'

'I wouldn't expect you to pay extra rent, my dear, not until you had got your little business going. After all, we've all got to rally round our brave boys and that includes giving them peace of mind about their families' welfare. But are you sure you want the responsibility of running a business on your own? Couldn't you get some sort of paid employment that could keep you and your little one until your brave husband returns home?'

"I was ready for that question as well." Nana said.

'No, Mr Vine. If I went out to work I would have to find someone willing to look after Simon for me and I think the poor child will need his mummy with him when he's not going to see his daddy for a long time.'

"I left a gap of a few seconds and then added the clincher to my argument."

'If he ever sees his daddy again, of course. None of us know what is going to happen to our brave boys over there.'

"And I lowered my head and dabbed my dry eyes with the frilly white handkerchief I had brought with me for just this purpose."

'My dear Mrs Drinkwater, I will give you every assistance I can.' said Mr Vine, coming out from behind his desk and helping me to rise. 'You decide what shelves and other things you need and I'll send Old Davy round first thing tomorrow to put them up for you. Tell me, what are you planning to sell in your shop?'

'I'm going to sell food, Mr Vine, all types of food, from vegetables to bread to tea. No matter what is happening in the world, people will always need to eat and therefore will always need a shop to buy food from.

'I agree with you, Mrs Drinkwater, people will always need to eat and, therefore, they will always need somewhere to buy that food. But from where are you going to get your stock?'

"I was ready for that question as well. It had been part of my planning process."

'We are right next to the railway station here Mr Vine and I have already been to see the warehouseman who deals with the goods trains. I have also arranged to buy goods from the ships as they dock here. I have my supplies set up and ready to start. I hope I have thought of everything.'

'It sounds to me as though you have, my dear Mrs Drinkwater, and I wish you every success in your venture. But how about capital? Do you have funds in place to purchase these items that you need?'

'I have some savings which I hope will be sufficient for my needs.' I said. I had no wish to start my new business on capital borrowed from someone else. The profits were going to be for me and Simon, not for paying back loans at huge rates of interest.

'You have thought of everything.' Mr Vine said, sounding almost disappointed. 'I wish you good luck and I hope your William returns home to you by Christmas, as all the politicians are promising.'

"So I'd taken the first step." Nana Lymer continued. "I'd climbed the first hill in my new life and I was standing on the summit, pleased with myself and very, very determined to succeed. I looked ahead at the vista of hard work and possible success which was laid out in front of me and I swore an oath to myself that I would not only keep Simon and I in comfort, I would end up keeping us in luxury. William had abrogated any feelings I had had for him when he had decided he was going off to war and this abandonment of us had made me lose any respect I may have had for him as my husband and as the father of my child. He was no longer part of my plans for the future. When, or if, he came home, he would find he was married to a different person."

Nana paused at this point and Victoria took the opportunity to ask if the old lady needed another drink.

"I think I would like another cup of tea and could you see if there are any biscuits going spare? This story-telling is making me hungry as well as thirsty."

"I'll make you a cup of tea and I'm sure I'll be able to find some biscuits." Victoria said. "Do you think we should stop for today? Do you think you are getting too tired to carry on?" Victoria was concerned that she was forcing her Nana to do more than was good for her, just to satisfy Victoria's curiosity, but she had to admit that Nana was much brighter than she had been over the last few months. Her eyes were bright and sparkling and there was a healthy pink glow to her cheeks that Victoria hadn't seen for a while. Perhaps she shouldn't feel guilty about this at all. Was it possible that she had given Nana a new lease of life? Should she feel guilty that she hadn't encouraged Nana to talk more before now? Had the old lady been missing out on meaningful communication? Whatever the truth was, Victoria made herself a promise that she would spend more time having proper conversations with her Nana.

While she was making the tea in the kitchen, her mother came through from the shop to take a break herself.

"Are you still sitting with Nana?" she asked, when she noticed that Victoria was making more tea and putting a plate of biscuits on a tray. "You don't have to stay with her now. She's unlikely to get out of bed and escape without someone seeing her during the day while we're in the shop. Don't let her blackmail you into staying with her all the time. She's good at manipulating people and you would be a walk-over for her."

"No, it's okay, Mam." Victoria smiled. "Nana's telling me what it was like when she was young and I'm enjoying listening to her. And I think it's doing her good to think back to her youth. She seems to be really enjoying it."

"That's as may be, but you've got revision to do for your exams, don't forget. You won't get decent marks if you don't do the work."

"I will get my revision done, Mam, but I've got all the Christmas holidays to do it in, so a couple of hours spent with

Nana won't make me fail any of them. We're both having a good time and it means you don't have to worry about her. Winners all round!"

"We'll find that out when we get your exam results, won't we? Don't get too clever for your own good, my girl. You go and sit with her, but make sure you are in this kitchen at 5 o'clock for your tea. I'm not having it spoilt because you forgot what time it was."

"Yes, ma'am, I mean no, ma'am, I mean I'll be here for my tea, I promise!"

Victoria grabbed the tray and sashayed past her mother as she aimed the tea towel at Victoria's legs, then climbed the stairs with the ease of youth. Nana was waiting for her as she entered the room, a huge smile on her face and a sparkle in her eyes. Victoria realised for the first time just how expressive Nana's face was. When she was happy and smiling her eyes lit up and she seemed to brighten any room.

"Tea is served, madam." She said, as she placed the tray across Nana's knees. "And I found some custard creams; do they meet madam's requirements?"

"They'll do I suppose." Nana answered, joining in with the role playing. "I hope that tea is in a silver teapot."

"Not likely, Nana. It's a brown pot and as plain as can be. But I poured the tea into a pretty china cup."

"You did, lass. You're a good girl. Now, do you want to hear any more of my life story today or are you bored with it?"

"I'm not bored at all, but you must stop when you get tired. I've got two weeks off school for Christmas, so I've got plenty of time to sit with you. We don't have to get through the whole story today."

"That's good, cos this story is going to take at least a couple of days to get through. I've never been one for using one word when I could use ten! So, where had we got to, pet?"

"You'd been to see Mr Vine, if he would let you use the house he owned but you were living in, to set up a shop to sell food from the parlour." Victoria looked very pleased with herself for remembering every detail of what Nana had told her. "You said his office was in Station Road. There's a solicitor's office still there, but it's called 'Vine and Miller' now."

"Yes, he'll be my Mr Vine's grandson, I would think." Nana mused. "My Mr Vine was a good deal older than me and I can remember his son taking over, but that would be just before the Second War. This one must be his grandson or even his great-grandson. It's a proper family firm, just how things should be, passed down from one generation to the next. It's the same here, with your mam and dad working in the shop downstairs, this was where I moved to, after my first shop on Albion Street."

"You owned this house and shop before Mam and Dad had it?" Victoria said. "I always thought they'd bought it after they got married, because wasn't Dad a joiner and working down the docks? I'm sure that was what he was doing."

"That's right." Nana agreed. "Your Dad was a joiner when your Mam met him, but after they were married the shop got so busy your Mam couldn't manage on her own. And then, of course, you came along, Bia needed the help in the shop and so Jack gave up working on the ships and worked in the shop full time. But we're getting ahead of the story, talking about that. If I'm going to tell you what happened, I need to do it in order, so that I don't get confused. But I must admit, I've got a better memory for what happened years ago than I have for what happened yesterday. Old age isn't being very kind to me, I'm afraid."

Victoria took hold of Nana's hand again. "Don't worry about it, Nana," she said. "Shall we carry on with the story? You'd been to see Mr Vine and he gave you his permission to open a shop in the parlour of your house. How long did it take for you to get set up and ready to start trading?"

"Not long at all, pet." Nana settled herself comfortably with her back resting against the pillow and took up the story from when she had visited Mr Vine.

"He was as good as his word, Mr Vine, I'll give that for him, and he sent Old Davy round at 7 o'clock sharp the next morning, ready to start putting up shelves for me. He had an old handcart that he'd pushed from Station Road and it was laden with wooden shelving, a couple of old tables and a pile of tools."

'Mr Vine said I had to come and put these here shelves where you want 'em, Missis.' he said, as I ushered him into the parlour which I had stripped of all furniture and fittings the night before. "And he wants to know if you can use these old tables. He seems to think you might want them as some sort of counter to serve from.'

"That was such a good idea and I felt stupid that I had congratulated myself on thinking of everything, but I'd never even considered what I was going to use as a counter! But Mr Vine had thought of something else."

'The boss said you can keep the cart as well, like.' Davy added, when he'd finished carrying everything into the parlour and he'd taken the cart round the back alley and put it in the back yard. 'He thought you might need it for collecting supplies, like.'

"That was another thing I'd not considered, just how was I going to carry goods from the railway station and the docks to my shop? I'd definitely not done the excellent planning I'd thought I had, but I wasn't above getting help from wherever it was offered, so I accepted the hand cart as well and resolved that, in future, I would try to look at a problem from every angle before I decided that I'd thought of everything!"

"That handcart was a godsend to me until I could afford a proper horse and cart, with stabling and fodder for the horse, so that was another element that Mr Vine added to my business empire. I think he must have had great faith in what I was capable of doing, because a lot of other people weren't overstruck on him and said he was mean, but I always found him open-handed and generous, with material goods and advice. I used him a lot, professionally, after I began to make money and I was always completely satisfied with his work and his bills. But

I'm getting ahead of the story now! Where was I? Oh yes, Old Davy had come to put up the shelves."

"He worked all morning, did Davy, and by lunchtime he'd transformed that parlour into a proper shop, with shelves and a counter made from two tables fastened together. The last job I got him to do before he went back to Mr Vine was to put up a sign next to the front window. I'd painted it myself the night before, on an old blackboard that Simon had played with. It read, 'Drinkwater's Grocers' in large letters so that passers-by could see it and know that I was in business. I was rather proud of that sign. It wasn't professionally done, but it was bright and cheerful and as good, if not better, than any sign outside any other 'house shop' in the town."

"Were you nervous, Nana? I mean, were you worried that the shop wouldn't be a success and that you'd wasted your savings on it? Savings that you could have used to feed and clothe you and Simon."

"I admit, I was rather nervous because I'd put so much time and effort and money into it." Nana said. "But I had to go through with it, I had no choice. It was either sink or swim and if that was going to be decided by the amount of hard work I was prepared to do, then it was only going to go one way. But I admit I was shaking the day I opened the shop. After Davy had left that first day, I went to get the handcart out of the back yard so that I could go and collect the supplies I'd ordered from the docks and the station. My next-door neighbour heard the noise I was making because I was finding it very difficult to manoeuvre that cart around the yard and she came to see what I was doing. I'd never had much to do with my neighbours, because I wasn't the sort to stand and gossip in the streets, but we'd always been civil to each other whenever we had met. Annie was a plump little body, probably in her mid-fifties then and she always kept herself to herself, like me. She was a widow, with a son who was about twenty years old, but he had a mental age of about eight. Peter, he was called and he followed Annie about, rather like Simon followed me. The difference between them was that he was a huge lad, with shoulders as broad as a barn door and muscles in his arms that would have made Popeye look skinny, but he was a gentle giant. He had no idea of his own strength and Annie often worried that some unscrupulous man would introduce him to boxing or some such thing and make a fortune out of him. She kept a very close eye on him because of this and I had rarely seen him out without his mother."

"Anyway, Annie came to the back gate and asked if I wanted Peter to give me a hand pushing the cart and I was so grateful for his help that I told Annie what I was about to do. I wouldn't normally have been so forth-coming but I felt she deserved an explanation of what I was doing with the cart, so I told her. Then Peter pushed the handcart to the station and the docks for me and when we got back to the house, I mean shop, Annie had already started to make the pies I had told her I was going to bake when I got back. She had a very light hand with pastry and I was amazed and incredibly thankful for her help. I had a lot more to do in order to be ready to open the following morning and having the baking taken off my hands was a god-send. But I was worried because I couldn't afford to pay her or

Peter for what they had done that day, but she brushed my apologies aside."

'I admire your determination and your hard work, lass, and I don't mind helping out a bit. I wondered what you would do when I heard that your William had signed up and I admire the fact that you haven't sat on your backside, bewailing what is happening to you, which is what a lot of women are doing at this moment. I also think that William was being selfish when he enlisted, although going to fight the Hun isn't going to make more of a man of him. He just hasn't got it in him and he should be old enough and man enough to admit that. I think you are worth ten of him, lass and, if I was in your position, I wouldn't be making excuses for him. But that's my personal opinion and you can tell me to mind my own business if you want.'

"I was very much taken aback by what Annie said, because I had expected that other people would all be agreeing with William's decision and it was such a relief to be able to drop the 'supportive little woman' front that I was showing to the world and be true to myself. I promised both Annie and Peter that, as soon as I had made any money, they would be well paid for helping me."

'Let's see what happens tomorrow, shall we?' were Annie's last words as she and Peter went home for the night. 'We'll be here first thing in the morning to give you moral support.'

At that point in her narrative, Nana Lymer paused because Victoria's mam had entered the room carrying a tray bearing Nana's tea.

"And yours is downstairs on the table waiting for you, Miss. So get yourself downstairs now."

"Ok mam, but can I come back after tea?" Victoria pleaded.

"I don't think so. Nana looks a bit washed-out to me, so I think she's had enough excitement for day. She needs to rest this evening and then have a good night's sleep. We'll see if she's up to it tomorrow. Go on, off you go."

Victoria had no choice but had to leave Nana and go and eat. She was concerned that she was asking too much for Nana to spend all day recalling the past but she felt that Nana looked much brighter than she had for a long time, even if her mother said that she looked washed-out. She would just have to curb her impatience and wait for tomorrow.

Chapter Three

"Why do you want to spend so much time with your Nana?" Victoria's mother asked the next morning when Victoria announced her intention of spending another day with her.

"I like listening to her stories about her youth." Victoria answered, fully aware that she wasn't giving a completely honest answer to the question, but wary of letting her mother know exactly what it was that the old lady was telling her. Her guilt made her over-compensate and she launched into a list of subjects which were all lies but were what she hoped her mother would believe and not be suspicious of. "She's telling me about the clothes she had when she was my age and what she liked to do. It was a really different world then and I'm finding it fascinating," she ended

Her mother glanced at her, disbelief written all over her face.

"I'm sure it is, but I would advise you not to put too much credence on what she's telling you, after all, there are days when she doesn't even know who she is, never mind what dresses she wore when she was a lass. Go and sit with her if you want to, but take all she says with a rather large pinch of salt. She always did have a very vivid imagination."

Victoria trailed upstairs, reluctant now to enter the room when her mother's words were ringing in her ears. Was Nana only imagining it all or had she really owned the shop like she said she had? Had she had a husband before Granddad Sam or was he a figment of her imagination? And what about Simon? He was the reason Victoria had been interested in the first place, what if he had never existed? She really hoped that what Nana was telling her was the truth, but how could she test that out without upsetting her Nana? Her mother had put doubts in her mind and suddenly Victoria wasn't sure that she wanted to listen to any more of her tales. She opened the door and stepped reluctantly into the room.

"Hello, pet, come to listen to some more of the story?"

Nana was sitting up in bed with a fluffy pink bed jacket round her shoulders and a large biscuit tin on her lap. Victoria hesitated only for a couple of heartbeats, but it was long enough for Nana to glance at her and recognise reluctance when she saw it.

"Don't tell me, your mother wanted to know what we were talking about and she told you not to believe a word of what I say." Nana suddenly sounded tired and Victoria's guilt washed over her like a cold shower.

"Yes, she did, but I'm not going to listen to her. I know that what you told me yesterday was the truth and I've come to listen to the rest of the story."

"Come and sit down, pet. I wondered if your mother would try to stick her oar in, so I've got some things to show you which will prove that I haven't completely lost my marbles."

In spite of the echo of her mother's warning still ringing in her ears, Victoria took her place next to Nana's bed and held out her hand to take the document which Nana was holding out to her.

"I think you'll find that *that* is my marriage certificate from when I married William and with it is Simon's birth certificate." Nana said, watching Victoria very closely as she perused both pieces of paper. "I haven't been lying to you, nor have I been making up stories to try and keep you with me. If you don't want to listen to a silly old woman witter on about her early life, that's fine by me, but I do think it's doing my conscience good to talk about what happened."

Victoria managed to feel guilty for the third time that morning.

"I want to know what happened, Nana." She said. "I really do. And I believe every word that you say. Mam isn't going to stop me from coming to see you, I promise."

Nana patted the hand that Victoria had laid on her arm in her eagerness to prove that she *did* actually want to be with her.

"Ok so, you tell me where we'd got to when your mam brought my tea last night."

"Annie and Peter had helped you get the shop set up ready to open the next day." Victoria answered promptly. "What was the first day like? Were you busy? Did you sell everything that you'd bought from the docks and the station?"

"Whoa, lass. You took in every word I said, didn't you? You don't have to prove yourself to me. But make me one promise."

Victoria looked Nana straight in the eye. "What do you want me to promise? I won't tell anyone what you tell me, I said that yesterday."

"No." Nana said. "No. I want you to promise me that the minute you get bored with me, you tell me. I don't want to force you to listen to me and I don't want you to fall out with your mother because of me. I want you to be here because it's what you want, do you understand?"

"Yes, I understand you. And I repeat, I'm here because I want to hear about what happened to William and Simon and you. So can we please go on with the story? What happened the first day you opened the shop?"

Nana smiled and squeezed the hand she was holding.

"Right," she said, thoughtfully. "The first day I opened the shop. Well, I expected that it would be fairly quiet on the first day. After all, there were other shops in the town that had been established for a few years and I didn't expect that their regular customers would suddenly stop using them and come to me, but it seemed that I was wrong. I unlocked the front door to find that there was a small queue of customers waiting for me to open and they piled in and began buying from me immediately. I had made sure that my prices were fair, because I'd checked what other shops were charging and I had a good selection of what people would want to buy. Annie's home-made pies went down a real treat with a lot of the customers and I decided that they were going to be a staple in my shop. I was very grateful when Annie came in and began helping me to serve these customers and she brought Peter with her, of course, who kept Simon occupied by playing with him"

"It was further on in the day, when I overheard two women talking as they waited to be served, that I realised they actually wanted me to succeed. Evidently, I was doing what a few of them would have loved to have done; I was providing for myself and my child without the benefit of a husband. I think that was where the Suffragette Movement had their core supporters – women who were sick of having to rely on often very unreliable men to keep them. This was before the Suffragettes got going properly, of course, but they tapped into a need that was already there. As the war moved on and more and more men went away to war, women provided the work force and did jobs that they would never have been considered able to do in the past. There was also more money about because the men working in our iron works were all working double shifts to help with the war effort and ordinary people had money to spare, for the first time ever. That was the reason why the pies and cakes went down so well. Women had the money to buy them instead of having to make them. It made life easier for a lot of women."

"By mid-morning, Annie went into the kitchen to make more pies because the others were selling so well and I carried on with serving customers. It was turning into exactly what I had dreamt it would be and Annie, Peter, Simon and I all danced a jig after we locked the front door for the night. I was able to give Annie and Peter some money for helping me and we ate the last of Annie's pies for our tea, all sitting round the table in the kitchen. Then Annie and I baked more pies and cakes to sell the next day and I fell into bed, exhausted but the happiest I had been for a long time."

"So it was a success, Nana." Victoria commented. "You were successful right from opening the shop on the first day."

"I suppose I was, but I didn't have time to stop and think about it. The next morning I was up while it was still dark to go and get more supplies, Peter pushing the cart and Simon running along beside us as we walked. Annie stayed in the kitchen and baked again, which was a good thing because the queues for pies were even longer on the second day and we made four batches all together that day and sold the lot. Those first few weeks shot past so quickly because I was always so busy, but the shop was turning into the little gold mine I had always hoped it would be. It wasn't all plain-sailing, of course, I made many mistakes in the first few months mainly because of my inexperience, but I learnt from them and moved on. I had a bit of trouble with some of the men who worked down the docks and who weren't too happy having to deal with a young woman, but they soon got used to it, particularly as I always took them pies or pasties which I gave to the ones who helped me."

"More and more men were seduced into the army and more women took over their jobs, giving up working in service and earning more money in the factories and driving buses than they'd ever been able to before. They wanted to spend that money, so I began running up skirts and blouses for them and getting in other little luxury items so that the girls wanted to spend their extra money in my shop. I also started making ginger beer and lemonade, because a lot of the work these women were doing was hot and thirsty work and they couldn't call in at a public house on their way home like their menfolk used to do"

"You must have been working all day and all night to get all that done, Nana." Victoria was amazed that this tiny woman had accomplished so much.

"I had help, don't forget. Annie was a godsend because she was prepared to work all hours to produce pies and cakes and pastries and when she came to the shop, Peter came with her. He was the muscle I needed to pick up supplies, but he also acted as a minder when I was out buying. I had to carry money around with me in order to pay for what I bought and there were a good few lawless men around the docks at that time, who wouldn't have hesitated to knock me out to get their hands on my money. I would have been a very easy target because, although I was

71

doing a lot of hard physical work and I was reasonably fit, I was only a smidgeon over five feet tall and skinny with it, because the hard work had sloughed off any excess fat I may have been carrying. Peter was a marvellous deterrent to any of those men who got the idea into their heads of relieving me of my cash."

"So Annie, Peter, Simon and I settled into a life of long hours and hard work, but it wasn't very long before I realised that I needed to take on another member of staff, because the initial rush had never subsided and we were running all the time to stand still. I didn't mind whether it was a boy or a girl that I employed, but I needed someone to run errands for me, to help with the baking and to stock the shelves. Annie and I discussed it but neither of us could think of anyone who fitted what we were looking for and I must admit I was starting to get a bit desperate. Then the right person dropped into my life out of the blue and I knew we were onto a winner."

"Couldn't you have advertised for staff? Didn't the local paper carry 'situations vacant' like they do now?" Victoria asked. "I bet you would have got loads of candidates if you'd put an advert in the paper."

"I probably would, pet, but I didn't have the time for interviewing loads of applicants. I just wanted to find the right person, which I did. I'd started taking 'orders' from women who were going out to work and who didn't have the time to stand and wait to be served in the shop. All they had to do was to drop a list of their requirements into the shop on their way to work and we would pack them up and Peter and I would deliver them that evening. It was cash on delivery mind, because I didn't work any other way. Nobody could run a tab in my shop, they had to pay up or they didn't get the goods, so if they didn't pay when I arrived with the order then that order went back to the shop with me."

"One morning, Annie took an order from a young girl, while I was giving Simon his breakfast and it was one of the orders Peter and I delivered that night. When we arrived, it was a man who answered the door, which in itself was rather unusual, because it was mostly women who dealt with me. He greeted our arrival with a huge smile and ushered me into the kitchen while he got the money to pay me. Peter stayed outside, keeping watch over the cart and the rest of the orders, because we didn't want anyone running off with it and also because he was very shy and didn't mix with other people very well."

'I'm Sam, Sammy Lymer,' the man said as he paid for his order. 'I think I know your husband, lass, William isn't it? Works in the iron works?'

"Granddad!" Victoria interjected. "That's how you met Granddad Sam!"

"Yes, that was the first time I met him." Nana agreed. "But let me continue or I'll lose my train of thought! I didn't want to talk to a stranger about William. It was late, I'd had a long day and I was finding it difficult to keep on pretending that everything was hunky-dory between me and my husband. I still had work to do when I got back to the shop because I had another batch of ginger beer to make and Simon would be wanting his bedtime story before he would settle down for the night. Annie was baking while she kept an eye on Simon, but she would be tired and ready to go home and I really didn't want to have to make small talk with a stranger, but he was a new customer and I wanted the repeat business, so I sat on my impatience and answered him."

'William used to work in the works, but he's away in France with the army, now. He's doing his bit for King and country.' I said, the false patriotic tone which was a part of my new persona coming easily to me because I'd used it so often before.

'I'd heard tell he'd enlisted.' Sam said. 'I'm foreman in the next section to where he used to work and I couldn't understand it when I heard he'd joined up. I thought they were only taking single men as yet, although I suppose *that* will change cos it's not looking too good out there. I've no wish to follow the colours, but I suppose I'll still be needed to make iron and steel for the ships and the guns, so hopefully I won't be conscripted. I mustn't say that to most people, though, you get called a traitor and a coward if you're not desperate to get over there and get your head blown off. But it must be hard on you, lass, looking after a bairn and working all hours as well. You must be exhausted.'

"I nearly buckled there and then under his kind tone, because I was so tired and I was used to people telling me what a wonderful thing William had done to enlist. Most people ignored the fact that I was working at least fifteen hours a day to keep William's wife and son in food and lodgings and praised what marvellous things William was doing. I knew conditions wouldn't be good for William in France, but he'd chosen the road he wanted to travel and hadn't spared a thought for Simon and me. It was all about William's ego and manliness, not patriotism or bravery, but I was getting heartily sick of pretending I was proud of him. And his army pay had never materialised either. We hadn't seen a penny since he'd marched off to war; we could have starved in a gutter. But I pulled myself together and refused to admit any of this to Sam Lymer who was a stranger to me, albeit a sensitive stranger. I pulled my public face back over the real me and smiled at him."

'It's not so bad.' I answered. 'I've got Annie and Peter to help me and at least I'm always there for Simon. If I'd gone out to work he would have had to be farmed out and I don't want that to happen.'

'I can understand that. My daughter, Alice, looks after her younger sister while I'm out at work. I lost my missis last year and I've worried myself sick over the two youngest ones ever since. Our George and Bill joined up a month ago, so there's only the three girls at home with me now.'

'Three?' I asked. He'd only mentioned two girls, so I wondered who the other one was.

'Aye. There's our Hannah as well. She's the one who brought the order this morning, on her way to work. She's started working for Dennison, the butcher, but I'm not happy about it. He's short-tempered and too handy with his fists that one and I don't want my lass working for him, not since I saw the black eye on his missis last week.'

'She's telling folk she walked into a side of bacon.' I said. 'But it's more likely to have been stuck on the end of her husband's fist. It's a shame *he* doesn't enlist so he could take his temper out on the Hun instead of his wife. I find him very unpleasant, even with his customers and I can understand why you aren't happy about Hannah working for him. But I'm looking for some more help in my shop. I could do with a lass to help make up the orders and to train at making pies and cakes. If your Hannah can turn her hand to that sort of work, then tell her to come and see me tomorrow and I'll show her what I want her to do. Do you think she'd want to work for me?'

'I'm sure she would, cos she's frightened of the pig butcher. I'm sure she would much prefer to work for you. She's a good girl and her mother trained her to bake, so she should be of some help to you.'

'Good.' I said. 'She'll be doing me a favour and she's best away from that butcher. Thank you, Mr Lymer.'

'Call me Sammy, lass, everyone does. Mr Lymer's a bit too formal, don't you think?'

'Ok, Sammy. Tell Hannah to be round at my shop at 7o'clock on the dot tomorrow. We start early in my shop!'

'She'll be there, bright and early. If you need any help from me, don't hesitate to let me know. I admire what you are doing, but with your lad away at the Front, you need to know that you've got back-up if you need it. Take care going home, Mrs Drinkwater.'

'Call me Bia, Sammy.' I said. 'I don't think I need to be too formal either.'

'Bia? That's an unusual name, isn't it? I bet you got some stick for it when you were a kid.'

'My full name is Abia, but I've always been called Bia. Nobody ever forgets my name, Sammy. Once seen, always remembered!'

"So, I left the house and Peter and I finished delivering the orders. Annie was pleased when we got home and I told her about taking Hannah on. She knew Sammy and had known his wife, Sarah, before her death.

'She had too many children, poor Sarah. I think she had fourteen, or something very close to that number.'

'Fourteen!' I choked. I couldn't believe my ears. 'Are you sure, because Sammy only talked about the three girls at home and two boys who enlisted, like William. That's only five.'

'I think that was half of what was wrong with Sarah. A lot of her children died young.' Annie said. 'Sarah had her heart broken so many times when they died, that it finally killed her. Only one of them died at birth, I think, the rest caught one of the childhood diseases and I think one of them was burned to death in a fire.'

'Oh my God. That poor woman! It was no wonder she died young.'

"I tried to imagine what it would be like to lose Simon through an illness or, God forbid, an accident and I couldn't do it. My heart went out to Sammy's wife and to Sammy. He was still living with all his losses and still managing to smile! My opinion of him rose even higher.

'Did you say Hannah is working for the pig butcher?' Annie cut through my thoughts. 'I hope he's not going to cause you any more trouble if he finds out that she's now working for you.'

"I had told Annie about Dennison making a pass at me and then being so rude and brutal when I had refused him. I had to admit that the thought of him causing trouble had crossed my mind when Peter and I were walking home, but I had decided to ignore it. Dennison might not be bothered about losing a shop girl and surely he must have an apprentice butcher working with him. There were lots of young girls looking for work at that time, so he would be able to replace Hannah fairly easily. I didn't suppose for one moment that he was as choosy as I was about staff, so a replacement wouldn't be hard to find. That was where I made one of the biggest mistakes of my life."

"But why, Nana?" Victoria asked. "Surely even someone as nasty as Dennison wouldn't do anything bad because one of his staff had left him and gone to work for you. That's a bit over-the-top, isn't it?"

"Oh yes. It would be an over-reaction, certainly, but I didn't allow for Dennison's state of mind at the time. There again, I didn't know much about him, other than that he didn't like having his advances turned down and that he turned nasty when rebuffed. I don't think anyone else would have acted any differently from me, given the same insight into his character. It's something I've considered deeply ever since, though. If I hadn't employed Hannah, would life have turned out the same? I just don't know. When I consider what else happened, I think it probably would have taken the same course. All I did was exacerbate it."

"Exacerbate what, Nana?" Victoria was beginning to feel she was losing track of the story at this stage, as though she had missed an important point.

"No, I'm getting side-tracked again." Nana shook herself mentally. "I've got to tell this in its proper order or it will all get too confusing for anyone to understand. Where was I? That's right, Hannah. That was how I got my third member of staff and Hannah turned out to be every bit as capable as her father had said. On top of that, she had a really sunny nature and she would set about tasks with a light heart, singing hymns as she worked. The old biddies who came in the shop liked her to serve them and she had a way with her that could turn any sour face into a smile, so she made life a joy."

"Some nights, Sammy would collect her at closing time and he would turn his hand to any job that was beyond Peter's capabilities, as well as having a fund of stories which amused Simon when he was crotchety. Despite the terrible accounts about the dreadful conditions that were beginning to filter home from the battlefields, life in our little backwater was happy and productive and I felt surrounded by good friends. And then William came home on a few days leave from the Front and he turned everything sour."

"Did you know he was coming home?" Victoria asked when Nana paused. "Had he written to you or did the army let you know?"

"No, he hadn't written to me at all and the army only got in touch if a soldier died or was badly wounded. I had had no idea that he was coming home, but I must admit that I had hardly thought about him once I opened the shop and I hadn't written to him. I didn't even know where I would have sent a letter. His home-coming was a complete surprise to me and not a welcome one at that."

"Why did he turn everything sour, Nana?" Victoria asked. "Didn't he like the fact that you'd opened the shop?"

"To say he didn't like me turning the house into a shop was a massive understatement. He walked into the shop one Friday morning, wearing his uniform, and looking as black as thunder when he saw the customers and the walls filled with shelves."

'What's going on here, Bia?' he growled. 'What have you done to my house?'

"Well, that got my goat straight away because I considered it *my* house now, not his. I'd earned the money to pay the rent on it and I'd done all the work. If Simon and I had waited for William to send money home, we'd have been evicted months before and probably have died of starvation soon after. I hustled him through the shop and into the kitchen, away from the curious eyes and ears of my customers in the shop. Annie was baking at the kitchen table and I asked her if she would go and help Hannah serve while I had a few words with William. Cheery as ever, she walked past William, patted him on his arm and said it was good to see him. He didn't have the grace to reply to her, he could barely contain himself until she was out of the room, before he launched into a blistering attack on me."

'What do you think you are doing? How dare you turn the parlour of my house into a shop, without even consulting with me? You have no right to do what you've done. When those customers have gone, you can lock the door and don't ever open it again.'

"His voice was so loud; I could imagine that they could hear it in the railway station, never mind in the shop in the next room. I was fully aware that all conversation had ceased in the shop and then I heard Hannah launch into a rousing chorus of 'God Save the King'. Silently, I thanked her for her presence of mind and her kindness to me for what she was trying to do before I turned on William."

"He was standing in front of the kitchen range, for all the world as though he was a country squire berating the hired help, with his arm raised and his index finger pointing towards the parlour. Despite my anger at the gall he had to berate me, I couldn't help but notice how ineffectual he looked, his weedy frame not filling out the uniform he wore. He had lost the extra weight he had carried before he left home and it made him look like a gawky adolescent in a temper. I had never been as angry as I was at that moment and I am sure if I had been carrying a knife I would have slit him open from his throat to his toes. I couldn't stop myself from answering him, but I had the composure to keep my voice so low that William had to strain to hear what I said, although my actions left him in no doubt as to my frame of mind. I had no intentions of feeding the hunger of the local gossips, many of whom were standing in my shop trying their hardest to hear the argument raging in the kitchen."

"My anger was so white-hot I pushed him backwards so that he landed in the easy chair next to the range and then I put my face so close to his we were literally nose to nose and then I hissed very quietly but with as much venom as I could muster,

'Don't you dare come back here, shouting the odds about your house, your parlour when, if it hadn't been for me opening this shop, Simon and I would have been out on the streets and no parlour for you to come back to. That shop has kept us housed and fed since you trotted off to play soldiers when you didn't have to and it's a bloody good job I opened it. Now get this clear

– I've paid the rent on this place since the day you enlisted. I've worked long hours doing back-breaking work to make this shop successful and you aren't coming back here trying to throw your weight around and thinking you can boss me about, because you can't.'

"I kept poking him in his chest as he cowered in the chair in front of me, but I really felt like taking the poker to him and if he'd said any more I may well have done so. I had a reputation to uphold in the town and I wasn't going to be the subject of spiteful gossips, spreading the word that my husband didn't like what I'd done while he was away fighting the Hun. I didn't want to lose any customers through his attitude, or have my reputation as an honest businesswoman besmirched."

"He did feel inadequate, didn't he, Nana?" Victoria said. "No matter what he did, you would always turn out to be the strongest person in your relationship and he couldn't cope with it. You were way too strong for him."

"Yes, I came to that conclusion eventually, but I was too stupid to realise it at the time. I was only concerned about the shop and Simon, so I defended myself in the only way I could, I argued with him and I came out on top again. I think if I had still loved him, I may have taken a more conciliatory tone with him, but any love I had had for him had died the day he had enlisted in the army and I was only concerned about me, Simon and the shop."

"The fire had gone out of William as I towered over him and he stopped shouting at me. He wriggled in the chair until he could get his hand in his pocket, pulled out some folding money and waved it in front of my face.

'I've kept the money for you.' He said. 'Pay the rent with it and then you can close the shop.'

'You just don't understand, do you?' I answered. 'I don't want your money; you keep it and spend it however you like. The shop will continue, you aren't going to ruin it. You are going to put a smile on your face and you are going to speak to all of the customers in my shop as though you are really proud of me. And, you will continue to toe my line until you go back to the Front, which, as far as I am concerned, can't come soon enough. Do you understand me?'

"He mumbled his agreement, by now totally cowed, but his visit into the shop was halted when Simon came into the kitchen from the back yard and stood just inside the door, staring at his father. William stood up and held out his arms for Simon to run into them, as he had done since Simon had learnt to walk, but the child wouldn't move. He stood in the doorway and no matter how William urged him he wouldn't go near his father."

'He can't remember who you are.' I told William. 'He's only three and he can't recognise you in a uniform.'

"I think it was Simon's reaction to him that curbed William's temper tantrum more than what I had said to him but, whatever it was, he behaved as the proud husband for the rest of his leave. Simon was more comfortable with him once he had changed out of his uniform and, by the time his leave was over, he'd started calling him 'Daddy' once again."

"It was only after William had left to return to his unit that I realised I had never once asked about the war and what conditions were like at the Front. William hadn't volunteered any information, in fact he had hardly spoken to me after the first day, and I hadn't been interested enough to ask. But it spoke volumes for the change in our relationship. The marriage was over in all but name and I had no regrets about it. Annie and Hannah both knew that it was very rocky relationship that we had, but both of them avoided the subject. It took less than a day for the ripples that William's presence had made in the pond of our lives to settle back out again and we carried on as before.

Chapter Four

Victoria was impressed with how well her Nana had dealt with William's anger, but she felt incredibly sorry for her that her husband couldn't appreciate the work and effort his wife had put into running the business. As Nana finished telling her about William's home leave, her mother shouted up the stairs for Victoria to come down.

"I'm sorry, Nana, but I'm going to have to go downstairs. Mam sounds cross and I don't want her to refuse to let me come and sit with you."

"That's ok, pet." Nana said, who was ready for a nap before her lunch anyway, although she would never have asked Victoria to leave. "You go downstairs. I'll have a nap and perhaps Bia will let you come back this afternoon. Remember, you only come to see me if you want to. I'm not forcing you."

"I'll be back as soon as mam lets me, but it might be later on this afternoon because the shop sounds busy. She might want me to stack some shelves or serve some customers. I'll see you later."

When Victoria got downstairs it was to find her mother in an atrocious mood, the shop heaving with customers and her father juggling serving customers and boning a side of bacon because they were running low.

"How long do you intend sitting upstairs with her?" her mother snapped at Victoria as she made her appearance in the kitchen. "It's nearly Christmas, the shop's heaving with customers, I've got lunch to make for four people and you are just sitting on your backside having a lovely chat. Do you intend giving me a hand or not?"

Victoria couldn't cope with her mother when she was in this mood and she knew that no matter what she said or did her mother was going to carry on moaning about it for a few weeks to come.

"I'll go and serve then." she said, knowing that it was a waste of time trying to justify what she had been doing. She hoped that her easy acquiescence would divert her mother's bile, but it was a vain hope. Her mother's voice followed her as she opened the door from the kitchen into the shop. This was the most dangerous part, because if her mother was in a really foul mood, she would follow Victoria into the shop and spend the next five minutes continuing her diatribe, despite the number of customers who were providing an audience. Victoria hated it when that happened because it was excruciatingly embarrassing to have her faults highlighted in front of customers, even though a few of them would grimace at her and soundlessly convey that they pitied her. Victoria would much rather do without the pity and not have her character stripped bare in front of witnesses. Thankfully, her mother decided that she was too busy to waste time pointing out her daughter's faults to the world and his wife that day and Victoria was spared the public humiliation.

With the ease born of long practise, Victoria worked hard serving the customers and made it possible for her mother to prepare the midday meal for them, but her idea that she may be allowed to spend the afternoon finding out how Nana had managed in the earlier shop was baulked by the conversation at the dinner table.

"You'll have to work in the shop this afternoon as well, Victoria." Her mother said as she cleared away the plates. "Go and get Nana's plate and then you can restock the Christmas display, there's a lot gone from it this morning and I want the stock shifting. The more there is on display, the more will sell."

"When I've finished that can I go and sit with Nana again, please?"

"No." Her mother was adamant. "You can stay and help your Dad because I'm going to get my hair permed for Christmas and Keith can't come in this afternoon. He's taking his mother Christmas shopping." This last was said as though Keith had no right to be doing anything as frivolous as shopping with his mother. Victoria sighed inwardly, because she knew that the afternoon was now spent and it would be the next day before she would get the next instalment of Nana's story. She knew better than to show her disappointment, however, because her mother would take that as a criticism and feel duty bound to explain, at length, just exactly how her daughter was misguided.

So, Victoria spent the afternoon working in the shop, after rushing upstairs to explain to Nana why she wouldn't be with her the rest of the day. Her Nana accepted it with resignation, knowing full well how impossible it was for Victoria to shirk her responsibilities and not wishing to interfere in the mother/daughter relationship. Privately, she abhorred Bia's irritability and wondered where she had gone wrong in her child-rearing that she had produced a person who was capable of such venom.

It was the next afternoon before Victoria got the opportunity to snatch another couple of hours at Nana's bedside, arriving with tea and biscuits and the news that her father was insisting that she be left to her own devices for the whole afternoon, for which Victoria was extremely grateful.

"I know Mam gets very tired," she explained as she settled herself onto her chair, "but I do wish she wouldn't take it out on me. It's not my fault that the shop's busy and she'd be complaining if it wasn't. Sometimes I just can't do right for doing wrong."

"Never mind, chick. At least you're here now and we can go on with the story. I must tell you the whole sorry tale before I die and, at my age, you never know when that could be. I don't want to die before I've finished it, because there's more than one reason why I'm telling you all about it."

Nana refused to be drawn into explaining this cryptic comment, but launched straight into the next part of the saga.

"William went back to his unit in the same frame of mind as he had been in when he arrived home. He still didn't agree with me running the shop, but he realised that there wasn't a lot he could do about it and it did relieve him of any responsibility for Simon and I. After he'd gone, life settled back into the regular pattern we had established since we opened the shop, hard work and long hours, but all made joyous by Simon's happy presence and the comradeship of Annie, Peter and Hannah.

An added bonus was that, for the first time in my life, I was earning enough money to have extra left over after all the bills were paid and I thought long and hard about what I was going to do with this money. I had no intentions of wasting it on fripperies or of putting it into a bank to sit and earn little in the way of interest. It was going to have to join in with the team and work hard for its living, just like I did. I wanted to use it to make mine and Simon's futures even more secure, but I couldn't decide what was the best way of making my money work for me. There were a couple of options I had considered; I could open another shop in another part of the town, but I would then need a manager and more staff or I could invest the money into a different type of business altogether, but I didn't have any experience of any other types of business."

"You didn't want to let go of the reins of your shop, if you had to work in another business." Victoria declared. "I can understand that. I wouldn't want to have to pass the running of any business of mine to someone else; because I wouldn't think that anyone else could do it as well as I could."

"You are a very clever girl, Victoria. Much cleverer than I was at your age, or even when I was older than you. You have the very rare ability of analysing why a person does what they do. I think you will make a very good teacher because you will want to know how and why children learn and how to motivate them so that they do learn from you."

"So what did you decide to do?" Victoria asked, uncomfortable with the praise that Nana was giving her because she wasn't used to being praised in any way. "Did you decide to invest the money in another business?"

"There was a lot to consider before I made a decision about it. We had got to a point in the war where the enemy was going all out to sink the merchant ships which provided our island with a lot of its food. I think the Hun had reasoned that if they could starve us out then that would ensure their victory, but in the end, they only succeeded in forcing the United States into the war, because they sank a lot of American shipping. But I had known that my income would drop if their tactics succeeded and I had already negotiated deals with a couple of farmers who farmed the land on the outskirts of the town, to buy their produce as it was harvested. I had contracts lodged with Mr Vine so that they couldn't renege on them, but I was still worried that, at some point, my income could drop sharply as the result of shortages and I didn't want all my eggs in one basket."

"How did you decide what to do then?" Victoria wanted to know.

"Well, one evening, Annie and I were discussing the effect that enemy action could have on my business when Sammy Lymer called in to collect Hannah. He had taken to dropping in regularly when his shifts allowed and I had grown so used to his easy presence that I included him in the conversation as though he was a member of our little family."

'If I were you, lass, I'd think on why I started selling groceries in the first place and look for a business that would fit that same criteria.' he said, when I asked him for his opinion on the matter.

'I decided to open a grocery shop because people would always need to eat.' I answered immediately. 'And also, it was a subject which I could understand fully. I couldn't have opened a solicitor's office, for example, because I'm not trained. But I don't see where I can go from here, apart from opening another grocery shop in another part of the town and then I would have to get someone in to manage it, which would mean more expense and less profit and there would still be the same problem of supply and what would happen to my business if the supply lines were cut off.'

'I mean that you should continue along the line of what will people always need?' Sammy smiled. 'Look around for other ways of making money that won't depend solely on supply but that will provide the answer to the question of what people will always need. They will always need food to eat and…'

'They'll always need somewhere to live.' I finished for him. 'You're right! And if you take that argument to its conclusion, they will always need clothes to wear as well.'

'Yes, well I hadn't gone as far as your last point, but I was ahead of you on the subject of housing. So much so that I'm arranging to buy a house in Cromwell Road which I intend letting out at a reasonable rent. I've been doing so much extra work since this war started and with George and Bill away and Hannah working, I've got a few quid put by that could be better spent on bricks and mortar than sitting in a bank. That way, I'll always have an income, should anything stop me from being able to work.'

"I fully agreed with Sammy that investing in property would be a very sensible thing to do and, when he told me the price of the house he was arranging to buy and the rental return he could get on it, it didn't take me long to work out that it was a bigger return than my money was earning in the bank. The drawback was that I had never owned a property in my life and I didn't have the first idea on how to go about buying one. I had never collected rents before either, but I knew that I didn't want to have to do that because it would make me especially vulnerable if I was walking around the town carrying a large amount of money. There was also the question of what I would do if a tenant didn't pay their rent. If someone didn't pay for their shopping, I wouldn't let them take the goods out of my shop, but if a tenant didn't pay the rent, I would need a man to deal with them."

"The answer to all those questions was sitting next to me at my kitchen table and I wasted no time in letting him know what I was thinking."

'Why don't we buy the house in Cromwell Road together?' I asked. 'We could go fifty-fifty with the cost and you could do the rent-collecting.'

"I knew as soon as I saw Sammy's reaction that this was what he had wanted all along and I had given him the perfect introduction. I stopped talking and realised what I'd said. For all I knew, he might not have been the good friend he had always appeared to be; he could have been working himself into my good books with the express purpose of fleecing me out of all my money. I knew that what I was thinking would be written all over my face because I had never been any good at dissembling, so I turned away from Sammy because I didn't want to hurt his feelings when he had been so good to me. His next words had me spinning back round to face him immediately."

'I wouldn't buy anything with you as a partner...' he began.

"My face flamed and I drew myself up to my full height, ready to give him one very large piece of my mind, when he finished the sentence he had begun."

'...until we had drawn up a proper legally-binding contract with that tame solicitor of yours, so that you could be assured that everything would be above board and legal.' he finished.

'Sam, I am so sorry. Was it *that* obvious what I was thinking?' I asked him, blushing again that he knew how distrustful I was of other people."

'It's obvious that you've been let down by someone, lass,' he answered. 'It's not my place to question what's happened in your life, but if we are going to go into business together, there's no harm in making sure that everything's above board and watertight, for both our sakes. I wouldn't take offence at anyone being sensible about a business arrangement that's to protect both parties. And I want you to take time to consider what we are about to do, so that you don't feel that you are being forced into parting with any money.'

"Sam was right, of course, we had to ensure that our partnership was legally set-up and that both of us had a way out of it if we decided that we didn't want to continue the business." Nana continued. "I also needed to view this house and decide whether or not I thought it was a viable proposition, so I made an appointment with the agent to go and look round the house the very next day. I was pleased with what I saw, in that the house was in good repair and, although it was only small, it would make a good home for a newly-married couple. Sam was waiting for me at the shop when I got back after viewing the house and he was very eager to hear my thoughts on it. I told him that I still wanted to join him in buying it and so we made an appointment to go and see Mr Vine and make our partnership legal."

"We set up a joint bank account and agreed that the rent would be paid into the account weekly, any repairs that needed doing would be paid for directly from this account and that Sammy and I would then have a half share of the money that was left, although, in practise, neither of us wanted to take money out on a weekly basis. Mr Vine drew up the legal documents for this and Sammy and I both signed copies of them and lodged them with Mr Vine. That afternoon, after we had closed the shop for the day, Annie, Peter and Hannah joined Sammy, Simon and I and we had a slap-up meal in the kitchen, to celebrate our new business venture."

'I'm very pleased to be going into business with you, Sam.' I said as we sat round the range after we'd eaten.

'The feeling is mutual, Bia.' Sam replied. 'I think we should have a toast to our new partnership to begin it in the right way.'

'I'm afraid I've only got either ginger beer or lemonade to use to toast our business with, but if either of those is good enough for you, I will happily join you in toasting our new partnership.' I told him.

'Ginger beer is good enough for me.' Sam smiled. 'Come on, fill your glasses everyone. To mine and Bia's new business venture and let's hope it proves to be very lucrative.'

"And was it, Nana?" Victoria couldn't resist her need to know how everything had turned out. "Did you make a lot of money from renting out the house?"

"Nobody makes a lot of money from renting out one house, darling. But it was a good start and it soon blossomed into bigger and better things, which I will explain as we get through the story. But I must keep to the chronology of the tale; otherwise I might miss important points out of it, which may be vital in understanding the whole. I know you want to jump forwards in time, but I'm too old to be able to cope with that. You'll just have to bear with me and we will both reach the end of the tale together. But, before we go any further, don't you think it's time for a tea break? I could really do with wetting my whistle."

Victoria jumped up immediately to go and make tea for her Nana, but she crept down the stairs with her heart in her mouth in case her mother was in the kitchen and she demanded that Victoria had to work in the shop. Luckily, the kitchen was deserted and she set the kettle to boil and was rummaging in the cupboard for biscuits to go with the tea when she heard the door open. She whirled round with an excuse ready on her lips to try and head her mother off before she could get into her stride, but it was unnecessary because it was her father who had entered.

"It's ok." He said, raising his hand to stop her blurting out the excuse she had ready. "I'm not going to insist that you come and work in the shop. You stay with Nana and keep her company and I promise I won't tell your mother that I've seen you."

"Are you sure?" Victoria felt she should ask, but she really didn't want to work in the shop that day.

"Yes, I'm sure. Keith's here today and it doesn't seem as busy as it's been the last few days. Most people have got their Christmas shopping done by now, so it's not as frantic as it was. Don't take any notice of your mother, she just gets herself worked up at this time of year and she always takes it out on us. Go on; take that tea upstairs before it goes cold."

With a light heart, Victoria picked up the tray and made her way back upstairs. Nana greeted her arrival with a sweet smile.

"I was beginning to think you'd been waylaid by your mother." She said, carefully choosing a biscuit to dip in her tea.

"No, I saw Dad and he told me to come back up here. Keith's working today and Dad says it isn't as busy as it's been the last few days. He said Mam always takes it out on us when she's busy and tired."

"She always makes sure everyone knows how she's feeling, that's right enough. But enough of today, let's go back to the war."

"Ok, Nana, I'm ready and waiting." Victoria curled her legs beneath her and concentrated all her attention on her grandmother.

"Right, where was I? Oh yes, the first house I bought with Sam. The partnership turned out to be every bit as lucrative as we had hoped. In the first twelve months, we bought another three houses to go with the one we had bought in Cromwell Road and we rented them all out to couples with young families. Sammy always made all the arrangements when we bought another house, although I always insisted that we both viewed them and decided if they were right for us or not. Sammy negotiated the price with the owners; he dealt with any maintenance work which needed to be done and he found the tenants and collected the rent from them."

"To the rest of the world, all the houses belonged to Sam Lymer and the only person (apart from Annie) who knew of my involvement was Mr Vine when he drew up the contracts and I knew he wouldn't break his professional silence and reveal my joint ownership. I was adamant that no-one else would be privy to my business secrets because I didn't want anyone to think that I was profiting from the fact that the country was at war. I always kept very quiet about the extent of my little business empire, even after the war had ended, because I didn't feel that it was anyone else's concern. I've always been a very private person."

"Just how big did your 'little business empire' become?" Victoria was amazed at the idea of this tiny old lady being a captain of industry, it just didn't seem likely. Her mother's warnings swam around in her mind again and she hoped her incredulity wasn't showing on her face.

Nana Lymer gave her a very sharp look.

"Don't deride what you don't know, young lady," she snapped. "For a girl who came from a poor home, I did very well for myself. That's exactly the sort of comment your mother would make. I would have thought better of you."

Victoria was immediately contrite, because she had also heard the echo of her mother's dulcet tones in what she had said and she wasn't proud of it.

"I'm sorry. I shouldn't have said that. Please go on with the story."

"That's ok. Now, where was I? Oh yes. We had moved into 1915, by the time we had bought the other three houses. The war hadn't been over by Christmas 1914, as all the newspapers and the politicians had said it would be, in fact, it didn't seem to be going very well at all over in France and the Low Countries. There was a lot of bad news coming from the Front and we were beginning to hear about the terrible conditions that the troops were living and dying in over there. There were lists of soldiers killed and missing in the newspapers and life was pretty unbearable for the families of the soldiers left behind in England. I had heard nothing from William since he had gone back after his leave, although I must admit that I hadn't really expected to. But I didn't know if he was still alive, although I supposed the army would have let me know if he had been killed or badly injured, or if his silence was because he was still sulking with me over my opening the shop without his permission. I was very busy working in the shop all day and trying to make sure that Simon had plenty of my attention as well, so I'm afraid I didn't really think about him at all. It was very much a case of 'out of sight out of mind'."

"When we were first married, we had lived with his parents and I soon learned that he would sulk if he thought he wasn't getting the attention he thought he deserved. I put this down to the fact that his mother spoiled him like a child, waiting on him hand and foot and even anticipating his needs so that he never even had to look for the newspaper; she would be there holding it out to him when she thought he wanted it. When we moved to Albion Street and set up house on our own, I took the first opportunity that came my way to explain to William that he couldn't come first anymore because I had Simon to care for. He was only a baby and his wants and needs came before anyone else's, even mine and that the sooner his father accepted that the better. William took great exception to this and managed to sulk for almost three months. In fact, he only stopped sulking when he made the decision to enlist."

"So, I took the absence of letters from William as proof that he was indulging in a huge sulk about the shop and put all thoughts of him from my mind. As I said before, I was very busy with the shop and Simon and the four properties and so forgetting about William wasn't difficult. But I did have something else on my mind. I was looking about for a new house to buy, not one to rent out, but one that all our family could live in and that would have larger shop premises than the one I currently rented from Mr Vine. It was ridiculous that I was a landlady, yet I didn't own the house I lived in. And in saying 'all our family' I was including Annie and Peter as family. I was so close to both of them by this time that I didn't want to leave them behind when I moved."

"Both of them earned a salary from me, but I was aware that a large proportion of that money was swallowed up by their rent and I knew that Annie repeatedly did without things that she needed in order to feed and clothe Peter. I knew what it was like to love your child to distraction, but most children grow up and live independently of their parents. It was unlikely that Peter would ever do that and I had a vision of Annie working until she dropped dead, in order to care for him. Added to that, Annie was now like an older sister and a mother all rolled into one for me, so I looked on her as my family and families look after their own."

"You would have needed a big property to have enough bedrooms for all of you and have space for a shop." Victoria said, her practical side to the fore.

"It wasn't only the size of the property that was important." Nana continued. "I needed more space for both the living and business parts of our lives, but I also needed the new house to be in the right position in the town. I didn't want to move any nearer to the docks area, even though it would be easier for collecting goods from the ships and trains, but that part of town was becoming more and more dilapidated and the 'rougher' element had moved into it. I also needed the new house and shop to be on a street that people used as a thoroughfare, so that the shop would pick up plenty of passing trade. Houses in the areas I wanted to move to were at a premium and I was aware that I was going to have to pay quite a hefty sum of money in order to get what I wanted, always supposing that I could actually find what I was wanting."

"That was where Sam came up trumps again. He had called in to tell me about a house he had found near the railway station which he thought would be ideal for us to buy, so I had to tell him why I didn't have the spare cash for it at that moment. I was reluctant to confide in him, because I did like to hold my cards close to my chest, but I believed in honesty between partners so he deserved to know why I was holding back from another business commitment."

'What sort of property are you looking for?' he asked, when I had confided in him my reason for not buying another rental property.

'I need one that's big enough for Simon and I, but also has room for Annie and Peter, because I don't want to leave them behind. Added to that, I want a property that has a bigger shop floor, so that I can carry more stock with space somewhere for a storeroom. I also want it to be on one of the main streets so that I can catch any passing trade, but not too far from where we are here on Albion Street. I don't want to lose the customer base that I've already built up.'

'You've certainly put some thought into this Bia and your list of criteria is a pretty long one, but I think I may have the answer for you.'

"I could hardly believe it. I had been searching for weeks for a property that fitted my wants and here was Sam, telling me he knew of somewhere within two minutes of my mentioning it."

'I've heard that Mrs Rudge is giving up running the corn shop on the corner of Queen Street and King Street. She's selling up and going to live with her daughter in Normanby. You can't blame her; she must be seventy if she's a day and its heavy work shifting bags of grain around. Anyway, there's the shop and a kitchen downstairs, four rooms on the first floor and two more on the top floor. That would give you ample room for you and Simon and Annie and Peter could have the whole top floor.'

'But how do you know so much about it?' I asked him. 'It's not been advertised or anything or I would have seen it.'

' Old man Rudge took me up into the attics one day, years ago, to show me his collection of fishing rods, cause that's where he used to store them.' Sam said with a knowing smile. 'I reckon he thought he would be able to sell me a few, but I just wasn't interested. Fishing's never been an interest of mine, I would be bored stiff in half an hour. But you should go round and see her before anyone else steps in in front of you. I'm sure you would be able to negotiate a good price for it because she's desperate to sell. That place is far too big for her since her old man died.'

"I could have kissed Sam at that point because that shop was exactly what I was searching for. I used to collect grain from there for my Dad's chickens when I was a kid and I knew how big the shop was. It was like a cathedral in comparison to the house in Albion Street, with three large, plate-glass windows which fronted Queen Street and King Street. I would have ample scope for making wonderful window displays which would attract customers into the shop. Added to that it was on one of the main streets which led down to Middlesbrough Road, so anyone going to the big shops would pass mine before they got there. It was an ideal location and once I'd given it a new coat of paint I was sure it would be bright and airy. I also remembered that it had a large back yard, with plenty of room for storing any overflow from the shop, if Sam would build a shed for me."

"But that's this shop, Nana. That's where we are now, you've described it exactly how it is. So you owned it?" Victoria couldn't believe what she was hearing, having always believed that her parents had bought it from the Rudge family before Victoria was born.

"That's right. I won't go into all the ins and outs of buying the place, suffice it to say that by the end of May 1915, I was the proud owner of 24 Queen Street with three floors of rooms (including the shop) and its own large back yard. 'Drinkwater's Grocers' moved with us and the business continued to flourish, with Annie, Hannah and I working our socks off, stocking shelves, baking pies and pasties, making soft drinks and starting a home-cooked meat section. The whole place constantly smelled of hams and legs of pork being roasted in the oven in the kitchen. Peter said the house always smelled like Christmas to him and, although Annie and I smiled at what he'd said, we both had to agree that he was right."

"I paid a local decorator to whitewash the whole building from top to bottom and even broke my own rule about not going into debt, by buying a new settee and chairs from Vaughan's furniture shop on what was locally called the 'never-never'. In other words, it was on credit and I hated every minute that I owed that shop money. I scrimped and saved so that I could pay it off in five weeks, because I hated owing anyone money. I promised myself I would never get into debt again and I never have. That once was enough for me."

"Annie and Peter moved to Queen Street with Simon and I, just as I had hoped that they would and it worked very well for all of us. Simon and I shared the first floor and Annie and Peter had the top floor. We very rarely used the sitting room above the shop, because we all liked to sit around the kitchen table at night, talking and playing games with Peter and Simon. We were very busy once we had moved because I don't think I lost a single one of my old customers, Queen Street was very close to Albion Street, and we did attract a lot of passing trade. I always made sure that my prices were fair and I often sold items that other shops didn't stock, particularly as I had so much storage space since Sam had built the sheds in the back yard."

"Sam had bought my old house from Mr Vine, saying that he was doing so to stop anyone else using the parlour to open a shop in competition to mine and when I'd built up some capital again, I gave him half the cost so that Albion Street

became one of our jointly-owned properties, once again rented

out to a family with a son away at the Front.

Chapter Five

"1915 passed very quickly for us and it wasn't long before we were celebrating our first Christmas in Queen Street. I must admit that I did occasionally think about William and wonder where he was and what he was doing, but I didn't ever dwell on thoughts of him. I knew that he wouldn't know that we had moved house and I did wonder if I should try and get in touch with him to give him our new address, but I didn't know where to send a letter. And thinking about sending him a letter always brought me to the same point – it wasn't *our* new house, it was *my* new house and shop and I didn't want him in it."

"I can understand why you felt like that, Nana." Victoria interrupted. "He wasn't pleased when he came home on leave to find that you were managing very well without him, just think how much worse he would have been to discover that you'd bought a bigger property. You would have shown that not only could you manage without him, but that you were extremely successful without him. It wouldn't have done his ego any good at all."

"Very true, pet. But I had moved on in the way I felt about him. When he first went off to war, I was extremely angry with him. When he came home on leave and was so petty and childish over what I had done, I was angry with him, but, by the time I moved into Queen Street, that anger had dissipated. In truth, I no longer cared what mood he was in because I was now indifferent to him. I certainly wasn't hoping that the war would end soon, because the end of the war would signify the end of my life as a single woman as William would return home and I didn't want him back. And I would never have dared to say that to anyone at that time. It not only made me unpatriotic, but it made me a heartless, unfeeling wife."

"I'm sure you were never heartless." Victoria was shocked that her grandmother could have thought about herself as an unfeeling woman. "You were caring for your son and for two other people who weren't part of your family. Nobody could ever have accused you of being heartless and unfeeling."

"I don't know whether anyone else would have accused me, but it was enough for me that that was how I felt. I know Annie was aware of how my feelings for William had changed, but she didn't judge me, so that eased my conscience a bit and then, as we moved through 1916, everyone's thoughts turned to the war, because it was going so badly. When our troops began fighting on the Somme, the newspapers were full of as much detail as they were allowed to publish and they were also full of the lists of the dead. It began to seem that every person in England had lost someone on the battlefields of France and Flanders. There were enormous amounts of telegrams sent to households around Britain, all carrying the terrible news that a son or a father or a brother had died. Some women wouldn't answer the door when the telegraph boy arrived, as though keeping that terrifying piece of paper out of the house meant that their sons or husbands wouldn't be dead."

"I couldn't imagine what it must have been like to learn that your son had been killed on a battlefield, it tore at my heart to even think about it. There were nights when I couldn't leave

Simon, even though he was fast asleep in his little bed, and I would sit holding him tight, praying that this war would be over before he reached the age to go off and fight. I wondered how many other mothers, with boys older than mine, who were whispering that very same prayer as they watched over their sleeping children, all hoping that the war would end before it claimed any more lives."

"It must have been horrendous, Nana, for all those mothers and sisters and wives and then it happened again, less than twenty five years later." Victoria's eyes had filled with tears at the thought of so many deaths.

Nana Lymer patted the hand which had reached out to her as the tears began to fall.

"So much loss and death and destruction. Could it ever be justified? I often wondered about that, particularly when we went to war for the second time. I know many people found solace in religion, but that has never been an outlet for me and the older I get, the less tolerance I seem to have for those who put all their hope in a god. But I was telling you about what it was like at home when our troops were fighting on the Somme. If I keep on getting side-tracked, I'll never get to the end of the story."

"As I said, the newspapers were giving out quite a lot of information on what was happening over in France and many people were beginning to read more into the official reports than they had done before, going on the numbers of soldiers who were being killed and seriously injured. There were also long lists of the missing and convalescing soldiers who were fit enough to return to their families were letting civilians know that 'missing' often meant blown to pieces, so that no trace remained."

"Everywhere that people gathered, be it on street corners, in public houses or, as in our case, in shops, the conversations were always about the war; what was happening and where, who had been killed, who was missing in action etc. etc. etc. You wouldn't have thought it was possible for there to be that many conversations all based on one theme, but that was how it was. It was an all-consuming passion that ate away at the lives of everyone left at home, so that all of everyday life was based on what was happening on the other side of the English Channel.

"It was during one of these discussions that Mrs Horner told us that she had heard that the pig butcher's only son had been killed, on the second day of action on the Somme. Until then, I had known so little about Dennison that I didn't know that he even had a son, but gossip throughout the rest of that day soon filled in all the details. Young Albert was not only the only son, he was also the only child in the Dennison family, a point which made me grieve even more for his mother, given that she had no other children to turn to. The reason for this was revealed when Mrs Horner's cousin, Mrs Battersby, confided in the whole shop that Mrs Dennison had fallen with a second child when Albert was two years old, only to have it beaten out of her when her husband had been told that his wife was extremely friendly with the coal man. Not one of the gossips who were discussing this snippet of information actually believed that the mousy Mrs Dennison would have attracted the attentions of the tall, handsome coal-wagon driver. They all firmly believed that Mr

Dennison had picked up the tale when he was drunk and had misunderstood what was being said. All agreed, however, that the resulting injuries suffered by Mrs Dennison had put paid to any hopes she may have had of having further children."

"Did she go to the police?" Victoria asked, appalled at the idea of such a brute beating a pregnant woman.

"People didn't go to the police in those days." Nana explained, "If she had, they would probably have arrested Dennison, but she would have been too frightened of him to press charges, worried about what he would have done to her when he got home. She knew it was safer for her to keep quiet about it, but she must have suffered both physically and emotionally. I must admit, I was sickened when I learnt the true character of the man, but I was so thankful that Hannah wasn't still working for him."

"Over the next few weeks, Dennison was the subject of much of the gossip in the shop; in fact his actions often made the subject of the war slip to second place in people's minds. He had taken the death of his only child very badly, his neighbours all spreading the word that he was to be overheard every night, bellowing about his loss to any who would listen and that he had taken to regularly frequenting the Red Lion bar and consuming huge amounts of alcohol. This made him even more aggressive than he usually was and he began taking it out on his wife. It soon became unusual to see her without a black eye and cuts and grazes on her face where he had been using her as a punch bag, but the worm turned eventually (when he broke her left arm) and she upped and left him one evening when he was drowning his sorrows in the Red Lion."

"He returned home that night to find his wife gone and to discover that she had taken the contents of the shop till and his strongbox, leaving him penniless and punch bag-less. It was said that his rage was terrible to behold, a statement his neighbour took great delight in expounding on, given that he had once been on the sharp end of Dennison's fist when he had remonstrated with him for hitting his wife. Dennison had taken his meat cleaver and hacked at the marble meat slab in his shop until the cleaver had shattered, leaving pits and hollows in the marble surface."

"Dennison's behaviour then became a problem for us. When he had sobered up, and word on the street said that *that* had taken three full days, he realised that he no longer had a willing slave to provide for his every need, both in his shop and in his house. What he wanted was his young servant girl back, so he high-tailed it round to Sammy's house, demanding that Hannah return to her rightful employment at once, which Sam told him would only happen when Hell froze over. Sam could be quite intimidating in his own way, and because he was defending his daughter, it didn't take Dennison long to realise that he wasn't going to bully Sam into forcing Hannah to return to him. But both Sam and I were worried that Dennison might take it into his head to waylay Hannah on her way to or from the shop and we both knew that Hannah wouldn't be able to fight him off. Sam, because he was working shifts in the iron works, wasn't often at home to be able to deliver Hannah to work and then collect her at the end of the day, so we decided that it would be best if Hannah stayed with me and didn't have to walk the streets at all."

"We both hoped that Dennison would calm down after a couple of weeks and that things could return to normal, but we didn't allow for Dennison's state of mind. I truly believe that the man was bordering on insane and that he should have been committed for the sake of public safety because, three days after calling at Sam's house, he called at the shop."

"The first we knew of his arrival was when the shop door was slammed back against the doorjamb with a force almost strong enough to shatter the door frame and Dennison entered my shop, screaming that he wanted his shop-girl back, he wanted her back now and he would flatten anyone who got in his way.

"Every person in the shop turned to see who was causing such a commotion, then shrank back against the shelves to keep out of Dennison's way. I was in the kitchen behind the shop, with the door open so that I had a clear view of what was happening from where I was standing making pastry for the next batch of pies. My blood ran cold when I saw who it was who was causing the disturbance, but I breathed a sigh of relief when I remembered that Hannah was upstairs doing some housework for me. The only member of staff in the shop at that time was Annie and I knew she would do all she could to stop Dennison getting through to the kitchen. I could also tell that the pig butcher hadn't seen me, because he was making sure that Hannah wasn't hiding behind one of the displays."

"Making as little noise as possible, although it was doubtful whether Dennison would have heard a bomb explode above the noise he was making, I tiptoed through to the back yard, where Simon and Peter were filling the cart with the boxes of orders for delivery that afternoon."

"'Simon,' I hissed at him, as quietly but as forcefully as I could, 'go upstairs to my bedroom and you ask Hannah to lock the door so that you are both safe inside my room. Don't open it for anyone except me. Do you hear me?'

"Simon opened his mouth to question why I was asking him to do something so unusual, but there was a massive crash from inside the shop and he paled and then ran as fast as his little legs could carry him, through the kitchen and up the stairs. I offered up a short prayer that he would do as I had asked and that Hannah would have heard the noise and guessed what was going on. Only pausing long enough to check that Simon was on his way to safety, I then turned to Peter."

"'Run to the iron works and ask the gatekeeper to get Sammy. Tell him Butcher Dennison is on the rampage and we need him here at the shop. Don't give up until the gatekeeper gets Sammy Lymer. Do you understand?'"

"I could have screamed at the slow way in which Peter absorbed my request. He was wide-eyed and obviously afraid because of the crashing noises now emanating from the shop and he stood and stared at me. God forgive me, but in my panic, I took hold of his arm and shook him like a dog shakes a rat. It was too much for Peter and he turned his troubled face to me, his mouth turned down and starting to tremble."

"'Get to the ironworks and ask the gatekeeper to get Sammy Lymer. He's urgently needed at the shop. Do you hear me, Peter?'"

"And I shook him again, my fear communicating itself to him. I'd never laid a finger on the lad until that moment and he was only used to smiles and soft-spoken requests coming from me. He stared back at me, his pet lip trembling as he tried in his oh-so-slow way to understand why I was being so rough with him. I could feel the panic and alarm rising in my chest as more noise came from the shop and it was at that moment when the pig butcher appeared in the kitchen, spittle covering his face and his hair sticking out all round his head. He glanced around the kitchen, obviously searching for Hannah and me and then he noticed that the back door was open and he could see Peter and me standing in the yard."

"'Go, Peter, go!!'" I screamed at him, the time for whispering being past and, thankfully, the sight of the overweight butcher galvanised Peter into action and he set off through the open back yard gate, heading for the ironworks.

Dennison made as if to follow Peter, as if he thought Peter would lead him to Hannah, so I stepped across the yard until I was standing facing him as he moved out of the kitchen and entered the backyard. I was only inches from his swinging fists, but I was overwhelmed by the anger I was feeling at his intrusion of my home and I stood my ground in front of him, oblivious to the fact that I should have been scared to death of him. I should have been cowering away from those massive fists which had already killed his own unborn child, but my own fury was so white-hot within me that he should dare to enter my inner sanctum, unbidden, that I threw caution to the winds."

"I stood, ramrod-straight and in total control of every muscle in my body, and stared him straight in his eye, something which I later learnt that his wife had never managed to do. I then addressed him as though we had met on our way into church."

"'And what can I do for you, Mr Dennison?' I asked, in a very restrained and quiet manner. 'Do you need some stores which I can supply or have you come for some of my famous pies? If so, please come back into the shop and we can serve you where I serve all my customers' and I stepped closer to him and continued to stare straight into his bloodshot eyes. From that distance, I was very aware that he stank of alcohol, bad breath and unwashed body and clothes and it took a great deal of resolve not to shudder and step away from him. I knew, however, that my attitude was affecting him in a way to which he was clearly unused and it was in my interests to keep him off balance. It may have been my quiet tone or the fact that I was so close to him, but whatever it was, the bluster seemed to go out of him a bit and he shook himself like a dog before he replied."

"'I've come for my servant-girl, Mrs High and Mighty,' he said when he managed to remember where he'd left his mouth. 'You stole her from me and I want her back. She's coming with me now, whether you like it or not.'"

"His voice rose as he got to the end of the sentence and he started remembering both why he was there and that people were generally afraid of him. By that time, however, I was in such a white-hot rage with him that I did what no other person had ever done before to him in the whole of his stupid, stinking, fat life. I stepped even closer to him, so that my nose was within half an inch of his and I was almost overpowered by the stench from his mouth, body and clothes. It was nausea-inducing but my fury so intense I overrode my sense of smell as well as my fear."

" 'You get off my property this instant and stop acting like a schoolboy bully in a playground with me, Mr Dennison.' I said, putting as much sarcasm as I could muster into saying his name, but still not raising my voice above a church-pew-during-a-funeral whisper. 'Take your drunken brain home for a rest and don't you ever come threatening me again.'"

"My voice was so quiet and controlled that the pig butcher couldn't decide whether he had heard me properly or not, but he took a step backwards to give himself breathing space and the time to try and think up an answer. Something, I don't know what it was, made me step towards him so that we were once again nose-to-nose."

"'Don't even think about it, Mr Dennison.' I said, as quietly as before. 'Get off my property and go and sober up before you do something you will later regret.'

"I could hear that a crowd had gathered behind me, at the open backyard gate and I prayed that if the butcher turned violent then they would stop him before he did me any real damage. I couldn't rely on anyone to intervene when he started causing me pain, I could only hope, but that didn't stop me. I continued to step forward every time he retreated and I continued to let him know that I wanted him off my property. He was finding it very difficult to understand that I wasn't going to buckle under his bullying attitude, I think because he was so used to his poor little wife cowering in front of him. The fact that I didn't let him intimidate me was what was holding him back from letting his fists fly, so I continued to press forwards, but, at the same time and with a detached part of my brain, I was trying to work out where I went from there. We would eventually run out of back yard and when his back was up against the wall, he could turn nasty again."

"What did you do next?" Victoria was horrified at the thought of the pig butcher hurting her grandmother.

Nana Lymer smiled at Victoria's shock.

"I was at a loss as to what to do next and I was terrified that he would turn violent again if I gave him chance to think and then inspiration struck me. In the same formal but soft voice I had used all along I said,

'I am very sorry about the loss of your son and I couldn't begin to imagine the grief and misery which you must be feeling. But that wasn't my fault, nor was it Hannah's and you won't feel any better for taking your anger and despair out on us. Peter has gone for the constable, Mr Dennison. Don't you think it would be wise if you left before he arrives? You could get into very serious trouble for brawling in the street and, just think on, you can't run your business if you are in a police cell.'"

"That was where I made my first mistake in dealing with the pig butcher. Mentioning his business reminded him of the reason why he was there in my shop and the spittle flew from his slack mouth and splattered across my face as he yelled at the top of his voice.

'I can't run my business without someone to work for me and you've stolen my servant girl. I want her back or I'll break every shelf in your shop and then I'll break every bone in your body.'

"I didn't think it was possible to get any angrier than I already was, but feeling the filthy wetness hit my cheeks and having him screaming abuse in my face froze my rage even further. It was so intense an anger that my sensible brain ceased to function and I acted purely on instinct when he prodded his meaty stinking forefinger into my chest as he threatened to break my bones. I could clearly see his ugly red-veined face, but it had a scarlet aura around it that hid everything else from my view. I could see his huge, round, slobbering, drunken, ugly face, but I was blind to the rest of the world. He had dared to prod me in my chest and I couldn't stop myself from responding as all reasonable thought left my head. I lifted my hand until it was level with his chest and I jabbed my forefinger into an expanse of flabby, dirty shirt-front, at the same time screeching at the top of my lungs for him to 'GET OFF MY PROPERTY.'

"I don't know whether it was shock that I had dared to poke him or surprise because my voice was suddenly so loud right in his face, but he took an involuntary step backwards. I don't kid myself that it was because I was strong enough to topple him with one finger, drunk as he was, or that he was frightened of me for even a single second, but step back he did and the tin bath which should have been hanging on its hook on the backyard wall but for some reason wasn't, caught him behind his knees and his legs buckled under him and he fell backwards into the bath. Because it hadn't been hanging on the wall, the bath had about two inches of cold rainwater in the bottom of it and this fountained out around him as his heavy body dropped into it, splashing me from head to foot with a shock like ice."

"What the cold water was doing to Dennison's nether regions, I neither knew nor cared, but the cold was enough to tip me over the edge into absolute fury and I grabbed his wet hair and shook his head until his teeth were rattling like hailstones on a tin roof, screaming all the time for him to 'GET OFF MY PROPERTY.'"

"I stopped shouting and let go of the butcher's hair when I realised that I could hear laughter coming from behind me and I turned to see a crowd at my open backyard gate, all convulsed with laughter at Dennison's plight. Sammy and Peter were just pushing their way through the crowd and both were grinning from ear to ear at the sight of the overweight lump sitting in our tin bath, still snorting from the shock of his fall and his impromptu bath."

"'Are you all right, lass?' Sammy asked, as soon as he was close enough for me to be able to hear him over the laughter and jeers of my neighbours. 'I never thought the drunken bugger would come here trying to lay down the law with you, even though I did think he might try going after our Hannah.'"

"'I'm all right, Sammy.' I answered, although I had to admit that I was feeling pretty shaky, more from the anger I had felt than fear, although I wasn't sure.'"

"Sammy turned to Dennison, who was just starting to climb out of the bath, all the fight having gone out him, what with the shock of his fall, the cold dousing he had had, and the jeers and catcalls of the neighbours."

"'You ever try coming after my Hannah again, Dennison.' Sam said, 'And I'll run you through with my father's campaign sword he got in the Crimea. Do you understand me?'"

"But, before the pig butcher could answer him, a voice shouted from the gateway."

"'You've no right coming after women like that. You want to find someone your own size to pick on.'"

"There were cries of agreement from the gathered crowd out there and Mr Nugent, who lived next door-but-one to my shop, shouted,

'You try attacking Mrs Drinkwater like that again, butcher-boy, and we'll give you the pasting you deserve. We all know your lad's been killed at the Front, but that's not this lass's fault.

She's only trying to keep a roof over her head, while her lad's away fighting and you should be ashamed of yourself for trying to attack her. She's not the size of twopennorth of copper!'

"There were general cries of agreement at this statement and, to be honest, it was those which reduced me, finally, to tears. Annie came and put her arm around my shoulders and led me into the kitchen, away from the gathered crowd. Hannah had come downstairs with Simon, now that all danger seemed past and, sensible lass that she was, she was putting the kettle on for a restorative cup of tea."

"I almost collapsed onto the fireside chair while Annie and Hannah fussed round me and Simon buried his face into my aproned lap, aware that there had been a lot of shouting and banging and not sure if it was all over now. I cuddled him to me, whispering words of comfort which were as much for my benefit as his. Peter followed us into the kitchen within minutes, although Sammy stayed outside until all was peaceful again."

'"He's gone.' He announced, as he came through the back door and gratefully took the tea Hannah proffered him. 'Some of the lads from Westcough's brewery yanked him out of the bath and are escorting him back to his own shop. The crowd have dispersed now that all the excitement is over so I've locked the back gate. I'm going to come with you when you deliver the orders tonight, Bia, just in case the idiot takes it into his head to have another go, although I think he'll think twice about bothering you again now he's seen that so many people are against him. Let's just hope that he's learnt his lesson now and doesn't get it into his head to try that trick again.'

'"I don't think he'll try anything again.' I said, with far more confidence than I was feeling, nodding down at Simon who was still hiding his head in my apron. 'He's had enough of a shock to stop him ever coming back here again.'

Sam picked up on this immediately.

'That big baby won't come back for another cold bath, that's for sure. I don't think he likes having a bath, the spluttering he was doing.'

"Simon raised his head from my apron and smiled at Sammy."

"'Dirty man,' he said, grinning shyly at Sam. 'Dirty man doesn't like water.'"

'You are right there, Simon. That dirty man won't be having another bath for a long, long time.'

"I smiled at Sammy over the top of Simon's head, trying to show my gratitude for his instant understanding, but Sam just smiled and gave his head a little shake, brushing off the compliment. Hannah and Annie went back into the shop to serve the customers who were once more queuing for their groceries and Simon followed them. I could hear him asking for a sugar mouse from the jar as he sidled up to Hannah and there was the distinct sound of a large glass jar being lifted from the shelf and then opened."

"'Don't worry about him, pet.' Sam said, as he stretched his feet out towards the warmth of the range. 'Those brewery lads were a bit rough with him as they got him out of that bath and they carried him like one of his own sides of bacon to get him back to his shop. I've had a few words with some of your neighbours while I was out there and they'll keep an eye out for him reappearing at any time. But I think he's realised that he's not welcome anywhere round here now, so you and little Simon will be safe.'"

"'Thank you, Sammy.' I said, relieved that the pig butcher had been warned off in that manner, because I was still shaking from the shock of it all."

"'You've got a rare temper on you, lass, when you've got your dander up like that. I almost felt sorry for old Dennison, having you nose to nose with him. It's one of the funniest things I've seen in a long time, you poking him and him falling backwards into that bath! It's done me a power of good. I haven't had a laugh like that in a long time.'"

"'Well, I must say, I hope you enjoyed it! I must do it again so that everyone can enjoy themselves.' I said tartly, a bit put-out by Sammy's delight in watching Dennison get his come-uppance."

"'No, you don't have to do it again. I'm just trying to lighten the atmosphere a bit.' Sam said. 'I know how much it's shaken you to have him forcing his way into your house and none of us want it to happen again, but you mustn't dwell on it. Anyway, I've got to get back to work. They'll be docking my pay if I'm out much longer.'

"I knew he had to get back to the works, but I was extremely grateful for what he'd done for me that day. Even though I prided myself on my independence, it had been good to know I had someone close on whom I could rely in a crisis. It marked the next stage in our relationship. We were now very good, close friends."

Victoria had been silent all through this monologue, concentrating on what her grandmother was telling her but also trying to imagine what it must have been like to have faced down a bully like Dennison.

"Did he come back, the pig butcher I mean?" She asked. "Or did he learn his lesson and stay away from you and Hannah?"

Nana Lymer smiled a rather wan smile.

"He stopped bothering us about Hannah," she said. "But that wasn't the last I saw of him, not by a long way. But I'm tired now, pet. I think I could do with a little nap to recover from all this talking. Why don't you come back tomorrow and we'll talk about it then? Is that ok?"

Victoria felt incredibly guilty for keeping Nana talking when she was obviously tired. She berated herself for not keeping an eye on her and stopping her when she started showing the first signs of fatigue. Victoria could clearly see the dark rings under her grandmother's eyes, standing out starkly because her face was very pale. She tucked her up into the blankets and then tiptoed out of the room, silently promising that she would take

more care of Nana tomorrow.

Chapter Six

The next day was Christmas Eve and Victoria knew it was going to be a bad day before she even got downstairs. She could hear her mother's voice from the bathroom while she was cleaning her teeth, the decibel level and the screech level both pointing to one of her mother's bad moods. As she walked downstairs, hoping that her mother was only complaining to a delivery man, the decibel level rose and Victoria could make out the subject of her mother's diatribe.

"Why wasn't the bread ready for collection? Don't they know that it's Christmas Eve and the world and his wife will be coming in for extra bread to get them through the holiday? What am I supposed to tell the customers? Sorry, you'll have to wait till next week before you can have a loaf."

Victoria couldn't make out what her father said in reply. His deeper tone and the fact that he was keeping his temper remarkably well meant that she couldn't make out the words he was using, but she could tell that he was trying to be reasonable and to make his wife see sense. Victoria couldn't understand why he never shouted back at her mother or why he always kept his temper with her, but that was how it was. She opened the door and slipped into the kitchen, wincing as the volume coming from her mother rose even higher. She hoped that the tardiness of the bakery would keep her mother occupied but it was a vain hope as her mother turned on her the instant she got through the door.

"Don't be thinking that you can spend all day today sitting with her upstairs again, cos you can't. It'll be all hands to the pumps today. It's Christmas Eve, you know."

"Yes, I do know it's Christmas Eve and I also know that I'll have to work in the shop today because it will be busy." Victoria hoped to head her mother off at the pass, but she failed again.

"Too right you'll have to work in the shop. That's what keeps you in fancy clothes, you know miss. It's only right that you take your turn working with the rest of us. I can't be expected to do everything on my own."

Victoria's dad had had enough.

"You don't do everything on your own. I'm in there all day, every day, as well as you. I'm now going back to the bakery because the bread should be ready by now and I'll be back and have it in the display case before we open. Can we just get on with it, please?"

And he disappeared out of the side door, making good his escape before his wife found something else to complain about. He needn't to have bothered because Bia had found her next victim and wasn't going to let go of this one quite so easily.

"Right," she began. "You can take Nana Lymer her breakfast and then, when you've had yours, I want you out there in the shop ready to fill up shelves and weigh potatoes out ready for us opening. They'll all want extra veg today and we're not losing any sales just because the shelves are half empty."

"Yes, Mam." Victoria said, as she hoisted the tray bearing Nana's breakfast into her arms and set off for the stairs.

"And don't be spending too long giving her that tray. You only need to put it in front of her and she can do the rest herself." Her mother couldn't resist having the last word, even when there hadn't been any argument. Victoria sighed as she mounted the stairs, wondering if her mother would ever speak nicely to her or if that was a pipe dream never to be realised.

Nana was sitting up in bed waiting for her breakfast, the bed jacket wrapped tightly round her little frame and a heart-warming smile on her lips.

"Good morning, pet," she said, as soon as Victoria opened the door. "We won't be able to have our little chat today, will we? Your mother's on top form already and it's not eight o'clock yet. I could hear her from here."

Victoria smiled a little ruefully.

"We've no chance of getting even five minutes today. She was on the warpath before I even got downstairs. The bakery hadn't got our order ready when Dad went for it so she was declaring that we wouldn't have any bread and the customers will all go elsewhere. Dad's gone to get it now, though, cos they'd told him it would be ready before we opened."

"That's your mother, pet, always makes a drama out of a crisis, I often wonder where she gets the energy from to complain so much. Never mind, we should get some time tomorrow afternoon, after Christmas dinner."

"I certainly hope so, Nana, because I won't be able to stand being in the same room with her all day, not when the shop's closed and she can concentrate on putting right all my faults."

"I know, chick. I don't understand why she has such a down on you. It isn't as though you are a bad lass, trawling the streets and making a name for yourself. You go to school and do your homework when you should; you get good exam results and you work hours in the shop for very little reward. If you ask me, your mother doesn't know a good daughter when she sees one, but if she keeps harping on at you she'll push you away completely. You get back downstairs before she starts again and I'll see you tomorrow."

"Ok Nana. You have a rest today and get the next part of the story ready for me."

It was very busy in the shop all morning. Victoria didn't have chance to think about anything other than the customer she was serving. Every time one customer was satisfied, another appeared in their place and it was well after lunchtime before they even got chance to have a coffee break. They took it in turns to snatch a sandwich each for lunch, then, as the tide of customers seemed to be abating, Victoria filled every shelf she could find with every tin, box and tube she could find, so that the shop was still well-stocked. By four o'clock, the tide of customers had turned into a trickle and she was amazed when her mother stopped her from filling up the fridge with more cheese.

"That'll do, Victoria. I reckon that the rush is over now. Go and see if Nana is ok and you can stay with her till I call you for your tea."

Victoria was terrified that her mother would change her mind before she got out of the shop, but there was no screech following her as she climbed the stairs.

"It's quietened down in the shop so Mam said I could come and sit with you! Isn't that great?"

"That's wonderful, pet. Are you too tired to make a drink, only I'm dying of thirst?"

"Of course I will, Nana." Victoria said. "Shall I bring some biscuits up? To keep us going till tea-time?"

"You do that, pet. That sounds lovely. I'll get my thoughts in order because I wasn't expecting you today."

Victoria rushed back down into the kitchen, put the kettle on, got the cups and the biscuits and then hopped from foot to foot, willing the kettle to boil quicker so that she could escape

161

before her mother came into the kitchen and announced that she had changed her mind about Victoria sitting upstairs. But the coast was still clear when the tea was ready and Victoria carried it back up to Nana's bedroom and then settled herself down in her favourite chair for the next instalment.

"We didn't hear any more from the pig butcher after his bath and thoughts of him and what else he might do were wiped from our minds when there was an accident in the iron works." Nana Lymer began the next part of her story. "The first I knew about it was when one of the cooling towers exploded and the noise was heard all over the town. People went out into the streets to find out what had happened, but then a huge pall of black smoke, pushed by the strong wind, came from the direction of the ironworks and nobody could stay out in it for long. The smell alone was horrendous, but the black smoke billowed down every street in the town, whirling through every open door and window and leaving a layer of black ash over everything it touched. People who had run towards the works came back with their faces and clothes covered in it, coughing and retching as though they were going to bring up their insides."

"Some of the houses which were in the streets surrounding the works were damaged by the force of the explosion and three women and a child were killed by falling masonry. It was a terrible time for the town and even the War was forgotten while rescuers dug survivors out of the rubble and collected the dead from inside the works. Four workmen were killed altogether; bringing the total of the dead to eight, but the number of the wounded was a shock to us all. Over forty workmen were injured, some badly, some not so badly and that led to a lot of misery in the town. There was an investigation into what had happened and the report later produced blamed some of it on working practises. The war was using up iron and steel faster than the works could produce them and there had been corners cut to increase output, with the inevitable conclusion being the explosion."

"After the dust had settled, literally, there were families who had lost their breadwinner and families who were temporarily without income and the town pulled together to help them. There was a fund set up to help and all the businesses in the town made a donation, my little shop included, so that no-one would starve, but life was still very tough for a lot of people, coming on top of the families who had lost their breadwinners because of the war."

"One such family was the I'Anson family who lived at number 46 Queen Street. Mrs I'Anson had shopped with me from the day I had opened my first shop, spending nearly all her husband's wages, apart from what was needed for the rent, on food in my shop. Two weeks after the explosion in the works, when the rescue money had been doled out to the needy families, I was in the window of the shop, putting up a display of skirts which I had made for those women who were now working and didn't have the time to make their own clothes anymore."

"Mrs I'Anson, who was a tiny little thing who looked as though a good puff of wind would knock her over, passed the window about five times, but never came in. I was puzzled by her behaviour, particularly because she didn't have any of her five children with her and I did wonder who was looking after them for her. I had a lot of time for the I'Anson family, because the husband was a hard worker who always worked whatever overtime was going and didn't waste any of his money on drink. Mrs I'Anson looked after the children who were always spotlessly turned out and who were very well behaved. I didn't have to keep a close eye on any of her children when they were in my shop, not like some children who were trained in shop-lifting from an early age."

"Mr I'Anson had been wounded when the explosion occurred in the ironworks but, luckily, he had been hauled out of the rubble with only cuts and abrasions and a broken leg. The broken leg had been set, but would obviously take time to mend and, although the works were soon up and running again, it was going to be a while longer before he would be able to work (and get paid) again."

"All of this was running through my head as I continued to arrange the skirts in what I hoped was an attractive display in the window facing Queen Street. We were lucky in that we had another window on the other side of the shop which faced out over King Street, us being on the corner of the two streets, making my displays visible to anyone who walked past."

"The sixth time she walked past, Mrs I'Anson stopped right at the corner of the two streets and seemed to be making a decision. After a couple of minutes, and I must admit I had stopped work and was watching her; she turned about and finally entered the shop. She hesitated in the doorway and then spied me where I was perched on the window ledge, giving one of the skirts a good shake to make it look more attractive."

"Mrs I'Anson came towards me, looking as though she was heading into battle and by-passing both Hannah and Annie as she did so. When she reached me she stopped and, in a very quiet voice, asked if she could have a word with me in private. I could see that she had wound herself up for something which she obviously considered to be very serious, so I invited her through into the kitchen, so that we wouldn't be overheard. I closed the kitchen door behind us, which was something we rarely did so Annie and Hannah would know not to disturb us, and invited

Mrs I'Anson to take a seat at the kitchen table. When we were both seated comfortably, she stayed silent, wringing her hands together and glaring at them as though they had a life of their own and she couldn't control them."

"'You wanted a word with me, Mrs I'Anson,' I prompted her, when the silence between us had stretched to a couple of minutes. 'Please, you can say what you want to me. It will remain private between us; you have my word on that.' I could tell that she had no idea where to begin, but her hesitation was making the whole situation worse for her and I was beginning to feel very uncomfortable."

"'I, I er need to ask you a favour, Mrs Drinkwater,' she finally said, continuing the hand-wringing and still not raising her face from them. 'You'll have heard that my Bert was one of the workmen injured in the explosion?'"

"I knew that she wasn't expecting me to answer that so I just nodded and she continued with her tale."

"'We got some money from the fund which was set up to help people like us, but it wasn't a huge amount and, not to put too fine a point on it, we've now spent it all. I think I've spent it wisely but the fact remains that it's now all gone and I've got the children to feed.'"

"I noted that she only mentioned feeding the children and she rose even more in my estimation, because it was obvious that she put her and her husband's welfare right at the bottom of her list of concerns. I understood how she felt because I had always felt like that about Simon, as long as he was well-fed and happy, it didn't matter about me."

"'I wondered if you would take my wedding ring as payment for some food and hold it, so that I could buy it back from you when Bert gets back to work.' she asked."

"It had cost her a great deal to beg like that and I knew that she had only done it for the sake of the children. When she had finished speaking, her whole body slumped down on the chair and she looked like a condemned man. She was obviously expecting me to refuse to help her, but she wouldn't give up before she had tried everything she could think of to feed her children."

"I put out my hand and patted her on her arm."

"There's no need for you to lose your wedding ring, Mrs I'Anson." I replied immediately. "You can have your weekly shopping for as long as it takes Mr I'Anson to get back to work and then you can pay me back as and when you are able. I would do anything to make sure that my Simon is fed and provided for, so I fully understand how you must be feeling."

"The relief on her face was indescribable. It was though someone had lit a lamp behind her eyes and her joy shone out over me. She insisted on leaving her wedding ring with me, even though I told her I didn't need collateral for her loan and, to cut a long story short, when her husband got back to work, the first thing she did was to repay the money and receive her wedding ring back. I didn't charge her the full amount for her groceries because I knew life would be difficult for them even after Mr

I'Anson was working again, especially when I discovered that their landlord had insisted on having all of his back rent paid in full. The next time one of mine and Sammy's houses came available, I offered it to the I'Ansons at a rent lower than what they had been paying for number 46 and they moved happily into it."

"That poor woman!" Victoria exclaimed. "How could her landlord expect her to be able to pay their rent when her husband had been injured? You were very good to her, letting her have the food cheaper and then finding them somewhere to live."

Nana Lymer shook her head.

"I wasn't being a saint, Victoria," she answered. "I admired that couple because they put their children before themselves, the same as I did, and I had no intention of making a profit out of their misfortune. I wouldn't have been able to live with my conscience if I had done that. But I haven't told you about the I'Ansons to make me look good, I've told you because it had a bearing on what happened to me next."

"I don't think that Mr or Mrs I'Anson told anyone else how they had been helped, but word seemed to get round that I would take certain goods in payment for food when times were hard and it wasn't long after this that I found myself running a small pawn-broking business alongside the shop. I was very careful about what goods I would accept and from whom, because I had no intentions of being caught for fencing stolen items, but I regularly accepted wedding rings and other small items of jewellery, as well as things like silver tea sets or boxes and supplied food to the value of my estimation of their worth. I say my estimation of their worth because I had no specialist knowledge of gold and silver, but I made my estimations on the price of similar items in the jewellery shops' windows, always subtracting a percentage which I felt was added as the profit on each item."

"I later learned that I had underestimated the value of many items, but never because I wanted to squeeze extra money out of those experiencing hard times, it was always a genuine mistake on my part."

"Did people come back and collect their possessions when they had the money to pay for them?" Victoria wanted to know, finding it difficult to imagine what pawning an item of value would be like.

"Some people got their possessions back, others never did find the money and I soon amassed a very strange assortment of items which I stored in the strong box I kept in my bedroom. I intended that one day, when I wasn't quite so busy, I would sort them out and sell what I considered to be valuable items and use the money for Simon to go to a good school when he was older. In the meantime, the strong box had items added to it quite regularly and it became yet another string to my bow."

"Did anyone try to cheat you with these items, Nana?" Victoria asked. "You know, did anyone pretend something was gold when it wasn't?"

"Sometimes, pet." Nana Lymer smiled at her question. "For some reason that I've never understood, I was always pretty good at being able to tell what was real gold and what wasn't. Added to which, I didn't accept any items from those whom I considered to be villains or ruffians although, as I accepted items in place of payment for food, the ruffians tended to stick to the real pawnbrokers where they got cash for their goods. Usually, my customers were those who were genuinely in need, not tricksters out to make a killing. Anyway, that became my third business venture, albeit a venture I sort of fell into rather than one I had planned."

"Things were getting worse as far as the War was concerned and the big operations in France and Flanders were killing so many of our boys that there were few places left in the British Isles where there wasn't a roll call of the dead. To make things worse, the Hun were being particularly successful in sinking merchant shipping, which was affecting the supply of food. I had contracts with a few local farmers but I was afraid that there would come a time when there would be shortages and I had to have a contingency plan for maintaining my supplies. I decided that it would be a good idea to buy in as much nonperishable food as I was able to get hold of, but with that idea came the problem of storage."

"Our new place in Queen Street had more storage space than in my old house, but I needed more and that was when one of the warehouses at the dockside became available for rent. I thought it would be a good place to store food for various reasons; it was out of sight of most people in the town so I could fill it without anyone being aware of what I was doing; there was always a gatekeeper and the dock workers about so it was unlikely that any thieves would consider it easy game and, best of all, it was the ideal place for receiving goods which had arrived by ship or by train, the station being next to the docks."

"Sam knew what I was doing, of course, because I had discussed it with him before I paid the first rent on the building and he tramped the whole area finding other sources of supply so that we soon had a goodly amount of stock stacked in the warehouse. I got very friendly with the dockworkers and the gatekeepers because I always took pies, pasties and ginger beer for them whenever I went down there and they repaid me by letting me know whenever a shipment had got through the blockades, carrying goods they thought might be of interest to me."

"I always took Peter with me whenever I went to the docks because he was good protection for me and he loved to jaunt around the town. He had filled out over the last couple of years because he and Annie were eating a lot better since they had started to work for me and his shoulders had broadened with the extra exercise he was getting. He was as big as a barn door, but his brain hadn't kept up with his body's growth and, inside, he was still only a little boy. There were times when Simon could more easily understand what was being explained to him than Peter could, but he had made it his purpose in life to look after me and one growl from him could dissuade any sailor who thought he could try it on when we passed on the dock road."

"Another benefit I got from renting the warehouse was an idea which was planted in my mind by the man who rented the warehouse next to mine, Mr Sanderson. He was a grain importer who was very worried by the amount of ships being lost to the enemy, some of which had contained his grain as part of their cargo and it was now rotting on the seabed. One day, as I was commiserating with him over another such loss, he informed me that he was salting wealth away in case his business collapsed as a result of enemy action. I asked him if he was keeping the money in the bank, because it wasn't safe to have cash on his premises, but he wasn't keeping cash. He told me an old sea captain had advised him years before to always put his money in gems not in gold or stocks and shares. The price of both gold and stocks could (and did) vary enormously, but jewels never lost their value. An added bonus was that they were small and could be easily concealed either in a house or about the person."

"I mulled over that conversation in my mind for the rest of the day and that night, after Simon had had his bath and bedtime story, I took out the stash of jewellery which I had hidden in my bedroom. There wasn't a huge quantity, but I had a few gold rings, a couple of gold brooches and some bracelets. Quite a few of them had gemstones in their settings and although

I could recognise pearls, sapphires and rubies, there were a few which I couldn't identify. Don't run away with the idea that I had amassed a small fortune, because I hadn't, but I needed to know the true worth of the whole collection. I had given foodstuffs to the value I placed on them, but I had no idea of what I would get for them if I sold them."

"I resolved that the next day I would go to one of the big jewellers in the centre of town and ask them for a valuation. If they turned out to be worth a decent amount, I would work out some method of carrying them hidden about my person. Perhaps I could make a padded pocket which would hang inside my skirt and not reveal itself to the outside world."

"The next day, I visited the two largest jewellers in the town and asked them both for a valuation of my little pieces and they both arrived at a sum that simply stunned me. It appeared that I had an eye for gems, to add to my ability to tell real gold from fake and my little stash was worth a considerable amount. Word soon got round town that not only would I accept brooches and chains in payment for food, but that on occasions I would give cash for a jewel that I particularly liked. And I liked them a lot if they were worth money. I was very careful not to give too much money out for a piece of jewellery, but I was always determined to give what I considered a fair price, particularly if the recipient was a decent, hard-working member of the community. I never had the intention of making a huge profit out of the misery that the War had engendered which was why I kept my council over what I owned and I didn't live in an ostentatious manner. I have never in my life wasted money or bought items I didn't need. I left that sort of behaviour to those who made money on the black market out of people's misery."

"Times were changing rapidly through those first couple of years of the War. So many men had been killed or injured, so many households lost their breadwinners and women were now doing many horrendous jobs to help out with the war effort and to keep their families fed and housed. I was so grateful that I had had the foresight to start my shop when I did and, although I worked very hard and for long hours, I was ably supported by Annie and Peter and, of course, Sam and Hannah.

Because of my contacts in the dockyard and my contracts with many local farmers, I always had stock to sell and we suffered a lot less than many other businesses. Sam continued to find houses for us to buy to rent out and, during the whole of the War, we only evicted two families for non-payment of rent. Both of these families had husbands working in the iron works and earning good money and should have been able to manage their budgets well, but both sets of parents had taken to drink and thievery to support their needs for alcohol. It distressed me very greatly to have them evicted and I found it very hard to live with what I considered to be the guilt of throwing families onto the streets, but we had let them remain for a lot longer than any other landlords would have done. I had to remind myself that all that I did was for Simon and I had to put him before anything else."

"You couldn't let them live rent free, Nana," Victoria said. "It wasn't your fault that they were weak people and you couldn't carry everyone's burdens on your back."

"I know, chick, but the guilt ate at me for a long time. I couldn't help it."

"Did you collect a lot of jewellery Nana? Did you sell it all or did you wear some of it?" Victoria was fascinated by the idea of owning gold and precious jewels and secretly wondered if there were any gems hidden in Nana Lymer's possessions in that very room. Nana laughed at the questions.

"Wear some of it?" she said. "No, I was up to my ears in flour, potatoes and cooked meats all day, every day! I didn't have the time or the inclination for dressing like a countess. Anyway, those gems were for Simon's schooling so that he would get a good job when he was older and never have to worry where his next meal was coming from. They were a means to an end for me, not for decoration. Now, where was I with the story? Oh yes, I had rented the warehouse down near the docks."

Nana thought for a moment, trying to get the events of the early decades of the twentieth century organised in her mind before she continued her tale.

"In July of 1916, Mr Sanderson, the grain merchant, lost his son on the Somme and lost his appetite for life in business at the same time. His wife had died before the War began and his son's death meant there was only him and his daughter left of their little family. He couldn't face the daily grind and worry that his grain business consisted of, so he sold up and went to live in one of the small villages on the other side of Eston Hills. I can't remember which village, but that doesn't matter. He bought a smallholding and intended raising chickens there and pretending that the horrors of war weren't happening. I felt sorry for his daughter, who I felt deserved a bit more out of life, but I couldn't imagine how terrible it must be to lose a child, so I wished him well in his new venture and carried on working."

"Three days after Mr Sanderson had left, Peter and I were down at the dockside, supervising the unloading of some stock from a ship which had just berthed when I saw someone open the door of Mr Sanderson's warehouse. I glanced across to see who was my new 'neighbour' and realised that it was the pig butcher who was locking the door. I tried to get into my warehouse before he saw me, but he turned his head as I moved and I couldn't pretend that I hadn't seen him. I stood still, unsure of what to do next, but he took that decision out of my hands and started walking towards me. I wondered whether I should lock myself into the warehouse until he had gone, but I had to admit that I hadn't heard any scurrilous gossip about him since he had been man-handled out of my backyard, so I dithered on my warehouse doorstep, watching him as he strode across the roadway between the buildings."

"'Mrs Drinkwater.' He said, lifting his cap as he stopped in front of me. He seemed to be sober and was speaking civilly, so I took my cue from that and answered in the same fashion."

"'Good afternoon, Mr Dennison.' I answered politely. "Have you taken the empty warehouse, then?"

"He stepped towards me to continue the conversation and I had an overwhelming desire to back away from him, but the pride which had made me face him down in my backyard now kept me standing my ground."

"'I'm expanding my business, Mrs Drinkwater. I've been quite successful since I stopped drinking and I've bought out Mr Sanderson's interest in the grain store. Food is at a premium in these bad times.'"

"I couldn't agree more." I replied. "That has been my stock phrase since I started my business, people will always need to eat, no matter what is happening in the world. I'm glad you are having a successful time, Mr Dennison." I inclined my head at him and then turned to go, but his next words brought me up short."

"'I've got you to thank for it, Mrs Drinkwater. You gave me more than a soaking that day in your backyard. You made me take a long, hard look at myself and I didn't like what I saw. I have been working extremely hard to redeem myself ever since.'"

"I didn't trust him." Nana continued, with a grimace on her face as though she had sucked a lemon by mistake. "The words slipped too glibly off his tongue for them to ring true and, let's face it, a leopard never changes its spots, however much it tries to hide in the undergrowth. A lifelong drunken bully doesn't become a pillar of society overnight. But the proof of his redemption would be how he coped the next time life took a swing at him, not an occasion I intended to hang around to find out. At that moment, Peter arrived at my shoulder to tell me that the stock was now all in the warehouse and we could go home. I thanked him and turned back to the pig butcher."

"'I hope you continue to be successful, Mr Dennison." I said, but the butcher wasn't listening."

"'I see you've still got that young bull hanging around, then,' he commented."

"I heartily disliked his tone as he nodded at Peter and I sprang to his defence immediately."

184

"'Peter is a very good worker, Mr Dennison.' I said. 'And he's good protection for me in this part of town. He always comes with me when I come here and he wouldn't let anything happen to me.'"

"I didn't think it was a bad idea to let the pig butcher know that I wasn't ever alone when I came down to the docks, because all my nerve-endings were screaming at me that Dennison was trouble with a capital 'T'. As we walked away from him, I distinctly heard him mutter under his breath that he wasn't the only one who needed to change, that I could learn a lesson on that subject as well. I chose to pretend that I hadn't heard him, although my heart was fluttering uneasily at his comment. My uneasy feelings at his proximity to my warehouse were strengthened as we walked out of the dock gates a few moments later, when the gatekeeper asked if I'd seen my new neighbour."

"'All sweetness and light, isn't he?' he said, when I answered in the affirmative. 'I wouldn't trust yon bugger with the church bells, I wouldn't. I don't care how many people he

185

tells that he's off the drink, that doesn't mean it'll last. One of Satan's angels, that one, you mind my words. There'll be more trouble from him before long, or my name isn't Tom Taylor.'"

"I muttered a quiet agreement, hoping against hope that I wouldn't have to see too much of Dennison, but Peter's next words frightened me the most."

"'Why did that man sit in our bath, Mrs D? All those people laughed at him and he was very cross. He said you had a lesson to learn, I heard him, when you started to walk away from him. What did he mean? Are you going to go to school, then?'"

"I forced myself to laugh and assured him that I wasn't going anywhere, but the cold fingers of fear touched my spine and wouldn't let go, not even when I was sitting in our famous bath that night, up to my neck in hot water."

Chapter Seven

"The thought of the pig butcher and his threats hung over me for more than a week. It didn't matter what I did during the day to take my mind off him, this lesson I was going to learn was always at the forefront of my conscious thought. I worked all day thinking about it and I couldn't sleep at night for the pictures which rose, unbidden, every time I closed my eyes. I worked until every bone in my body ached for lack of sleep, but as soon as I tried to sleep, his face rose up in front of my mind."

"Then, something else happened which managed to push all thoughts of the pig butcher out of my head. William came home. He came home minus an arm and with some terrible wounds to his legs, but he was carrying a chip on his shoulder that could have been crafted into a table, six chairs and a Welsh dresser, with enough wood left over to complete a wardrobe and dressing table."

"Oh my goodness! How had he been injured? And why was he carrying a chip on his shoulder? It wasn't *your* fault that he'd been wounded, was it?" Victoria was furious for her grandmother, having to endure the tantrums of her husband just because she was better able to cope with life than he was.

The bedroom burst open as Victoria's mother slammed into the room.

"Get off your backside, lady and get down those stairs to help me do the tea. I've been shouting for you for a good ten minutes and you just ignore me and carry on doing what you want. It's not Christmas yet, you know. There's a lot of hard work to be got through before *I* can have a nice rest like you!"

Victoria didn't argue; that wasn't something anyone did when her mother was in one of her moods and it was obvious that she *was* in one of her moods. She said a hurried goodbye to Nana Lymer and then went straight to the kitchen and began peeling potatoes for tea.

"You are too hard on that girl, Bia, you'll lose her one of these days, you mark my words." Nana had often tried to make her daughter less aggressive towards her only child, but it was a pointless exercise. She often didn't say anything because she had a shrewd idea that it could have the opposite effect of what she intended and that Bia would be even more harsh with Victoria. To divert her attention away from the girl, she made an announcement she had been mulling over for the last few days. "I'm going to get up tomorrow and have Christmas dinner with the rest of the family at the table."

Bia was immediately against this. She had no wish for her mother to take up the reins of her life once more and start interfering in the running of the shop. As far as the general public were concerned, Bia and Jack owned and ran the shop and if her mother began mixing with the customers there was a good chance that she would remind everyone that, in fact, *she* still owned the property. When her mother had taken to her bed the previous year, after falling when she had been on one of her midnight strolls around the town, Bia had thought that she would never get up again and she had lost no time in letting the neighbours know that she and her husband had bought the business from her mother. If Nana Lymer decided she was well enough to come downstairs, then Bia's story could be scuppered.

"And what if you fall again, trying to get down the stairs?" she quickly said. "If you break a bone at your age, it could finish you off for good."

"I'm prepared to take that risk because I'm bored with living in this bedroom and only seeing you and Victoria, even though I love chatting to her. I would like to have some quality of life back, before I get too old to enjoy it."

"Do you think *I've* got any 'quality of life'?" Bia shouted at her mother. "I spend all day working my fingers to the bone in that shop, as well as running up and down stairs to care for you and you want to get up to improve your 'quality of life'. What will happen if you fall again? I'll have even more work to do, that's what will happen, but you don't care, do you?"

"Of course I care." Nana knew that she was losing the argument before it had really started. "I think I would make less work for you if I could come downstairs and help in the kitchen. I'm not an invalid, you know."

"You might not be an invalid, but you're doing your best to make me into one." Bia said. "If you didn't have me to look after you, then you'd have to go into a home and you wouldn't want that to happen, would you?"

"Ok, Bia. You win. I won't come downstairs tomorrow, but I'm not stopping in bed all day. I shall get dressed and sit in my chair."

"You do that." Bia's reply was terse. "You do what you want, just don't make any more work for me. I'll go and get your tea, and then you can rest. I want our Victoria to help me prepare the vegetables for tomorrow, so she won't be visiting you any more today."

Nana Lymer stayed where she was after Bia had slammed out of the bedroom, wondering what she could do to make life a little better for Victoria. She pondered for a while and then came to a decision; although she wouldn't be able to put her

192

plan into action without a little help from Victoria herself and it would have to wait until after Christmas.

Victoria was also wondering what she could do to alleviate the pressure she felt from her mother, but she couldn't see any way out of the situation until she was old enough to leave home. She hoped she would be able to do that when she went off to college to do the teacher-training she was determined she was going to do after she had finished her A-levels. But that was over two years away, because she would be taking her O-levels the following June and then there would be two more years of study before she could apply to train to be a teacher. Could she spend the next two and a half years with her mother? The constant sniping was reducing her confidence in herself and the older she got, the more it intensified, making her less and less sure of herself. If only her mother would stop pointing out her faults all the time.

Her mother entered the kitchen at this point and Victoria bent her head to her task of peeling potatoes, waiting for the comment which would inform her that she couldn't even peel potatoes properly. She didn't have long to wait.

"Why do you have to leave such a thick layer of potato still attached to the skin?" Her mother complained. "If I've told you once, I've told you a thousand times that you are wasting good food! Do it properly!"

"Yes, mam. Sorry, mam." Victoria mumbled, putting her head down so that her mother wouldn't see the red suffusing her face, a redness that appeared when she was angry, not ashamed. Her mother, however, didn't miss the blush that had coloured her daughter's cheeks and it satisfied her that she had the power to provoke that reaction in the girl, misreading the blush for shame rather than anger.

Christmas Day was fairly peaceful in the house, without the constant banging of the shop door and the chatter of the customers. Victoria helped with the breakfast, exclaimed her delight at every present and then helped prepare the meal, hoping she could get through Christmas Day without the carping criticism of her mother. It worked so well that Bia allowed her to go and sit with her Nana after they had finished the washing up and Victoria sped to her bedroom before her mother could change her mind.

Nana was in her armchair, wearing her dressing gown because she hadn't managed to dress herself without any help and Bia had made it very clear that *she* wasn't going to help her that morning.

"I didn't think you would be allowed to come and see me today, not after the paddy your mother was having yesterday." Nana said, beaming at Victoria as she placed a cup of tea and two mince pies on her little table.

"No, I thought I wouldn't be able to come and sit with you for the rest of the holidays, but Mam is in a better mood today. Dad says she gets very tired working in the shop and that's why she loses her temper so easily."

"Your father is a saint." Nana replied. "But we can go on with my story, now you are here, but only if you want me to, don't let me force you if you would rather be doing something else."

"Nana, why do you think I'm here? I can't wait to find out what happened when William came home."

Victoria sat herself on a little stool next to Nana's chair.

"Right. William suddenly arrived home without any warning and missing an arm. What happened next?"

Nana stared off into space, remembering how she had felt when William had opened the shop door and stepped inside.

"The first we knew about William's return was when the cart from the railway station stopped outside the shop one morning and Billy Pinkney jumped down from the driving seat and trotted round to the back. He'd been doing the job of station porter, driver and handyman since his older brother, Peter whose job it had been, had gone off to war with the rest of the patriotic crowd. He seemed to be struggling with something and I was racking my brains, trying to remember if I had ordered a bulky item which would have been sent by train, when I realised that it was William that Billy was helping down from the back of the cart."

"I went cold to my bones when I realised that William was back home. I could feel a cold drip like an ice cube slithering down my backbone and I wanted to blot him out of my sight. I was acutely conscious of the gaggle of women who were all waiting to be served and I cringed at the thought of what he would say when he came into the shop."

"His left coat sleeve was swinging empty as he landed on the pavement and he clutched Billy's arm as though he wasn't capable of walking the few steps from the cart to the shop. Billy was only a small lad and he struggled to keep

William on his feet until he got him to the shop door, but William had no trouble flinging open the door and making a dramatic entrance into the shop."

"'I'm back, Bia and back for good this time,' he shouted, as he gazed round at my customers. 'Come and give your war hero the cuddle and kiss he deserves and I'll tell you tales of the war that you won't believe.'"

"I came out from behind the counter and made my way through the customers towards him. They were all watching us very closely, to see how I would take his very obvious disability, so I didn't disappoint them, flinging my arms around his neck and weeping copiously into his shirt collar, as though I'd been longing for his return since the moment he had set off for France.

"'What happened to you?' I asked, when he finally let go of me and used his one remaining arm to steer me towards the door through into the kitchen and privacy.

"'I'll tell you later,' he replied, turning and winking at the women who were all hanging on his every word. 'We've got some catching up to do, if you get my meaning.'"

"A roar of laughter met this remark and I smiled sunnily up at him, all the while cringing inside at him saying something so crass to me. I was a very private person and that sort of comment didn't suit me at all. We passed into the kitchen where Annie and Hannah were working alongside each other, making pies at the large kitchen table. Simon was sitting on a stool at the end of the table, vainly trying to steal some of the brambles they were putting in the pies. He stared in surprise at the one-armed man in uniform but, once again, he didn't recognise his father, although William didn't seem to be aware of that this time. He busily ushered Annie and Hannah out into the shop."

"'Take the little scrap with you and treat him to one of those sugar mice I saw in a bottle on the shelf,' he said, 'And remind him that his daddy has come home for good this time.'"

"He closed the kitchen door against the stares of the customers and immediately dropped the bonhomie, glaring at me where I stood next to the kitchen range."

"'You've moved up in the world then, Bia?' he sneered. 'Got your own property and a nice little business now, eh? Hoped I'd never make it home again, did you? Did you think the Hun would do for me and that you'd never have to see me again?'"

"He was closer to the mark than he realised. I had rarely given him a thought since the last time he had come home, but when I had thought about him, I had hoped that he would never come back from the war. My mind had always baulked at the idea of him being killed, I wasn't that insensitive, but I had hoped that he would never come home. I hadn't put this hope into words, refusing to think about what could happen to him, but I didn't want him back and it now looked as though that hope had been dashed. He was back for the long term, because even our man-starved army wouldn't take him with only one arm and obvious damage to his legs. I wasn't sure how many of these thoughts were showing on my face, so I busied myself opening the oven door to check on the pies inside and to hide my eyes. His next words pulled me up sharp."

"'You could have written to me, to let me know that you had moved house. I told Pinkney's lad to take me home, only to find that someone else was living in my house and I had to ask where my wife had moved to. Can you imagine how stupid that made me feel? I'm a returning war hero and I don't even know where my wife has gone. You didn't want me to know that you'd moved house, because you hoped that I wouldn't be able to find you when I came back. Admit it.'"

"I was furious with him, firstly because of his attitude but mostly because he was too close to the truth for comfort. I hadn't wanted him to come back and I didn't know how I was going to cope with having him around all the time. It was obvious from the minute he got off the station cart that he wasn't going to be able to go back to work in the iron works and the thought of having him getting in my way all the time was anathema to me. But I was going to start how I meant to go on with William; I was my own woman and he needn't think that he was going to rule the roost in this house."

"If I'd intended that you would never find me again, do you think it likely that I would only have moved a few streets away from where I was living before? Don't you think I would have left the town and moved miles away so that you would never be able to find me? I could have changed my name, moved to another town and you wouldn't have known who or where I was, so you can stop using that tone of voice with me."

"'I don't like having to be told where I live by a snotty little boy!' he whined. 'In future, you will discuss all your plans with me before *I* decide what we are going to do. Is that clear?'"

"I wasn't having any of this and he needed to be told pretty sharpish."

"I told you last time you came home that this is my house and my business. I've worked for them, I've earned them and you don't have anything to do with them at all. If you think you can come home and start shouting the odds about what I can and cannot do, then you've got another think coming. I make my own decisions and that's the way it's going to stay. Do you understand me? Or do I have to make it clearer for you?"

"I couldn't stop myself from shouting at him. I knew he'd come home wounded and plenty of people would say he was a war hero, but he wasn't going to have any control over me or my businesses, a lesson he was going to have to learn pretty quickly. I wasn't the delicate little wife who depended on her strong husband for every little thing. I was an independent woman with a head for commerce and I wasn't prepared to give that up. But I wasn't too sure where I stood legally and if William got it into his head to hire a lawyer and fight to control my life, I had a terrible feeling that I was going to come off the worse."

"He drew himself up to his full height, ready to start laying down the law to me, but the effect on his weedy frame, which hadn't thickened out any, was just to make him look like a bantam cock and I couldn't help laughing at his ruddy-tempered face. This infuriated him and he started to pull off his jacket, struggling with the buttons, hampered by the loss of his arm."

"'Look, look what I've lost, fighting for King and country in that hell hole in Flanders. I've fought like a lion for freedom for all; I'm not fighting you at home as well. You'll do as I say or, God help me, I'll beat you to within an inch of your life. Do you understand me?'"

"He was screaming by the time he got to those last words and spittle flecked across his cheek and onto his uniform jacket. I knew he was very close to losing any self-control he had left, but I wasn't frightened of him. I had faced down Butcher Dennison, who was as big as a barn door, this little, weedy bantam cock wasn't going to get the better of me. Something else I had learnt in my battle with the pig butcher was never to give any ground to a bully so I took the initiative immediately. I snatched up the large knife which Annie had been using to cut up the meat for the pies which were in the oven at that moment and shook it under William's nose. I was as coldly calculating as I had been when I had pushed Dennison into the tin bath and my voice was barely above a whisper when I spoke.

"'Don't you dare threaten me, William. I didn't make you enlist in the army that was your own idea, so it's not my fault that you've been injured. You left us to sink or swim without you and now you are complaining because we didn't sink. Would you have preferred it if you had come home and Simon and I had starved to death while you were away? Would that have made you feel better or more manly?"

"I think he actually raised his remaining hand to strike me, but I shook the knife under his nose again and he suddenly slumped into the fireside chair, all the brashness draining away from him. The tears started to course down his cheeks and he fumbled with a handkerchief to wipe them away."

"'Of course I wouldn't have wanted you to starve to death,' he said as he rubbed his face with his hand, 'but I didn't expect that you would have made such a success out of running a shop. I thought you would have been desperate for me to come home and provide for you and Simon, not managing so well without me. I feel as though you don't need me anymore and I don't like it. I'm the man in this family and I should be the one who runs the business, not you. You should be waiting for me to come home every night, with a good meal ready for me and wanting to know what I've done during the day.'"

"'That little scenario is all in your head, William.' I told him. 'I've never played the helpless little woman role and well you know it. I'll be dammed if I'm going to start playing it now. I was the one who started this shop. I was the one who worked bloody hard to make it successful and, if you can't cope with that idea, then it's just hard luck. I have no intentions of giving up what I'm doing. Lucky for you that I can provide for Simon now that you've lost your arm, otherwise we'd be in a big hole again, wouldn't we? You should be able to do some work in the shop, even with only one arm, so you should still have your self-respect, but don't you ever threaten me again. Do you hear me?'"

"'I won't,' he murmured, still struggling to keep the tears from falling. 'I've had a terrible time over there, Bia. You've no idea how dreadful it is to be up to your thighs in mud and dead bodies, waiting for a sniper to find your position and shoot you when you least expect it, listening to the cries of the wounded laid out in No Man's Land, screaming for their mothers to come and save them. I was so afraid all the time that sometimes I couldn't move when the orders to advance were given. I couldn't make my legs support me, let alone make them run into a deathly barrage of gunfire.'"

"'Why did you do it, William?' I asked him. 'Why, if you were so frightened of being a soldier, why did you go and enlist when you didn't have to? You could have stayed at home and then none of this would have happened.'"

"As I said this, I realised that I wouldn't have wanted him to stay at home. If he hadn't enlisted, I wouldn't have started the shop or started buying houses with Sam Lymer, everything would have been the same as it had been before the war and I would have been bored with it. The thought of going back to that kind of life filled me with dread and I realised how long my own journey had been. William's reply took me by surprise, not only because I had forgotten what I had asked him when the wave of realisation had flooded over me, but also because of what he said."

"'You were always the strong one in our relationship, Bia, and I always thought you despised me for my weaknesses. I thought that if you saw me as a soldier and knew that I *was* brave, then I could live up to you and not feel inadequate any more. But, when I came home last time, you had started a business and were doing very well without me and it just made me feel even more inadequate than ever. And I wasn't even a brave soldier, because I was so scared all the time. I wanted to lash out and it was you I chose to turn on, like the stupid idiot I am. This whole mess is all my fault, you're right, and now I've spoilt everything.'"

"The tears started to course down his cheeks again and he was lost in a morass of self-pity and self-loathing, which I found stomach-turning and pathetic. I couldn't stop myself from giving him a shake and telling him to pull himself together, even though I knew that that probably wasn't the best way to deal with him. I couldn't pretend that I felt sorry for him because he was a grown man, he should have realised that war wasn't going to be easy and pleasant. He was reaping what he had sown and now he had to get on and make the best of what life had to offer him."

"I was thunderstruck by his revelation that he had only enlisted to prove himself to me and that he had known that I was the stronger of the two of us. I had never analysed our different strengths and weaknesses and hadn't realised that he had, coming up with conclusions which I would never have drawn. An inferiority complex seemed a very strange reason for enlisting as a soldier, but it was what he had done and now we both had to live with the consequences."

"So we started the next stage of our lives together, but it was a very uneasy truce that we had called between us. William was often in great pain from the wounds to his legs and his missing arm and was very difficult to live with, although he was lucky that the shop produced enough income for us to be able to afford pain relief for him. I found him plenty of work he was capable of doing in the shop, while trying to keep him away from the financial side of the business, but he was regularly uncivil to Annie and Hannah and sometimes downright rude to customers. He had very restless nights when his legs pained him and the missing arm seemed to cause him equal pain and I spent many a night making up the doctor's painkilling draughts and providing hot drinks. When he wasn't in pain, he often woke screaming in the night having had nightmares about his times in the trenches and, again, I would provide hot drinks and try to settle him back down again."

"Those were the nights when he often woke Simon and Annie, although Peter and Hannah both managed to sleep through all but the worst of them. If Simon was awoken, then he had to be soothed back to sleep, because his father's cries frightened him badly and I often wondered how I managed to stay on my feet, never mind work a full day in the shop, the lack of sleep was so draining. If it hadn't been for Annie and Hannah, I think I could have gone under at that time, but they both helped me so much, even to the point of ignoring William's rudeness when he snapped at them."

"That was also the time when I was grateful that Sammy had found these premises on Queen Street for me. There were enough rooms upstairs for William to have his own bedroom, ostensibly to stop him disturbing anyone else in the night, but really because I couldn't stand the thought of him sharing my bed. Whenever he touched me, my skin crawled nearly as badly as it had done when Dennison had made his advances to me and I always made an excuse to step away from him."

"Throughout all this, Sam Lymer was my rock. He was placid and easy-going, with a quick wit and the capacity to make me laugh, even when I was at my lowest ebb. William often walked into a room and caught me laughing with Sam over some tale he was telling and, although Sam did his best to draw William into the conversation and share his humour with him, William was always temperamental when Sam was around. It came to a head one Sunday when William made a disparaging remark about Sam as we were all sitting round the kitchen table, eating our Sunday lunch. Hannah was very upset and rushed out of the kitchen, heading for her bedroom, closely followed by Annie who was intent on comforting her. Before she left the kitchen, Annie stopped at the door and turned on William, something she had never done before."

"'You are a very small-minded man, William,' she said, 'and you have no right to try and belittle someone who has a generous spirit and a kind heart, particularly in front of that man's daughter. It's time you matured enough to appreciate those qualities in another human being.'"

"I was amazed at Annie, because she had previously always treated William with respect, but he had gone too far even for her. William, as usual whenever he was criticised, immediately began sulking and wanted Annie and Peter to leave our home. Quietly, I reminded him that this was my house and Annie and Peter's home and would remain so for as long as I had breath in my body; nobody would be evicted on his whim. What he said next left me speechless, not a state I usually inhabited."

"'You are having an affair with Sam Lymer! I should have realised this when I first came home. I *must* be stupid if it's taken me this long to realise what you are doing.'"

"He wanted to carry on, working himself up into a frenzy but I brought him back to earth with a bump."

"'Don't be so ridiculous, William.' I snapped at him. 'Sam is and has been a very good friend to this family. Without his help, I wouldn't have managed half as well as I have done, but we have never done anything reprehensible in the whole of the time I have known him, mainly because I am a married woman and he lost his wife last year. He still grieves deeply for her, but he throws his energies into working hard, caring for their children. He also has two boys who are fighting in those trenches that you have nightmares about, but he hides his worries and presents a happy face to the world, something of which you have no conception. Annie is right, you are incredibly small-minded, but I would also add that you are a poisonous little worm. Now, get out of my sight before I say even more.'"

"He stormed out of the room and then out of the house, leaving me shaking with anger at his behaviour. I apologised to both Hannah and Annie on his behalf, knowing full well that he would never think of apologising himself and then set about the tasks of clearing up in the kitchen and getting the baking started for the next day. My mind wandered as I worked, kneading the dough for the bread, but I stopped short when the thought rose into my mind that I *did* admire Sam a great deal. He was a real man, tough and intelligent, but also sensitive and caring and William didn't compare very well at all."

Nana Lymer faltered to a stop, reliving in her mind the worries and joys of that time of her life. Her recollections of her feelings of that day were crystal clear, more so than the more recent past and she was re-living the happiness she had felt when she had realised that what she felt for Sammy Lymer was more than mere friendship.

214

"Are you ok, Nana?" Victoria asked, worried about the far-away expression on her grandmother's face.

"Ok?" Nana replied. "I'm more than ok, I've got more happy memories than any woman deserves, but where had I got to? Oh yes, the problems I had with William when he returned from the war. Those problems were soon surmounted by even bigger ones. I found out what the lesson was that Butcher Dennison wanted me to learn. But I think that will have to wait until tomorrow. It's tea-time now and I'm tired. I think I need a snooze and your mother will be wanting you to help with making the tea. We'll carry on again tomorrow, if your mam allows it."

Victoria had to accept that that was all she was going to get that day, but she was worried that her mother wouldn't let her sit with Nana the next day, not when she had spent the whole afternoon with her. The shop would be closed again the next day because it was Boxing Day, so nobody would be doing any work apart from preparing meals. If she helped her mother cooking lunch she might manage to snatch the afternoon with her grandmother.

Chapter Eight

For a reason Victoria couldn't fathom, her mother was in an incredibly good mood the next morning, singing as she prepared breakfast and not requiring any help at all. The reason behind it became apparent after breakfast was over and Victoria had started the washing up. "Have you got anything planned for today, Victoria?" her mother asked, as she passed the plates over for her to wash. "Have you got homework to do for school or anything?"

"Nothing that I've got to do today." Victoria replied, wary at her mother's pleasant tone of voice. "I've got revision I've got to do for my mocks, but I don't intend doing any of that today. It is Boxing Day, after all."

"Yes, I think you should have a rest from schoolwork today. Your dad and I have been invited to have lunch at the Welsh's new house in Great Ayton and I wondered if you would look after Nana Lymer for me so that we can go. You wouldn't be interested in looking at their new house, but I would like to go and I can't if there's no-one to look after Nana."

"Of course I'll look after Nana." Victoria replied, absolutely ecstatic that she wasn't expected to spend any time with a family she really didn't like. She couldn't bear that her mother, unusually for her, saw the Welsh family as the perfect family with a wonderful home and was extremely jealous of them. A visit to their house usually produced a shopping spree when her mother would acquire items which she had seen at their house, convinced that they were the epitome of good taste and worth acquiring. Victoria had found their old home incredibly ostentatious and disliked the articles her mother would buy in her desire to copy them. She had no desire to visit their new home and would much rather spend the afternoon with Nana, free from any interruptions.

So, by two o'clock, her parents had set off on their trip and Victoria was free to make tea and biscuits and take them up to Nana's bedroom.

"Victoria!" Nana exclaimed when Victoria entered her bedroom carrying a tray. "I didn't think we would get two days of freedom!"

"Mam and Dad have gone to see the Welsh's new house and she wanted me to stay at home and look after you. So I'm here, ready for the next part of the story and I've brought tea so it doesn't make you thirsty, talking to me."

"You're a good girl, you really are. I just hope my story lives up to your expectations. Now, where had we got to?"

"William had come home wounded and was taking it all out on you. You were working your socks off, trying to keep the shop going and look after Simon, as well as spending many hours during the nights helping William through his pain and his nightmares."

Victoria was pleased that she could explain it all so well.

"Yes, pet. Life was difficult at that time. It was January 1917 and the snow lay thick on the ground. The winds seemed to be coming directly from the arctic, they were such lazy winds."

"Lazy winds?" Victoria interrupted. "What's a lazy wind?"

"A lazy wind is one that can't be bothered to blow round you, so it blows straight through you; it's as cold as that." Nana explained. Victoria smiled. She had experienced a 'lazy wind' the week before when she had been shopping in the town. That wind had blown through all her layers of clothing, obviously too lazy to blow round her.

"As I said," Nana continued, "The winds were very cold and very strong, it snowed regularly and there were bitter frosts at night. I often thought about those mothers' sons who were huddled in trenches in France and Flanders, waiting to be blown to smithereens and shivering with the cold and the fear. I also thought about their mothers and wives, sitting in their homes and worrying about their husbands and sons and praying for them to come home in one piece, or even slightly less than one piece, like William."

"William continued with his pain and his nightmares and his bad temper and his maudlin self-pity, all regularly spaced throughout the day, every day and I tried to hold it all together, often feeling so stretched out with the strain and the tension that, if anyone had plucked my strings, I would have twanged like a heavenly harp."

"Simon breezed sunnily through all our lives, always happy and smiling, always so loving, my ray of sunshine when everything else seemed so dark. Annie watched and listened and took note of all that went on between William and I, but she rarely spoke of it and, if she did, it was to let me know that she was always there if I needed a shoulder to cry on. Good friend that she was, she knew that if she had shown me pity and sympathy I would have dissolved in front of her and not been able to continue. She and Peter and, of course, Hannah and

Sammy, kept me sane at that time and I thanked God every night for sending the four of them to me."

"Hannah sang her way through every day, hymns, marching songs and even some questionable tunes and lyrics that she picked up as she went around town. I knew her father had this same capacity for enjoying life and he also hummed and sang his way through every day, although I knew he was extremely worried about his two boys who were fighting over at the Front. He hadn't heard from either of them for a long time and, occasionally, he would let slip that he was worried about them, although he always quoted 'no news is good news' whenever anyone asked him if they had been in contact with him."

"The shop was doing well, despite the fact that there were shortages of some foodstuffs. I had held the farmers to their contracts, so I usually had the basics available in my shop and the boys who worked at the docks were very good about letting me know if a ship berthed carrying any goods which they thought would capture my interest. Some things were very difficult to get hold of because the enemy were sinking a fair amount of merchant shipping, but we managed to always have something to sell."

"Sam and I continued to buy houses whenever we had the resources available to pay cash for them and we made a tidy sum in rents, so I knew we would always have something to fall back on should the enemy succeed in sinking the bulk of our shipping and we couldn't continue to stock the shop. What sort of a state the country would have been in if that had happened was something none of us wanted to think about, but we had to plan for all eventualities."

"I was still gathering a few pieces of jewellery when families hit hard times and needed to exchange their valuables for food. I was always fair over the value I placed on these items, although I did always factor a profit into what I gave in exchange. The size of the profit sometimes depended on whether I thought the owner of the jewellery would ever come back to redeem their goods and I must admit I was swayed by the person who wanted to pledge their goods against some food. I wasn't a real pawnbroker in that I never gave money in exchange for items, I always used food as my currency and that kept most of the drunkards away. They didn't want to pawn items for food, they wanted to pawn items for cash, so they mostly avoided me, although some did come to me in desperation and ask if I would give them money."

"The items which were never redeemed stayed in the belt round my waist that Annie had made for me and, when that got too full, I kept them in a strong box at Mr Vine's. He never knew what I was keeping in there, but he was a true professional and never enquired. When I found I was holding something I didn't like I would go to one of the main jewellers in the town and swap it for gems, following Mr Sanderson's advice and the jeweller began letting me know when he got an item in stock that he thought I might like."

"This was a part of my business of which William was unaware, although Sammy knew that I was squirreling jewellery away. William knew that Sam and I owned and rented out houses, but he didn't ask for any details about them partly, I think, because Sammy was involved in it and partly because he was frightened that I would refuse to reveal any information about them. He was right in his thinking because I had no intentions of ever letting William know just how much I was worth in case he attempted to appropriate any of it. He had taken to drinking to relieve the pains in his legs, but he only had what money I paid him when he worked in the shop. When this ran out he had to stop and I think it was only lack of funds that stopped him from drinking himself to oblivion every night."

"This was the year that Simon started school and William made it his task to take him and collect him every day, so that he was always out of the shop at these times. I noticed that people brought their items for pawning when William wasn't around and I wondered why they did this. Was it because they knew that William wasn't party to what business deals I did or was it because he was often unpleasant with customers, particularly if they refused to let him serve them and asked for me? I didn't know, but it served my purpose to not have him hanging around when I was valuing items and he was never given access to the book in which I kept my records of the items pawned and the amount of food handed over."

"January moved slowly into February, with no let-up in the horrendous weather conditions. The snow still lay deep on the ground and bitter frosts froze the water supplies and made walking a nightmare on the slippery ground. If you went outside you were wrapped up in so many layers of clothes that movement was almost impossible, yet the cold managed to get through to your bones and made them ache as though you had climbed mountains. I didn't want to have to go outside, but one day I got word from one of the dock labourers that a ship from America had arrived, with a consignment of meat on board. He had kept some aside for me and wanted me to go and move it into my warehouse."

"I knew I would have to go, because I didn't want to miss the opportunity of having good meat to sell, but Peter wouldn't be able to go with me because he was at the dentist's. He had been having a lot of trouble with one of his back teeth and Annie had wrapped his face in a warm scarf and bundled him off to the dentists to get it removed. I hesitated about going down the docks without Peter, but it was the middle of the day and I had never had any trouble whenever I had gone there before, so I went on my own. I left a message with Hannah for Peter to follow me down when he got back from the dentist and set off on my own."

"At the dockside, the labourer was waiting for me with a pallet of meat and, because I was alone, he happily helped me carry it into my warehouse and store it in the large cupboard I used for keeping meat. Then he left, taking with him some meat pies and ginger beer I had brought for him and his mates and the payment for the consignment of meat. I was alone in my warehouse; checking through my stock and collecting a couple of small items which I wanted to take back to the shop. It was only seconds later that I heard the outer door slam and I shouted to Peter that I was in the cold-store area. He didn't reply, but I heard his footsteps as he crossed the floor towards me, so I turned to ask him to take some of the items I was holding. It wasn't Peter who was standing there, but Butcher Dennison, grinning evilly at my discomfort. It took me a few seconds to recover from the shock of seeing him there, but I managed to croak a perfectly respectable 'Good day to you'."

"'It *is* a good day, Mrs Drinkwater,' he answered. 'I've been waiting for just such a good day to come along for quite some time and now it's happened. You and me, here together and alone. I have been anticipating this since I bought the warehouse from old Sanderson. You've kept me waiting a long time, Mrs Drinkwater.'

"I'll admit it; he was terrifying me, blocking my exit from the warehouse and standing far too close to me for comfort. I shivered at his smug tone and I didn't miss the leer on his face as he spoke to me, but I wasn't going to let the bully get the better of me."

"''I'm unlikely to be alone for very long, Mr Dennison,' I said, hoping my voice wasn't betraying the fear I was feeling. Had it wavered as I spoke to him? 'Peter is on his way here as we speak, so we won't be alone for very long.'"

"I hoped that the mention of Peter would make him think again about whatever it was that he had planned, because it would have been obvious to a blind man that he had something in mind."

"'Long enough for what I want to do, Mrs Drinkwater.' He said, as he moved towards me and grabbed my head in both his hands. I was totally unprepared for this and he drew me, unresisting, into his arms while he kissed my cheeks and then my mouth, all the while whispering in my ear.

"'I know you want this as much as I do. That armless wonder won't be doing much for you, now that he's come home. Anyone can see that a red-blooded woman like you needs more than that snivelling excuse for a man in your bed and I'm here, ready and willing to step in where he fails. You need a real man like me to keep you happy.'"

"I was rigid with the shock of what was happening at first, but then the anger within me boiled up so that my rage was white-hot and I found I suddenly had the strength to free my arms. I grabbed hold of his coat to steady my hold and then I brought my knee up into his groin with as much force as I could muster. The shock and the pain from the blow made him bend over towards me but he didn't loosen his grip of my head and, as he straightened back up, he pushed me up against the wall of the cupboard and banged my head two or three times against the wooden planking. I saw multi-coloured stars explode around the edges of my vision and then a blackness began to draw in and I think I nearly lost consciousness at that point. It was the pig butcher's voice that brought me back to full awareness, as he began to whisper into my ear once more."

"'Do you like to fight for it then, Mrs Drinkwater? You like to have a bit of a rough about before you get down to the nitty-gritty, do you? That's fine by me. A little, delicate scrap like you can't do much to hurt me, you know, but it'll be fun while you try.'"

"The revulsion I felt for him was stomach-turning and I was very nearly sick there and then. I didn't have the breathe to say anything to him and I could feel my legs turning to jelly as he continued to whisper in my ear and breath in my face. I struggled again, trying to free my head from his hands so that I could pull away from him and breathe clean air instead of his fetid breath, but he banged my head against the wall again and this time I did black out. It was only for a second but long enough for my legs to give way completely and I slipped down the wall."

"The pig butcher thought I was acquiescing to his demands and aided my descent to the floor by kicking my feet out from under me, never letting go of his hold on my head. I landed awkwardly onto my shoulder and the pain was so intense, it cleared the fuzziness in my head and I became fully aware of my surroundings again."

"Dennison threw himself on top of me, squashing the breath out of my body and compounding the injury in my shoulder. He let go of my head but put one of his hands round the front of my throat, squeezing hard enough to cut off the bulk of my air supply while he tugged at my skirts, trying to pull them upwards with his other hand. I tried desperately to struggle, but he was so heavy that I was pinned to the floor and couldn't even raise one knee. He began whispering into my ear again; saying such horrible and vulgar things that made me feel so sick and dirty and I couldn't do anything to stop him. His hand was winning its battle to pull my skirt up to my waist and then he grabbed hold of my underclothes, to try and separate them from my body."

"His cheek was touching my face as he concentrated on what he was trying to do and the smell of him was so unspeakably foul that I could feel the nausea rising in my throat and that made me panic. I knew that if I was sick I wouldn't be able to even turn my head to the side to expel it and there was a good chance that I would choke. The anger I was feeling was turned into white-hot fury that he could dare to do this to me and I reacted as an animal would if it was cornered."

"As he continued whispering into my ear, he rubbed his filthy unshaven face against my cheek and I opened my mouth and bit down on the only part of his anatomy that I could reach – his earlobe. I could taste the iron-like flavour of his blood as I clamped my jaws together and he let out a high-pitched squeal that would have rivalled any that came from the pigs that he slaughtered. He bucked about on top of me as the pain he was feeling reached a crescendo but I didn't let go. I was being ruled by a purely atavistic savagery that had risen in me because of what he was trying to do to me and all I wanted to do was cause him as much pain as I could. The blood from his ear was dripping into my eyes and across my face as I clung grimly on and it ran into my mouth as I continued to bite down as hard as I could. I didn't let go until he was lifted bodily off me and I could see Peter behind him. Peter was holding Dennison as though he was a human battering ram and he used him as such, banging his head two or three times against the warehouse wall, in much the same way as the pig butcher had slammed mine."

"Peter had been in a great deal of pain with his rotten tooth and I think he took all of that pain and frustration out on Dennison. I scrambled to my feet, righting my clothes as I did so and then gently placed my hand on Peter's arm, speaking to him in as soft and gentle a voice as I could manage at that time. Peter always responded better if people were calm and quiet with him, but it took a tremendous amount of self-control not to scream at this point."

"'That's enough, Peter" I said, 'that's enough. Put him down on the floor, there's a good lad.'"

"Peter stopped using Dennison as a battering ram and looked at me, puzzlement clouding his eyes and his mouth drooping in case he was going to get into trouble. He didn't put Dennison down though and I knew it would take very little to push him over the edge and start him attacking the butcher again. I had to calm him down so that he didn't kill Dennison and then get arrested for murder. As it was, I wasn't sure if Dennison was still breathing, Peter had put a great deal of effort into the force he had used to bang Dennison's head against the wall, the pig butcher's eyes were closed and he hung limply in Peter's grasp."

"'Put him down, Peter.' I repeated, as calmly as I could, given that every nerve-ending in my body was screaming at me to stop Peter murdering the butcher. I lowered my voice even further and found the strength from somewhere to smile at Peter.

" 'Put him on the floor, lad, so I can check if he is still breathing and, if he is, we'll take him back to his own warehouse and leave him to recover on his own.'"

"Slowly, as if he might change his mind at any moment, Peter lowered Dennison to the floor and then stood back, staring at me.

'He's hurt you, Bia, you're bleeding,' he said, pointing at my face where I could feel the pig butcher's blood drying on my skin."

"'No, I'm not hurt, Peter, you arrived in time to stop him hurting me. This is from Dennison's ear because I bit him when he knocked me to the floor.'"

"Peter's face creased and he laughed at the thought of me biting Dennison's ear and making him bleed. I could have screamed in frustration because he had no idea that we were in danger every moment that we had this body on the warehouse floor."

"'Is this what he meant about teaching you a lesson, Bia?' Peter asked. 'You know, I heard him say that you had a lesson to learn the day he bought the warehouse.'"

"'Yes, yes it is what he meant, but I'll explain it all later.' I said. 'Now, I've got to check to see if he's still alive, Peter. You go and look out of the door and see if there's anybody about. We don't want anyone to see us moving Dennison back into his warehouse.'"

"With a mumbled 'Ok' Peter crossed the warehouse floor towards the door and I crouched down next to the prone pig butcher. He was still breathing, although his eyes were closed and his heartbeat, when I checked that, was as steady as a rock. He obviously had the constitution of an ox. I straightened up as Peter came back to report that the coast was clear.

"'Can we carry him between us?' I asked. 'If you take hold of him under his arms, I'll lift his feet and we should be able to get him back next door.'"

"'No need for you to try, Bia.' Peter said. 'I can carry him on my own.' And he pushed his arms under Dennison's prone body and lifted him easily off the floor, setting off for the door so quickly I was almost left behind. I ran to catch him up, so that I could check that the coast was still clear outside before we went out into the open. There was no-one about and the snow was falling again from a darkened sky. For the first time that winter I was pleased to see the snow, knowing that it would deter anyone from hanging around outside and possibly seeing what we were doing."

"It only took seconds for Peter to cross the space between the two warehouses, kick open the door and dump Dennison's inert form onto the floor. I made one last check that he was still breathing and that his pulse was normal before I followed Peter back into our warehouse."

"'Are we going home now, Bia?' Peter asked. 'I'm hungry and I can eat now that the pain has gone out of my tooth.'"

"'In a minute, Peter.' I answered, wearily. 'I've got to get rid of the bloodstains on the floor, so that no-one will know what happened in here. Then we can go home and you can have the biggest pie in the shop for what you've done for me today.'"

"Peter's face split into a huge grin and he lugged a bucket of water across to the cold store and scrubbed at the floor to remove the bloodstains. Meanwhile, I dipped the end of my shawl into the bucket and scrubbed at my face to eradicate the crusted blood which had pooled around my nose and run down my neck. The dried blood on my blouse could wait until after we got home; I could cover that with my shawl. In any case, in the blizzard that was blowing outside no one would be stopping to look at other people. If there was anyone out in this weather, they would be head down and as intent on getting home as we were. As soon as the floor looked as normal as was possible, I checked outside again and Peter and I set off for Queen Street, with me holding on to Peter so that the strong wind didn't blow me over."

"I felt as weak as a kitten, as though I had done ten rounds in a boxing ring with a prize-fighter, but I had to keep going so that we could reach the safety of the shop. As I had expected there were very few people about on the streets; the blizzard had seen to that and Peter and I reached the safety of our back alley without having to stop. I didn't dare go in through the shop in case there were any customers in there who might be able to see the bloodstains on me in the lamplight. We went in through the back yard gate and entered the kitchen with a cloud of snow billowing around us until we could close the back door against it. Annie and Simon were sitting at the kitchen table where she was encouraging him to eat his tea. One glance showed her that there was something wrong and she quickly herded Simon up the stairs to settle him in his bedroom with a toy before coming back downstairs to find out what had happened. The only other person in the kitchen was Sammy as Hannah was serving in the shop and, thankfully, William had brought Simon home from school and then headed straight for the Red Lion."

Sam took my shawl and looked in dismay at the bloodstains on my blouse.

"'What's happened, Bia?' he asked, pushing me down into the armchair next to the range. 'Have you had an accident?'"

"I sighed, unwilling to remember what the pig butcher had tried to do to me, but knowing that I had to talk about it to get the whole ghastly business out of my head."

"'It was the pig butcher. He saw me going into the warehouse on my own and he followed me in.' I began, but Sammy held his hand up to stop me while he unwrapped me from my shawl."

"'Keep it until Annie comes back downstairs and I can get Hannah to shut the shop. That way, you'll only have to tell it once.' He said. I knew he was right and, in any case, I didn't have the strength left to argue with anyone. Peter, who had been rummaging in the pantry, popped his head round the door and asked if he could have one of the pies. I smiled agreement although my stomach heaved at the thought of food. I struggled to my feet as Sam and Hannah entered the kitchen.

"'I'll have to go and change this blouse, Sam.' I said when he looked enquiringly at me. 'I'll burn it on the range because I'll never manage to get those stains out of it.'"

"'Good idea.' He concurred. 'You can tell Annie to come downstairs while you're there. Can you manage, lass?'"

"I'd stumbled as I'd stood up and his voice was full of concern for me."

"'I'll manage, Sam.' I answered, although the effort to mount the stairs seemed almost gargantuan and I wasn't sure that I would manage."

"I collected Annie from Simon's room and we gathered around the kitchen range while I told the others everything that had happened that afternoon. It was a painful and embarrassing story and I really didn't want to tell anyone, but they listened

with sympathy and encouragement and only gave their opinions

when I had faltered into silence after relating the tale of the

journey home. I had been ripping my stained blouse into shreds

as I had talked, taking my temper and my hurt out on the material

and when I had finished I leant forward and pushed the torn

fabric into the heart of the fire. It burned brightly, illuminating

the faces of the four people as they sat around me. My heart

suddenly expanded with the love I had from them all and I felt

better than I had done all afternoon. In the silence which fell

between us we were all conscious of Peter's champing jaws as he

finished demolishing the pie I had given him and looked around

him for more to eat."

"'I don't think that'll be the last we see of the pig butcher.'

Sam said, looking more serious than I had ever seen him before.

'He'll not take it lightly that you bested him like that, although I

think it unlikely that he will make any official complaint. He'd

be hard put to explain why he was in a position for you to bite his

ear, but he'll want his pound of flesh for it, all the same.'"

"'There was nothing else I could do, Sam.' I said. 'I couldn't let him rape me and I didn't know that Peter had arrived. If I had known, I would have just waited for him to move Dennison, but I thought it was fight or be raped and I preferred to fight.'"

Sam's face turned a deep purple as I said this and he clenched his fists at his side.

"'I could throttle the bastard for what he tried to do to you, Bia,' he said."

"'No, Sam,' I cried. 'You mustn't do anything to him. He would run to the police immediately and you could end up in prison for a very long time. I don't want you to get into trouble because of me. Think about your children. They need you and so do we. Please, don't try to punish him for what he did to me.'"

"Hannah added her cries to mine and Annie roundly told him that he was best to keep his distance from Dennison, that he would get his just deserts in some other way."

"'The man's evil,' she declared, 'and he'll end in an evil way, you mark my words.'"

"I had to smile at Annie's vehemence, she was so convinced that good would triumph and evil would be punished."

"'Keep smiling, lass,' Sammy said, 'you've got such a bonny smile and it's not often that you get the chance to use it these days.'"

"'Is it any wonder, Sam?' I asked. 'All I want is a happy and safe home for me and Simon and all I seem to get recently is trouble.'"

"'I know, lass,' he commiserated, 'but things will turn out fine, just you wait and see if I'm right. But we need to get yon bugger warned off before he tries anything else. I wouldn't trust him with St Peter's keys, I wouldn't, so we need to get it sorted. Trouble is, I'm not sure what to do for the best so that none of us suffers. But I think the first thing is for you to have a good night's rest, Bia, and we can face tomorrow when it comes.'"

"I was so exhausted by then that I readily agreed, leaving Annie and Hannah to put Simon to bed and to prepare the shop for the next day. I awoke around midnight when William came home from the Red Lion and made a very noisy pantomime out of trying not to wake anyone. It was only then that I realised I hadn't given a thought to William all the previous day. I hadn't missed him when I got home and I knew that there was no way on God's earth that I was ever going to tell him what Dennison had tried to do to me. It was at that point that I realised I depended on Sam for support, but I only looked on William as a burden I had to bear through life. I was as likely to turn to him for sympathy and support as I was likely to fly to the moon. 'When hell freezes over' was my last thought before I slipped into an exhausted sleep."

Nana stopped speaking, her thoughts back in that cold night during the Great War. Victoria took hold of the delicate hand that lay on the chair arm and rubbed the back of it with her palm. Nana Lymer's gaze came back to the present and she smiled at Victoria's worried frown.

"Don't worry, pet," she said. "I'm not going to go into a decline over what that mound of blubber tried to do to me. He got what he deserved and I'd do it again if I had to. I wouldn't change what I did to him because what happened next would have happened anyway, me biting his ear didn't make him do it. What he did next was because of what William had done, not me, and I have never forgiven William for it. I never will forgive him, not if I live to be a hundred."

Victoria couldn't make any sense out of this garbled explanation, but she could hear the venom in her grandmother's voice and wondered exactly what had William done. But she wasn't going to find out that day because she heard the side door open and her mother and father moving into the kitchen. When she would be able to listen to another part of Nana's story was in her mother's hands and those hands could be incredibly volatile.

Chapter Nine

The next day was a normal working day after the excitement of the Christmas season and Victoria wondered what her mother had planned for her to do. She was concerned about Nana Lymer because she had looked so frail the day before when she had related what the butcher had tried to do to her and Victoria was worried that she wasn't strong enough to relive such terrible events without it harming her in some way. It was with a sense of panic therefore that she heard her mother explaining to her father that Nana Lymer was very tired that morning.

"What's wrong with her?" Victoria asked her mother, worried that she was the cause of her grandmother's fatigue.

"Just old age, I should imagine," was her mother's curt reply. "She's not getting any younger and she's bound to have her off days. I just hope that she isn't going to start wandering again, because I don't need the hassle of searching for her in the middle of the night, not on top of everything else I have to do."

"Do you want me to sit with her again, so that she's not on her own when she wakes up?" Victoria offered, wanting to watch over the old lady.

"I thought you had revision to do for your mocks? Christmas is over now so it's time you started it."

"I can revise in Nana's room the same as if I'm sitting in my room. If she's asleep she won't disturb me, will she?" Victoria suggested.

"That's true." Her mother considered the offer, loath to give in too easily to something that Victoria wanted to do, but aware that Victoria's presence in her grandmother's bedroom would save her from having to run up and down stairs to check on the old lady's health.

"Go on then," she conceded, "You might as well do both jobs at once and it'll give me time to get the shop sorted out for the New Year rush. But you get your revision done, my lass, don't be wasting time talking to the old girl. I've told you before what a romancer she is, you can't believe half of what comes out of her mouth."

Victoria couldn't understand why her mother had such a low opinion of Nana Lymer. She wouldn't dare speak to Bia like Bia spoke to *her* mother and Victoria wondered how old her mother had been when she had begun being so off-hand with Nana. Why hadn't Nana stopped her? She thought it was unlikely that *she* would ever dare be so rude.

Victoria collected her English Literature folder and one of her set books from her bedroom and then tip-toed across the landing and slowly opened Nana's bedroom door. The old lady was fast asleep in the large double bed; making hardly a mound in the bedclothes she was so tiny. Victoria's face was creased with concern as she gently moved a lock of hair which had fallen across Nana's face. The big brown eyes opened at her touch and made Victoria jump.

"I thought it was your mother, that's why I was pretending to be asleep." Nana said, dimpling at Victoria. "Has her ladyship given you permission to sit with me again?"

"Yes, she's worried about you being so tired, so she said I could come in here to do my revision and watch you at the same time." Victoria answered. "But she said you weren't very well and I was worried that you were upset about what you were telling me yesterday. You don't have to tell me anymore, not if it's going to make you ill."

"It's not making me ill, I just couldn't be bothered listening to your mother whinging about her hard life, so I pretended to be asleep." Nana confessed with a grin. "She has no idea how hard it was for my generation during the Great War, she thinks I've had it easy all my life."

"Haven't you told Mam what happened to you?" Victoria was dumbfounded that Bia knew nothing about her own mother's early life because she had grown sick of listening to her mother complain about *her* early life and conditions in the Second World War. Most of her mother's reminiscences had been about her older brother, who had been the family favourite (according to Bia) and how he had consistently tormented her when they were children. She reckoned that she had regularly been punished for retaliating against this tormenting, although her brother was never punished for being the instigator.

"Your mother has never been interested in anyone else's point of view." Nana answered tartly. "She was a bad tempered little girl and she grew up into a bad tempered woman. I've told you before; your father is a saint for tolerating her moods and her rudeness. I often wonder how Sam and I managed to produce such a miserable child, he was always so sunny-tempered and he had a marvellous sense of humour."

Victoria had to agree. She had never heard her mother laugh at anything, although she had never given the matter much thought before, accepting that, in general, mothers didn't laugh. Nana Lymer interrupted her musings.

"Have you got time to listen to more of my story today, or should you be doing your revision for your exams?"

"I've got plenty of time, Nana." Victoria said. "I've got the rest of this week and all next week to revise in and, in any case, it's only the mocks we are sitting when we go back, the real exams aren't until June. But you mustn't tell me any more if it's making you tired and upset."

"Rubbish." Nana said, emphatically. "It's been the most fun I've had in the last ten years. It's all too long ago for it to be upsetting me now. Anyway, there's another reason for me telling you what happened and you can help me with that. Will you run an errand for me tomorrow and not tell your mother what I've asked you to do? If she knows what I'm asking, she'll do anything in her power to stop it and it's vital that I see him."

"Of course I won't tell Mam." Victoria said. "See who? And why? And what do you want me to do?"

"I want you to go to Mr Vine's office in Station Road and ask him to come and see me. I want you to make an exact time for the appointment and I want you to let him in through the side door while your mother is working in the shop. That way, she won't know he's here and the deed will be signed, sealed and done before she finds out about it. Will you do that for me?"

"Of course, Nana." Victoria replied. "But Mam wouldn't want to stop you seeing your solicitor. Everybody has the right to see their own legal representative, that's what those two world wars were fought for."

"You are right, Victoria, but your mother wouldn't see it that way, I know. At least, not in my case she wouldn't. If it was happening to *her* we'd never hear the last of it, but I'm a different kettle of fish all together. Anyway, on with the story. Are you sure you want me to go on with it?"

"Sure?" Victoria squeaked. "Of course I want you to go on with it. I want to find out what happened to the pig butcher after you bit his ear. Did you bite any of it off or was it still attached to his head?"

"Oh I didn't bite any of it off. I think I *would* have vomited if I had done that." Nana Lymer shuddered at the thought of having part of Dennison in her mouth. "Over the next couple of days I was very unsettled, never sure if he might have gone to the police over what Peter and I had done to him. But Sammy was right in what he said. Dennison would never have let anyone know that he been bested by a slip of a lass and a lad who 'wasn't all there' as Peter was so horribly described. After a few days had passed I calmed down and stopped expecting the police to turn up at any moment."

"Within the week, however, the gossips began talking about Dennison's accident, putting forward various ways in which he could have come by the injuries he had sustained. I wasn't sure at first whether he had been in another 'accident' or if the injuries the gossips were talking about was what I had done to his ear. I didn't want to make it obvious that I was extremely interested in these injuries, so I tried to be very casual when I asked about them and it wasn't long before I realised it was the injury to his ear that I had bitten that was the subject of all the gossip."

"I tried to be nonchalant in my attitude when Dennison was discussed, but anybody who knew me well would have known that I was hiding something. Thankfully, those people who knew me well, like Annie and Sam, already knew what had happened and weren't likely to share their knowledge with anyone else. So none of the gossips knew that it was I who had caused Dennison's injury and they were all ready and eager to discuss what had happened to him. It was reported that the pig butcher had once again turned to drink to compensate for what he thought were the hard blows that Fate had dealt him and that he was becoming more and more aggressive and intolerant every time he was seen in one of the local hostelries. He wasn't opening his shop anymore, so it was only a matter of time before he ran out of money to fund his drinking binges and I shuddered to think what he would do then. I hoped that he wouldn't come looking for me again."

"The weather didn't get any better, in fact half way through February it got a lot worse. The snow which had fallen earlier in the winter had never melted because the temperature was so low and then gale-force winds began to blow, so cold they felt as though they were coming straight from the arctic. It didn't matter how many layers of clothes you wore, that wind could pass through anything and there were a few cases of frostbite among people who worked outside. The dock workers were particularly hard hit because that cold wind was coming straight off the sea, with nothing to take the edge off it. Every time I went down to the warehouse I took flasks of hot tea and soup with me and I wished that I could do the same for all the soldiers who were huddled in trenches, trying to stay alive in that horrendous weather."

"Although the daylight hours were starting to get slightly longer it didn't make any difference to the weather and when snow fell, it made even the middle of the day a dark, depressing time. William was suffering a lot of pain in his legs, because the icy conditions seemed to make every nerve ending susceptible and he was taking a lot of the painkilling drafts that the doctor prescribed for him. Unfortunately, they didn't seem to work when the pain was at its worst and he began drinking in order to numb it, spending nearly every night at the Red Lion. I didn't consider that it was a good idea for him to depend on alcohol so much, but his absence every evening made home life a lot more bearable and Simon soon stopped asking where his Daddy was. William stayed sober long enough each day to take Simon to school and then to fetch him home again, leaving for the Red Lion as Simon was having his tea. He would roll home about midnight, when I had already gone to bed, but as long as he was up in time to take Simon to school, I didn't question what he was doing."

"One Friday, during the second week in February, William set off to collect Simon from school as usual. It had stopped snowing, so when they got home he announced that he wanted to take Simon down to the market on Nelson Street and they would both have hot chestnuts from the cart which came every Friday. I agreed because Simon was so eager to go to the market with his Daddy and if it kept William out of the Red Lion for another couple of hours, then all to the good. It was already getting dark when they set off and I did wonder if it had been a good idea after all, but the market stalls always had lanterns lit and I thought Simon would probably enjoy the atmosphere of the bustling market as much as he would enjoy the chestnuts"

"I lit the lamps in the shop that day while Hannah continued to serve customers, but then the steady stream of eager buyers dried up and it gave me time to look outside. It had started to snow again and even as I watched, the tiny flakes of the first shower got bigger and bigger until they were the size of golf balls, flying horizontally past the window and forming a curtain through which it was impossible to see. As I stood staring out of the window, Sammy crashed through the door in his haste to get in out of the storm."

"'By, it's rough out there, lass,' he said when he had shaken the snow off his face so that he could see again. "Looks like its set in for the night again. I don't think I've ever seen so much snow in all my life. I've never known a winter like this one.'"

"I agreed with Sam but my mind was concentrating on Simon and William. I had expected that they would have been home by now, because it wasn't that far to the market and if they were only buying chestnuts, it wouldn't have taken very long. It was completely dark outside by that time and most people had returned to their homes. No-one would want to go outside again on a night like that."

"We closed the shop and I set about making tea for us all, expecting Sammy to say that he would go home to sort a meal for his other two girls, but he didn't. He hung around in the kitchen and was unusually silent, while I bustled around him, setting the table for us all to eat. I couldn't speak because I was far too worried about Simon and his whereabouts, although I saw the glances being exchanged between Annie and Sam. It was Peter who put my worries into words, however, when he innocently asked, 'Where's Simon? Why hasn't he come home for his tea?'"

"That was the final straw for me. I dropped the serving spoon I had been holding and swung round to look at Sammy."

"'Do you think something's happened to them?' I asked, my voice quivering with the fear which was clutching at my stomach."

"'What time did they go out?' Sam asked. 'It can't have been too long ago because Simon was at school today, wasn't he?'"

"'Yes, Simon went to school and William brought him home after school tonight. Simon wanted to go and get hot chestnuts from the stall at the market, so William took him there. But the market will have ended ages ago. They will have packed up and gone when the snow got heavier, because all their customers will have gone home. I thought William would have brought Simon home long before this.'"

"I dropped onto a chair and rested my head in my hands. My brain was whirling with thoughts of all that could have happened to them and I could feel the panic welling up inside me, threatening to escape and take all my self-control with it. Sam sat down next to me and took hold of my hand, forcing me to look at him."

"'Don't panic, lass,' he said, very quietly and calmly. 'They've probably taken shelter in one of the pubs near the market place and they're waiting for the storm to pass. When the snow stops, they'll likely come straight home.'"

"'You don't believe that any more than I do.' I replied. 'Something's happened to them and that's why they haven't come home.' I had an overwhelming sense of doom, even though my sensible side was agreeing with Sammy that they would have taken shelter somewhere out of the storm and that they would return home when the snow abated. In my mind, William and Simon's disappearance had something to do with Butcher Dennison and once that connection had formed, I couldn't separate the two."

"I stood up and began pacing the kitchen floor, my mind jumping from Simon to the pig butcher, back and forth, back and forth until my brain was reeling with the worry and I was almost running round the kitchen. It was Annie who put into words what we had all been thinking."

"'Hannah and I will stay here, in case William and Simon come home. Why don't you three go round by the market and see if anyone has seen the pair of them?'"

"Sammy showed that he was nearly as worried as I was because he didn't hesitate. He was pulling his coat on almost while Annie was still speaking and stopped only long enough to urge her to lock all the doors and not open them unless he or I spoke to her. I was as quick as Sammy and wrapped myself into my thick winter shawl and donned my gloves while Annie shoved Peter's arms into his coat and pulled a woollen hat onto his head."

"We set off into a complete whiteout, unable to see the hands in front of our faces as the snow whirled round us, deadening all sound apart from the wind and hiding all the familiar landmarks such as houses and roads. In order to walk along King Street we had to join hands in a line and Sam felt his way along the house fronts so that we knew we were going in the direction of Lorne Terrace and the market. I was the middle one of the line of us, with Sam on my left and Peter tugging my hand on the right side of me. The gusting wind was so strong that it was only these two anchors that stopped me from being blown over and I worried how we were ever going to find anyone in those terrible conditions. A picture of soldiers huddled down in trenches while the snow raged around them popped into my mind and for a second I almost believed that I was seeing the front line of a battlefield, until the wind gusted again and the snow formed white pillows in front of me. I learnt years later that it is possible to have mirages in a whiteout, the same as people have in deserts."

"We made our way slowly along King Street until we came to its junction with Middlesbrough Road, turned right and crossed over this main road and continued down Lorne Terrace towards the market place. It seemed to have turned even colder since we had left the shop, with the wind coming straight towards us as it blew in from the North Sea, laden with snow and carrying the bitter chill from the Russian steppes. Many people say it can be too cold to snow, but that night was the coldest I have ever known and the snow was unrelenting as the wind whipped it against our bodies."

"There were very few people about because the weather was so bad and those who were outside were hurrying as fast as they could with their heads down against the wind, intent on reaching home and shelter. Sam had to grab at arms as they went past in order to ask them if they had seen William and Simon. The answer was always in the negative and, by the time we crossed onto Station Road without any trace of them, my apprehension had reached fever pitch. I had a fear on me unlike anything I had ever experienced before, although I would have been hard put to have justified why I was so fearful. It was animal-like in its intensity and it made me want to sit down on the pavement and howl my fear to the skies."

"I tried to keep this fear to myself, but as we passed the bright lights of the Red Lion, I could see an answering fear in Sammy's eyes as he held my arm to stop me moving on."

"'I'll go in and see if they are sheltering in here,' he yelled above the noise of the wind, nodding towards the public house. 'I can ask if anyone has seen them if they aren't there.'"

"Peter and I waited outside in the cold. I wouldn't have been seen dead inside a drinking establishment like that and I knew that Annie wouldn't allow Peter inside a public house since one of his contemporaries had taken him in as a joke two years before and Peter had drunk beer until he was sick. It was so cold, standing there in the snow and the wind and my inner voice was screaming at me that something terrible was going to happen which I needed to stop, but I didn't know where to go to stop it. I didn't care if William was dead drunk in a ditch, as long as Simon was safe. If I could only find Simon and take him home, where we could be warm and safe from any harm."

"Peter could feel the fear coming off me. He could often sense the distress of others because his own senses were so simple and clear cut and they didn't drown out the feelings of others. He stroked my hand as we stood, linked, waiting for Sammy to come out of the Red Lion, hopefully bringing Simon with him."

"But that was not to be. Sam came out of the Lion alone, shaking his head when I asked if anyone had seen William and Simon. We continued to tramp along Station Road until we reached the Lord Nelson public house. This time, Sam just nodded in the direction of the front door and I nodded back. He went inside, once again leaving Peter and I huddled together in the wind and the snow. I tried to think about all the poor Tommies sitting hunched together in their trenches as the wind whistled above them and the snow did it's best to bury them before the Hun killed them, but I was all out of empathy that night. I could only think about Simon and how much I loved him. Even Butcher Dennison and what he had done to me couldn't penetrate my brain that night. There was a refrain going round and round in my head – Simon, Simon, Simon. Please be safe, my baby, please be safe."

"Sam came out of the Lord Nelson and, once again, he was alone, shaking his head at me as I looked at him in hope. So we set off again, quartering the streets around the market place, only stopping at each public house so that Sam could go in and enquire if anyone had seen William and Simon since the market closed and only getting negative answers. Peter and I stood and let the wind and the snow whip our faces as we waited with less and less hope at each bar."

"I hadn't realised how many streets there were in our town or how many drinking establishments and by the time we had tramped each street and visited places like the Cleveland Bay and the George IV, my face was frozen into a rectal grimace and my arms, legs and feet were so cold I could no longer feel them. Eventually, as we reached the corner where King Street crossed Middlesbrough Road for the second time that night, Sammy stopped and held me back. As we hesitated on the pavement, I realised that it wasn't snowing quite as heavily as before and the wind had dropped to only gale intensity."

"'We're going back to the shop now, Bia,' Sam said. 'I want to go and get Jenny and Alice and leave them with Annie before we go out again. I don't want them in the house on their own tonight. We can have something hot to drink to warm us up before we go out searching again. We can't carry on until we've thawed out a bit.'"

"Every nerve in my body was screaming 'No! No! No!' to this. I couldn't stop searching until I'd found Simon, but I knew that Sam was right about us getting something hot inside us. We wouldn't be able to search if we were frozen to the bone. I could also understand that he was worried about his two girls, but the fact that he wanted them to leave their home and join Annie and Hannah in Queen Street, told me more than he had put into words."

"'You think that butcher Dennison is behind Simon's disappearance, don't you?' I asked him, although I already knew the answer. 'That pig butcher has got my baby and he's going to hurt him!'"

"'Don't panic, lass. It won't help us if you lose your head now.' Sam replied. 'I don't know if Dennison has got William and Simon, but I'm damned sure that he's involved somehow and I want my girls safe before we go out and track him down. I wouldn't put it past him to try and use my girls in some way, so I want to stop that happening.'"

"'You're right, Sam.' I agreed. 'I'm sure he's involved in this somehow and it isn't safe for your girls to be on their own. Let's go quickly. The faster we get to the shop, the quicker we can be out searching again.'"

"We walked as quickly as we could along King Street and back to the shop where Annie acted as instructed and wouldn't unlock the door until she was sure that it was Sammy who was on the outside of it. She ushered us inside and pushed me down into the chair next to the range."

"'Get us hot drinks, will you please Annie?' Sam asked, while he wrapped his coat tighter around his body. 'Make sure Bia and Peter get warmed through while I go and get Jenny and Alice and bring them back here. I don't trust that pig butcher. I'm sure he's got something to do with this and I want my girls safe before we go out searching again. I'll have something hot when I come back with the girls.'"

"'I've got hot soup on the stove.' Annie answered. 'I thought you'd need something to warm you through after you'd been out in this weather. Bring the lasses back here and I'll look after them until you find Simon.'"

"'Good lass,' was all Sam said, but he wrapped his arm around her shoulder and pulled her to him in a bear hug, saying all he needed to without words. He then put his hand on my shoulder and squeezed me, putting such reassurance into it that I felt strangely comforted. Then he put his head outside the door.

"'The snow has stopped and the wind's dropping even more. It'll be easier going when we go back out.'"

"He slammed the door behind him as he disappeared into the dark and Annie locked it once again. She moved across to me and helped me to unwrap the layers of my shawl before she pressed a mug of hot soup into my hands. I wasn't hungry, but common sense told me I needed the soup to thaw my insides and to sustain me when we started our search again, so I forced myself to drink it, even though it was a struggle to swallow. The panic inside me seemed to block my throat, it was so tangible."

"Annie had moved across to Peter and helped him out of his winter wrappings before passing him a mug of the soup. He was incredibly eager for it and drank it greedily, holding his mug out for more when he had drained it. As she bustled about refilling it, Annie looked over at me with such compassion in her face I wanted to cry."

"'We'll find them, honey,' she murmured. 'Sammy won't rest until he's got Simon back safe for you. Don't you worry about that.'"

"'I know he won't Annie.' I replied. 'But I've got such a fear on me tonight. Something really bad has already happened, I can feel it and it's sucking the life out of me. If something bad *has* happened to Simon, I won't be able to carry on without him. He's my world, my life, my reason for living and I know something's wrong.'"

"My voice had risen as I spoke, as the panic inside me started to leach out of me and Peter was watching me with worried eyes and a frown on his forehead, struggling to properly understand what was happening. Annie hurried over to me and sat on the arm of my chair, holding on to me and rocking me as though I was a child."

"'Nothing will have happened to him, Bia,' she said as she tried to soothe me. 'They'll have met someone and likely taken shelter in their house while the weather was so bad. Now that it's stopped snowing they'll come home. Just you wait and see.'"

"I leant against her and took what comfort I could from the shelter of her arms but I knew, deep down, that the damage had already been done. Inside me my heart told me that Simon was dead and I would only get his body back. I would never again hold him as he laughed, or stroke his soft hair when he was settled in his bed for the night. My heart was as frozen as the ground outside with the pain and the fear of what had happened."

"Sammy wasn't long before he was back with Jenny and Alice and he got them safely ensconced next to the fire before he would have some of Annie's hot soup. I had risen from the chair as soon as the girls came in and I was wrapped in layers of outer clothing ready to set out again, before Sam had started on his soup. Peter followed my lead and he, too, was well wrapped up against the bitter cold."

"Sam drank his hot soup so quickly that it brought tears to his eyes, but he brushed them aside and bundled himself back into layers of clothing."

"'The snow has stopped completely now and the wind's dropped too,' he said, before we took our leave of Annie and the girls. 'The sky is clearing and it'll be easier to see because it's a full moon out there now.'"

"For some unknown reason, these words of Sammy's twanged the same nerves in my body that thoughts of Simon twanged, although I couldn't understand then why they did so. I just nodded my agreement and turned and hugged Annie before we set out again into the night. The air was even colder than before, if such a thing was possible, but at least we could walk upright and not have to fight to make any headway against the wind. We re-traced our steps to the end of King Street and turned right, heading for Lorne Terrace and the market place."

As Nana paused to draw breath, Victoria heard her mother shouting her name from downstairs and she didn't sound as though she was in one of her more placid moods.

"I'll have to go Nana. Mam's shouting for me and I daren't make her wait otherwise she'll stop me coming back this afternoon," she said.

"Before you come back this afternoon, please go to Mr Vine's office and ask him to come and see me tomorrow. Don't forget, he's got to come during the day when the shop's open and he has to come to the side door where you will let him in. That way, we can get it all sorted out before your mother finds out. Good girl."

Victoria promised that she would go to make the appointment as soon as she had had her lunch and Bia was busy in the shop. She very much doubted that Mr Vine would drop everything to call on her grandmother but she would do her best to explain and just hope that he could come soon. It was the only time her grandmother had been agitated about anything recently and Victoria didn't want to upset her any more. With a final promise to go to the solicitors' office that afternoon and to make sure that her mother wouldn't see her go out, she ran downstairs to help her mother make the lunch. If she was biddable over lunchtime, Mam might agree to her spending the rest of the day with her grandmother.

Chapter Ten

Victoria was as biddable as she knew how to be that lunchtime, offering to do the washing up before they had sat down to eat and explaining how much revision she had got done while Nana Lymer slept. It was difficult, eating a meal with her fingers crossed, but she managed to do it and was rewarded by being given permission to sit in Nana's room all that afternoon. Having offered to do the washing up, she did have to do it in actuality, so it was after 2pm before she could go back into Nana's room, to let her know that Mam was in the shop and she (Victoria) was going to let herself out of the side door and head towards South Terrace, before making for Station Road. That way, she avoided going past the shop and so her mother wouldn't see her through the shop windows and want to know where she was going.

Victoria made her way to Station Road and went half way down it before she reached the solicitor's office. It was a place she had never been in before and she was overawed by the large studded door and the brass plate fastened to the wall. She hesitated on the doorstep, not sure if she should knock on the door or whether she should open it and walk straight in. Then she realised that she looked as though she was loitering by hanging around outside, so she turned the brass door handle and stepped through into a reception office. There was a lady sitting behind the reception desk who looked up as Victoria entered. She had a long, thin face, almost horsey in appearance and a pair of horn-rimmed spectacles perched on the end of her nose. Her hair was pulled back from her face into a tight bun on the back of her head and what little of the hair showed was all a steel-grey colour. She wore a dark cardigan over a white blouse, both buttoned up to the neck and unrelieved by any brooch or adornment of any sort. She looked up as Victoria entered and seemed to measure her against a standard, her tight mouth proving that she obviously deemed that Victoria fell way short of the expected level.

"Yes. Can I help you?" The receptionist's voice was sharp, as though she was ready and able to send Victoria away with a flea in her ear. Victoria quailed internally, but the thought of having to return home and confess that she had been too scared of the receptionist to ask for Mr Vine to visit, stiffened her backbone and prompted her to step up to the desk.

"My grandmother would like Mr Vine to visit her at home tomorrow." Victoria said, more loudly than she had intended because she was nervous of the reaction of the receptionist and was doing her best to hide it.

"Mr Vine does not conduct business in private houses, nor can he drop everything to answer a summons from all and sundry." The receptionist was definitely looking down her nose at Victoria now and evidently considered the conversation to be over, as she rose from her desk and started rifling through the filing cabinet which was against the far wall. Her cursory treatment made Victoria's blood boil and she forgot about being timid as her need to carry out her grandmother's request surfaced.

"My grandmother would like Mr Vine to visit her," she repeated, stepping closer to the desk.

"And I reiterate, Mr Vine does not visit people in their homes, especially not at short notice." Once again, the receptionist considered the matter closed and turned back to the filing cabinet.

"But my grandmother's housebound, so she can't come to this office." Victoria's voice was rising as she panicked at the thought of trying to get past this brick wall. "Her name is Mrs Lymer and she has been a client for a long time. Surely Mr Vine can make an exception when his clients can't manage to get to his office."

The filing cabinet drawer was slammed shut to emphasise that Victoria had now stepped completely over the unseen line, before the receptionist turned to face her. She opened her sneering mouth to deliver what would probably have been a very cutting remark, but stopped when the door leading to another office was opened and a man popped his head round. He was a tall, dark-haired young man with a pleasant face and he scrutinised Victoria with a smile.

"Did I hear Mrs Lymer's name mentioned?" he asked, stepping forward towards Victoria. Victoria heaved a sigh of relief and hastened to answer him before the receptionist stopped her.

"Mrs Lymer is my grandmother and she wants Mr Vine to visit her at home." She was gabbling, she knew that, but she was desperate to get the request spoken before the receptionist butted in and stopped her. "She's housebound now and she needs to see Mr Vine urgently, so he'll have to come to the shop."

The man held up his hand.

"I'm Mr Vine." He said. "If Mrs Lymer wants to see me, then of course I will visit her at home. She's back living in Queen Street, then? At the original shop?"

Victoria wasn't sure what he meant by 'the original shop', but he had said Queen Street so she nodded her head.

"Nana came to live with us a few years ago, when she got too frail to continue living on her own. I'm Victoria, by the way, her granddaughter."

Mr Vine shook Victoria's hand and smiled warmly at her.

"I can remember your Nana when I was a child. My father used to call in to see her regularly and he often took me with him as a treat. Your Nana made the best cakes in the town and she always had time to listen to a small boy's woes. I will be honoured to visit her tomorrow. Shall we say about 2pm? Do you think that would suit her?"

"She'll be very happy with that." Victoria answered, smiling back at him. "Can you come to the side door though, not through the shop? Nana doesn't want you to come through the shop." She wondered if she should say that her grandmother didn't want Victoria's mother to know that she was meeting Mr Vine, but refrained from so doing because it could lead to awkward questions, so she didn't explain any more, but Mr Vine was there before her.

"Mrs Lymer doesn't want your mother to know that I'm visiting, eh? I can understand that." He smiled again. "No problem. I'll come to the side door at 2pm tomorrow and no doubt you will let me in. Will you make a note in my diary Miss Talbot, please? I don't want to let Mrs Lymer down by forgetting our appointment. She was a favourite client of my father and I could fully understand why." He turned back to face Victoria, missing the sneer that had spread across Miss Talbot's face when she was requested to enter the appointment into his diary. Victoria didn't miss it, however and smiled sunnily at the acidic lady.

"I shall see you tomorrow then, Victoria." Mr Vine said, shaking her hand. "I'm very pleased to have met you."

He smiled again and then returned through the door into the next office. Miss Talbot sniffed disgustedly but there wasn't very much she could do or say now that Mr Vine had spoken. Victoria smiled at her and left the office feeling much more confident than she had when she had arrived. It crossed her mind that Mr Vine obviously considered her grandmother an important woman, or he wouldn't have agreed so readily to making a home visit.

She delivered the message that Mr Vine would visit the next afternoon at 2pm as soon as she had let herself in at the side door and crept upstairs to Nana's bedroom. She felt very guilty about keeping secrets from her mother, but she could understand her grandmother's reluctance to let Bia know that she was seeing her solicitor. Victoria still had no idea why her grandmother wanted to see Mr Vine, but instinct told her that her mother would not approve. Nana Lymer took Mr Vine's acquiescence as her right and Victoria decided not to mention the fight with the battle-axe receptionist before Mr Vine had appeared. She didn't feel that she had come out of that particular meeting with any degree of success and didn't want to contemplate what would have happened if Mr Vine hadn't appeared.

"Shall we go on with the story?" Nana asked, once Victoria had delivered her message and got herself settled in the bedside chair.

"Oh yes!" Victoria answered. "I want to know if you found Simon that terrible night. But don't tell me any more if it's going to upset you." Victoria had a feeling that the search for Simon hadn't ended happily and she was worried about how much this narration was going to upset Nana Lymer. It wasn't fair of her to try and force her grandmother into discussing events that had been so traumatic for her, not just to satisfy Victoria's curiosity.

"I've told you before, pet, all this happened a long time ago." Nana reassured her. "It's still very sad, but the old adage that time is a great healer is very true. Mankind wouldn't have survived if people never got over sad events and couldn't carry on with their lives, now would it? But, where had we got to?"

"Granddad Sam had collected Jenny and Alice from his house and brought them to the shop so that they would be safe from the pig butcher. You, Peter and Granddad Sam were going out again to search for Simon and William. The snow had stopped and the wind had dropped, so it was going to be easier to search." Victoria hadn't missed a word of her Nana's tale.

"You are a good listener! It's very flattering that you are so interested in what an old woman has to say."

"So, back to my tale," Nana continued. "Sam, Peter and I set off once again to search for William and Simon. The weather had definitely taken a turn for the better and it was possible now to see very clearly because of the full moon shining in the sky. A thought came unbidden to my mind; this was what they called a 'hunter's moon'. How apt that phrase was didn't become clear until later and then it became as clear as the night sky. It was still exceptionally cold and the harsh frost was making the millions of stars glitter like ice in the black sky."

"One or two people were now out in the streets because the conditions had improved, but they were still hurrying along to get home out of the bitter cold. They were more easily halted now, so that Sam could ask them if they had seen William and Simon and conversation was now possible because the air was so still and the noise of the wind had abated."

"The answers were still all negative. No-one seemed to have seen William and Simon earlier in the evening and every negative answer increased the words in my head which throbbed along with my heartbeat. 'He's dead, he's dead' echoed in my head with every beat of my heart and my legs walked to the same beat, marking out my fear and terror as we traversed the streets."

"I think Sammy could feel the fear emanating from me because he took hold of my arm and half-led me along. Peter was once again conscious of my mood and slipped his hand into my other hand, so that we trudged, linked, along the roads."

"We reached the market place which looked so strange minus its stalls and crowds of chattering shoppers and I made to cross it to get to the Red Lion so that Sam could go inside and ask after Simon again, but Sam held me back. He had seen what I had missed as I trudged, wrapped up in my misery, and he pointed to a figure which was searching through the rubbish left by the stallholders when they had rapidly abandoned the market at the onset of the storm."

"I stood still and waited hand-in-hand with Peter while Sam went over to the market cross and talked to the figure. He soon came back with the first sighting of William and Simon that night."

"'The tramp's seen them tonight,' he said. 'Come and listen to what he has to say.'"

We all walked over to where the tramp waited, his hands full of the detritus of that day's market. He confirmed what Sam had said."

"'Oh aye, I saw them, lassie. Yon lad's the one who lost his arm to the Hun. Him and the little one came out of the Red Lion when it had just started to snow. I remember them 'cos I asked him if he had any spare change, but he told me to go to hell and work for it. I'd thought he might have been a bit freer with his brass like, him knowing what it was like to suffer.'"

"I realised then that the tramp was standing rather precariously on one whole leg and one stiff wooden leg and remembered his story from my childhood. He'd lost his leg in an accident in the ironstone mines on the Cleveland Hills and life obviously hadn't been kind to him since. Now the poor old bugger was outside on one of the coldest nights I had ever known, trying to find food to keep himself alive. But his next words pushed all thoughts of his problems out of my mind."

"'Yon pig butcher was talking to them, outside the pub. He had followed them out of the Red Lion. I wondered if he'd been fighting recently, cos he looked a right mess, with one of his ears bandaged up and a scratch across his face.'"

"Sammy glanced at me when the tramp spoke of the pig butcher, but I kept my face expressionless although that wasn't a difficult thing to do. I was frozen to the bone because the night was so cold and the tramp's words sent an icy torrent of fear coursing round my body, finishing by impaling my heart with its icy spikes. What the tramp said next stopped my heart completely."

"'The men shouted at each other and then they went off together down Station Road towards the docks. The poor little lad had to run to keep up with them and he was crying as he ran.'"

"My legs failed me and I sank down onto my knees on the snowy, icy road. I couldn't get back up, so I stayed there and lifted my face to the sky, praying that my baby wasn't dead, that he was alive and unharmed, but I knew within myself that this was a vain hope. There was no Divine Being listening to my prayers that night, ready to deliver my child back to me. Simon was dead and I knew it. What the tramp had said had sealed his fate and all I could hope for was the chance of finding his little body so that I could take him home, before I laid myself down and stopped breathing."

"With strong but gentle hands, Sam lifted me back onto my feet and turned my face towards the docks. Then he released me and walked back to the tramp, speaking with him and then handing something over which the tramp looked at in astonishment."

"'Thank you, lad. God bless you. I hope you find the little one soon. It's not a night for a bairn to be out of doors, although I'd leave his father to rot in the cold.'"

"The tramp limped away as Sam re-joined Peter and I."

"'What did you give him?' I asked, amazed at the fact that I could sound so normal when my whole world had turned upside down."

"'Just some money.' Sam answered. 'The poor old bugger needs it more than I do. I worked in those mines when I was a young lad and I know what a hard life it was. And I came out of it whole and counted myself lucky to do so. He's suffered for years and it isn't right that he should be outside in this weather, scavenging for food and with no home to go to. Added to all that, he's the only person who's been of any help to us tonight. Are you ready to move on now, lass? Yon bloke said they headed towards the docks when they left the Red Lion.'"

"'They headed for the warehouses, Sammy.' I insisted. 'They weren't going to the docks, there's no reason for them to go there. Dennison lured William to the warehouse, I know it. For some twisted reason of his own, he wanted William and Simon to go to the warehouse where he tried to rape me last week.'"

"'Yes, I agree with you. For whatever reason of his own, he wanted William to go to the warehouse with him. I think it was just sheer bad luck that Simon happened to be with William at the time and so he took them both. I can't for the life of me work out what it is that Dennison wants though. That's got me beat.'"

"'I can, Sam.' I said. 'I know what the pig butcher wants. He's told William that it wasn't rape and he wants to show William where it happened. It's all twisted lies because that's the way Dennison looks at the world. William is daft enough to believe what Dennison was saying, so he's gone to the warehouse with him, taking my baby into danger. I'll kill William if Dennison's hurt one hair on my baby's head!'"

"My voice had risen again as the thought of William being so stupid and risking Simon's well-being seemed to have brought me back to life. I was desperate to get to the warehouse, not only to save Simon, but also to wreak my revenge on both men who had made my life a misery. Sam's voice cut through my thoughts."

"'Simon will be fine. Don't you worry about him, Bia, not even the pig butcher would harm a child. Come on, the sooner we can get to the warehouse, the sooner we can get Simon safely back home.'"

"I didn't want to waste time arguing with Sam because time was of the essence in this quest to get my child back, so we set off for the warehouse, walking more quickly now that we weren't searching the road as we walked. Peter was still holding on to my hand, although he hadn't spoken since we had left the tramp and I could feel him trembling as we walked along. I wasn't sure if he was trembling with the cold or if it was because he had understood what the tramp and Sam and I had said and he was fearful over what had happened to Simon. Simon was his

296

best friend. They played together and talked to each other as equals, although Peter had always looked on himself as Simon's protector as well as mine. If the pig butcher *had* hurt Simon, there was a good chance that Peter would want to exact revenge. Life was going to get a lot worse for Dennison if he had injured my baby, both Peter and I would be demanding our pound of flesh from him."

"I wasn't convinced by Sam's statement that Dennison wouldn't have hurt a child. I had seen into Dennison's eyes when he had tried to rape me that afternoon in the warehouse and I knew that not only was he an animal, but also that he was crazy. I had seen the mind behind those eyes that afternoon and I knew that it was twisted and black. He was capable of so much evil and wouldn't be fazed by the idea of murdering a child."

"I stumbled as we set off for the warehouse and would have fallen again if I hadn't been supported on both sides by Sam and Peter. Sam cradled my arm as though I might collapse at any moment and Peter held on to the hand on the other side, drawing comfort from me and pouring comfort back into me. Without them both, I don't think I would have managed to walk as far as the warehouse, although my need to hold my son burned brightly inside me. I gritted my teeth and, supported by both Sam and Peter, walked the length of Station Road and turned through the dock gates to get to my warehouse."

Mrs Lymer paused in her tale, falling silent as her mind relived the fears she had carried that night over sixty years before. Suddenly, it all felt as though it had happened recently and she experienced the stab to the heart that she had felt when she had heard that her small son was in company with the detested pig butcher. Victoria saw her grandmother's face drain of colour and she grasped her hand to steady her.

"Are you all right, Nana?" she asked, terrified that these memories had brought on a heart attack in the old lady. "Shall I call for the doctor or shall I go and get Mam?"

"There's no need for you to panic, pet. I'm quite all right." Mrs Lymer replied. "For a moment there, I could feel the pain that I felt that night and it shocked me that I could still feel the intensity of it. I thought it was all too long ago for it to affect me now, but obviously I was wrong. Be a good girl and go and make a cup of tea, will you? That'll put heart back into me again."

Nana Lymer smiled up at Victoria as she leapt up to do her grandmother's bidding. Victoria was seriously worried about her and contemplated asking her mother to come up and check that she was fine and not likely to keel over at any minute, but she restrained herself, deciding that she would call her mother if Nana didn't look any better when she took the tea upstairs. Luckily, no-one entered the kitchen while she was making the brew, so she was able to rush back upstairs the minute the tea was poured. Nana was sitting up in bed, looking pink and pretty as she always did and Victoria heaved a silent sigh of relief.

"You had me worried there, Nana," she confessed. "You went ever so pale and I thought you were having a nasty turn."

"No, pet." Nana answered. "Just being a silly old woman, as your mother keeps on telling me. It took me by surprise that I was affected by the thoughts of that night, which *is* silly because I've thought about what happened that night so many times over the years and it's been a long time since it bothered me so much. But we'll not get much more time today to tell the story. It won't be long before your Mam wants you to help her get the tea ready. Do you think she'll let you sit with me tomorrow morning, because we could go through some more of the tale before Mr Vine comes?"

"I'm sure she will." Victoria was convinced of this. "She doesn't have to think about you and if you need anything while I'm here, I can get it for you, so it makes it easier for her. I'm sure she'll be expecting me to stay with you all day tomorrow. I tell her I can get loads of revision done while you sleep, so she can't complain about it."

"The tale is nearly told, so it won't be long before you are free to do your revision. I don't want you failing your exams just because I wanted to tell you stories." Nana said.

"I'm revising at night, instead of watching the television, so you won't make me fail my exams. You can tell me your story with a clear conscience!" Victoria hastened to reassure her, wondering if it was such a good idea for Nana Lymer to be re-living that terrible past. One thing Victoria was sure of was that it settled Nana's mind to tell what had happened. She hadn't wandered during the night since she had started to tell Victoria what had happened to her during the First World War. With a stab of remembrance, Victoria realised that Nana had been asking for Simon the night that the policeman had found her wandering on Queen Street. Had she been so desperate to tell someone about what had happened that her mind had been trying to do it for her when she was asleep? But Nana had drunk her tea and was ready to begin again.

"We didn't see another soul after we had left the tramp," she continued. "I think the whole population of the town was at home, snug in their houses out of the bitter cold and with no mind to wander outside again on a night like that. The streets were deserted and it looked very strange when I was so used to seeing them thronged with people going about their business. There weren't even any sailors on shore leave from the ships tied up at the docks, even they preferred being warm on their ships to tramping around a frozen town."

"The night was now so clear that the stars alone were shining brightly enough to cast shadows of their own and the moon was almost too bright to look at. The stars were so sharp in that black sky, they looked as though you could pluck them from their moorings and use them as knives. It was as I thought about this that I wished I had thought ahead and brought a knife with me, so that I could use it on Dennison if he had harmed my baby. Then I remembered that I had a knife in the cold store inside my warehouse which was for cutting the large hunks of meat that came off the ships, so that I could convey them more easily to the shop. I hoped that my deduction that Dennison had taken William and Simon to *my* warehouse was correct, because it meant that I had a weapon ready to hand in there and I intended to use it. If he had taken them to his own warehouse, then I would be bereft of weapons. I determined that if we discovered that Simon and William weren't in my warehouse with Dennison, then I would collect the knife from the cold store and take it with me to Dennison's warehouse."

"The warehouse door was locked when we got to it, almost as though it was only doing its normal job of being a place to store food safely, but I knew better. I knew that my baby lay dead inside that place and that the pig butcher was waiting inside there for me to find him. He knew I would come looking for my child and he was in there, waiting patiently for me to turn up. William, I was sure, was still alive, but I knew deep within me that Simon was already dead. So, in a way, I was more prepared than either Sammy or Peter for what we were going to see once we got inside the warehouse."

"Sam tried to force the lock on the warehouse door when he realised that he couldn't open it, but Peter stopped him by putting his hand on Sam's arm and then gesturing for him to stand to one side. Peter clasped both his hands together, held them out in front of his body and then brought his joined hands down onto the lock with an almost gargantuan force. It was more than the lock could take and it splintered away from the door, the heavy metal crashing to the floor."

"The warehouse door stayed closed but then, before anyone could put out a hand to push it, it slowly swung open and revealed the scene inside. The interior of the building was lit by a lamp which stood on a table at the far side of the warehouse and there was a man standing next to it. In a chair to one side sat another man. They were both illuminated by the lamp and both recognisable. The pig butcher was the man standing and William was the figure sitting on the chair. In a little heap on the floor in front of the table lay a tiny form, its arms spread out and its head facing the far wall. Even though I couldn't see his face, I knew this was my baby and I felt my heart sink down through my body to my feet as I realised that he was definitely dead. All my predictions had come true."

"I moved forwards as though I was wading through a river, it was so difficult to walk. The blood in my veins had turned to ice as I looked at my baby and every step I took seemed to send these ice spicules through my veins, stabbing me in hundreds of places inside me. I could hear each of my heartbeats as I crossed the warehouse floor, the sound of them so loud I couldn't hear Sam and Peter as they entered the warehouse behind me. The pig butcher and William were both silent, staring at me as they waited for my reaction to my baby's death."

"As if in a nightmare, I managed to cross the floor until I reached Simon and then I collapsed onto my knees next to his tiny body. The hand that lay nearest to me was totally relaxed, the little fingers slightly curled, looking as though they would flex at any minute and prove that Simon was alive. I lifted the slight body and cuddled him to me, but his head flopped over backwards away from me as I held him. The pig butcher had broken his neck. He had snapped it as easily as snapping a twig and with as little compunction."

"Inside my head I was screaming and wailing but, outwardly, I was very quiet. I could feel my frozen blood still pumping round my body, every beat of my heart carrying daggers of ice through my bloodstream along my veins and I could feel the sharp puncture wounds they were making throughout my whole torso. Still on my knees and still holding Simon's corpse, I turned and looked at William and Dennison for the first time."

"William was sitting on the only chair in the warehouse, his one arm tied to the chair's arm by a red cord which was also looped tightly round his neck, making it impossible for William to raise his head fully without strangling himself. He had blood dripping out of his nose and one eye was already swelling where Dennison had obviously swung a punch at him. His wounds left me cold. I wouldn't have cared if Dennison had been stabbing him with a sword while I watched. I would have just turned away and concentrated on Simon."

"The pig butcher himself was sitting on the edge of the table next to the chair, swinging his legs out in front of him and grinning evilly at the three of us. I couldn't understand why Sam and Peter hadn't overpowered him between them, but then I realised that Dennison was holding the end of the red cord which was wrapped round William's neck. As I glanced at it, he gave a sharp tug which tightened it, causing William to gasp and gag with the pain and the lack of air."

" 'If yon two heavies come any closer to me,' the pig butcher growled, 'I'll really pull your husband's cord. I've wrapped his neck like a joint of pork, with all the knots in just the right places. When I pull the cord those knots will tighten, compress his airway and the armless excuse for a man will choke to death. Do you want to watch me do it?'"

"Oh Nana! The man was mad, he must have been!" Victoria cried. "What sort of a person not only kills a child but thinks other people will want to watch him strangle a man? You must have been absolutely terrified!"

"No." Nana replied. "I wasn't terrified at all. I was dead inside and when you are dead you don't feel anything at all. And I was determined that I was going to kill Dennison for killing my child. I wanted revenge and I wanted it while the white-heat of my anger was still raging inside me. Not for me the idea that revenge is a dish best eaten cold, oh no. I only had one thing to live for at that moment in time and that was to watch my son's killer as his life-blood drained from him."

There was silence between them as Victoria digested this thought and then both Nana and Victoria clearly heard Victoria's mother shouting from the bottom of the stairs.

"It's Mam." Victoria said, unnecessarily. "It must be tea-time and I promised I would help her cook it. But I can't go now! I want to know what happened next!"

"You'd better go now, Victoria." Nana said. "If you upset your mother now, she might not let you sit with me tomorrow and you've got to let Mr Vine in when he comes. He might ask for me in the shop if he doesn't get an answer at the side door and then your mother will never rest until she finds out what he's here for. You must go downstairs now."

"Yes, you're right, Nana, as usual." Victoria said. "But fancy having to stop at that point in the story! I'll never manage to revise tonight because I'll be wondering what happened next."

"Just bide your patience, pet. You'll hear the rest of it tomorrow, don't you worry! Now go, quickly!"

"Right! I've gone! See you tomorrow, Nana!" And Victoria grabbed her English books and shot down the stairs into the kitchen, where her mother was already throwing meat into a big pan on the cooker.

"It's a good job you came when you did, lady" was her mother's opening remark. "I told you to peel those potatoes for tea, so that we can eat at a reasonable time tonight and what did you do? Not what I asked you to, that's for sure. You might be on holiday from school, but there's still work to be done here."

"I'm sorry, Mam." Victoria managed to butt in when her mother had to stop to draw breath. "But I was revising this Shakespeare play and I was lost in what was happening. I really didn't hear you. I'm sorry."

"Humph!" Bia grunted, knowing that she couldn't complain about her daughter revising for her exams. "Well, you can get on with them now."

Victoria set to with a will, amazed at herself for daring to lie to her mother and secretly pleased that for the first time in her life she had managed to divert one of her mother's bad moods away from herself. Was she growing up? Would she reach a point where it didn't matter to her what her mother said to her, she would be able to ignore the jibes and not let them hurt her? It hardly seemed possible but, for the first time in her life, she had given her mother an answer and it hadn't been thrown straight back at her. Was it the confidence to do it that was lacking in her and not the capability? She wasn't ready to test this out, but she felt that she *was* growing in confidence and it was coming to her from her grandmother. She felt she had done a lot of growing up since Nana Lymer had started telling her what terrible things had happened to her when she was a young woman, but she had fought back against every knock that life had given her. Perhaps Victoria was imbibing some of her grandmother's courage as she absorbed her story. It was a thought that made her feel warm inside and provided a protective shell against her mother's taunts.

Chapter Eleven

The next morning, Victoria was up, dressed and had had her breakfast before her father came back from his early morning visit to the bakery to collect the bread and cakes to sell that day.

"You're eager this morning." Dad smiled at her. "Are you going to do some revision for your exams today? You've got to get good grades to be able to choose what you want to do at A-level and then there's university after that. Doesn't look like you'll be earning any money to put into the family pot for a long time yet!"

"Dad!" Victoria cried. "You don't mean that, do you? You know I've wanted to go to university since I started the Grammar school!"

"Of course I don't mean it, you daft ha'pporth." Jack grinned at his daughter. "I'm only kidding you. I'll be as proud as punch when you get your place in a university! Just think. My daughter, university educated and me hardly able to put two words together. You could end up running the country, you could, once you've got a degree. There'll be no stopping you."

"I don't think I want to run the country, Dad. Anyway, can you imagine it? A grocer's daughter running England! It's not very likely, is it?"

"Stranger things have happened, pet. And you've got the brains to be able to do it." Jack smiled fondly at the girl, wishing that her mother would be kinder towards her. The lass was clever and bonny with it, but she never pushed herself forwards because her mother had spent all her life knocking her down. Jack couldn't understand why Bia had such a downer on her only child, particularly when the lass was so biddable and pleasant. He'd heard about youngsters these days who went off on the back of motorbikes without telling their parents and got up to all sorts of things. Victoria wasn't like that, but to hear Bia you would think she was the worst daughter in the world. Jack sighed. He'd given up trying to understand his wife about two weeks after he had met her. He supposed he really should intervene when Bia was in one of her 'daughter-bashing' moods

314

but that would turn her bad temper onto him and he much preferred a quiet life. There were times when he thought he let his daughter down, but it was easier for him to say nothing and he had taken the easy way all his life. One day, though, Bia would go too far and he would have to put his foot down, but he decided to leave thoughts of that day until it arrived.

Victoria gave her father a hearty kiss on his cheek and then swept upstairs with Nana's breakfast on a tray. She was eager to find out as much as she could that morning before Mr Vine's visit, because thoughts of what had happened in the warehouse had been on her mind since the day before, when her mother had called her away from Nana's bedroom.

"Good morning, Victoria." Nana was sitting up in bed, wrapped in her favourite pink bed jacket, when Victoria entered the room. "Can you stay this morning or do you have to work in the shop?"

"I can stay, Nana," Victoria answered. "Mam says I can stay with you all day again, so that means I can let Mr Vine in

315

this afternoon when he comes. Are you up to telling me the rest of the story or will it be too painful for you?"

"To be truthful, Victoria," Nana answered, "I'll be glad to get it all off my chest. I've carried memories about that night around with me for more than half a century and the anger and the sadness have eaten away at me. I feel refreshed that I can finally get it all out into the open. Just let me finish this cup of tea and we'll begin again."

Victoria moved the tray with the breakfast pots on it and settled herself into the comfy chair next to Nana's bed, eager to hear what happened next. Nana finished her tea and then composed herself for the next instalment, eager to tell it but wary of rushing in and missing out any vital parts.

"The pig butcher thought I'd brought Peter and Sam with me to the warehouse so that I could use them as muscle to overpower him. That had been the last thing on my mind. They had come with me to help me, but as far as I was concerned, *I* was the one who was going to dish out the retribution that night.

316

It never crossed Dennison's mind that I was an enemy, because he tarred all women with the same brush. To him, all women were weak creatures who needed a man to get them through life and he didn't look at me as a source of danger. That was a daft thing for him to do, particularly after the embarrassment he'd had when he had fallen into our tin bath, but any tiny handle I could get on the situation was a plus as far as I was concerned. He would underestimate me at his own cost."

"When he threatened to choke William if Sam and Peter tried anything, both of them moved a step away from the butcher and William, as though to give Dennison breathing room. But I wasn't stepping backwards, no matter what the cost. He'd done his worst to me already; nothing else could come close to the pain I felt through losing Simon. As far as my involvement in the situation was concerned, the pig butcher had already played his trump card and the thing about trump cards is that you can only play them once. From now on, I had nothing left to lose which meant I was ready, able and willing to play any trick in the book to make Dennison pay for what he had done to my son."

"I didn't want to let go of Simon. What I wanted to do was to hold him close and just stop breathing, so that I joined him in that very attractive state of never having any feelings anymore, but I had to get my revenge first, before I could join Simon in death. And in order to get my revenge, I needed to be able to move about in the warehouse. With tremendous sadness, I laid Simon gently down on the floor, arranging his arms and legs so that he looked as though he was sleeping peacefully, then I slowly rose to my feet."

"'Why did you do it?' I asked. 'Why did you kill my child? What have Simon or I ever done to you that could justify you killing my son?'"

"I was surprised that I could speak and that my voice didn't waver at all. I didn't speak loudly but my voice was strong and steady and I drew strength from my ability to be able to conceal what I was really feeling. The ice daggers in my blood had all gathered in my heart and they crackled every time my heart gave a beat, but because my heart was so cold, the ice daggers couldn't melt and I thought I would have them until I died."

"I waited without saying any more. I waited for the pig butcher to tell me why he had killed my baby, because I knew there was more to this than the butcher's anger at my turning down his advances. Even a madman didn't kill because he had been spurned. Dennison waited before he replied, glancing from me to Sam and Peter and then down to William where he lolled on the chair."

"'I think you need to ask your husband why I killed your son, Mrs Drinkwater,' he said, giving the red cord a yank as though he wanted to encourage William to speak. 'I'm sure he'll be able to explain it all to you.'"

"I was thrown by this remark, because it was the last thing I was expecting. I was so sure that he had killed Simon and was threatening to kill William because of something he had imagined *I* had done, that telling me that William knew why he had done it threw me off kilter. I glanced across at William, assuming that he would tell me what Dennison meant, but William had his head hanging down and wouldn't look at me. I looked back at the pig butcher and saw that he was smiling to himself, although there was precious little humour in that smile."

"'Come on, William.' Dennison snarled. 'Your lady wife is waiting for an answer to her question. She wants to know why I killed her little boy and you know why I did it. I know you do. It's only polite for you to answer the lady and put her out of her misery.'"

"Dennison yanked on the red cord again but, although he groaned as his airway was squeezed, William still refused to say anything. I couldn't stand the tension of waiting in that dimly-lit room for William to speak, so I asked my question again.

"'Why did you kill my baby, Mr Dennison?' I said, my voice now emerging louder and even stronger than before. 'What reason can you possibly have had to justify murdering my son?'"

"'Don't you get shirty with me, Mrs High-and-Mighty.' Dennison sneered. 'Just because you think you are too good for the likes of me, you're in no position to demand answers from me. *I'll* decide what is and isn't spoken about in here, not you. Do you get that?'"

"I very nearly went for his throat then, but I was aware that I didn't have a weapon to use on him and he was too physically strong for me to be able to do any damage to him without one. But I could do what I had done before, in my back yard when I had faced down the bully in him, so I moved closer to him, never letting my eyes waver from his face and displaying the magnitude of the disgust I felt for him. He couldn't move backwards through the table he was sitting on, but he very definitely pulled away from me. To cover this moment of apparent weakness, he decided that he would speak and answer my question, although the sneering tone didn't change."

"'He doesn't want to tell you himself, so it looks as though I'm going to have to do it for him.' He jerked the cord again, so that William's head rose and fell, almost as though he was nodding agreement with Dennison's words. 'Has he ever told you how he lost his arm?'"

"Once again I was placed at a disadvantage. I had no idea how William had lost his arm. I had never asked him about it, partly because I didn't want to make him relive what would obviously be a painful memory and partly because I had shut out of my mind anything to do with the war once William had enlisted. William had never proffered the information himself and the time for enquiring about it had passed."

"But Dennison continued speaking, so I had to put all feelings of being at a disadvantage out of my mind and concentrate, because I didn't know when the opportunity would arise for me to wreak my revenge on the pig butcher. I was still acutely aware that a weapon in the form of my butchery knife was still out of my reach until I could get to the cold store and grab it, so I had to have all of my faculties working at full power so that I was ready to take any action that was necessary. I didn't want to miss any opportunity to strike because I may only get the one."

"Did your beloved husband tell you that he was considered a real hero when he was over there in France, fighting the Bosche? More importantly, did you believe him when he told you what marvellous deeds he had accomplished over there? Or did you think that these tales of derring-do didn't ring true coming from a little weasel of a man like him? What did he tell you? Answer me, woman!"

"He was working himself up into a real rage and I was sure that he would lose control altogether when he reached a certain point. I toyed with the idea of pushing him until all he *could* do was to lose control, but decided that it would be impossible to foretell any reactions he may have if he was tipped over the edge, so I answered his questions."

"'I've no idea what happened to William when he was at the Front.' I said, quietly but firmly. I had no intention of letting him think I was frightened of him. 'I have never asked him how he lost his arm and he has never volunteered that information, so if you think he has been telling us tales of 'derring-do' as you put it, you are sadly mistaken.'"

"'Oh, Mrs Hoity-toity! You still think you are better than me, don't you?' he snarled. 'Well, I'm going to educate you a bit about what your husband did while he was away at the Front and then, mebbe, you won't be quite so high and mighty.'"

"I looked again at William when Dennison spoke those words, but he still refused to lift his head and look me in the eye. I had no idea where this was leading, apart from the fact that it was obvious that William wasn't going to come out of it looking like a hero, so all I could do was play along until a resolution to the situation presented itself to me. I glanced over at Peter and Sammy who were still standing to one side of the table, far enough away for Dennison to be comfortable that they couldn't jump on him. Sammy raised his eyes to mine and leant forwards as though he was readying himself to spring on the pig butcher. Almost imperceptibly, I shook my head at him and his muscles relaxed and he eased himself back into a standing position. Peter was staring at Dennison as though in a daze and I wondered just how much of the situation his poor, sad mind had managed to understand. I muttered a silent rapid prayer that he hadn't understood any of it, so that his ignorance would prevent him from taking any action at all. His was too pure a soul for it to be sullied by having any contact with the devil who was literally pulling the strings at that moment. I knew Peter had a very strong sense of what was right and what was wrong and I didn't want him deciding that what the butcher had done was wrong and reacting in the only way he knew how, by attacking Dennison. It could take some time before Peter worked it all out in his head and I hoped that everything would be over and done with by the time his poor brain caught up with what had happened."

"I wanted to hear what the pig butcher had to say before any action was taken against him and, when action was called for, it was going to be me who took that action, nobody else. When the scales were weighed on the Day of Judgement, they were going to dip because I was sitting on them with all my sins; no-one else was going to weigh them down."

"'Doesn't look like your beloved husband wants to tell anyone about his courage, does it?' Dennison went on. 'Have you told anyone the truth of what happened to you or are you quite happy to just let people think that you are a hero?'"

"Dennison tugged on the red cord again and this time William's head lolled over towards him. He still wouldn't look up and he still wouldn't speak at all, no matter how much the pig butcher taunted him. I was heartily sick of the man's prevarication, because I wanted to understand exactly what had happened, before I could concentrate on killing the pig butcher."

"'Is anyone going to tell me what all this is about?' I asked. 'If William doesn't want to play your mind games, why don't you just get on with it and spit out what you are so plainly desperate to reveal?'"

"'All right.' Dennison said. 'If he won't tell you himself, then I'll fill you in on the details. Let's set the scene, so we all know what happened where and who did what to whom. I'm basing what I'm going to tell you on an eye witness account, which was given to me two nights ago when I popped into the Red Lion for a drink. In there, I met a young lad, a soldier, who was home on leave from the army. He'd had a very bad experience and, contrary to what the gossip tells us about the war, his commanding officer had recommended some home leave for him, to give him time to recover and rest before he went back to active duty. Davy, his name is, Davy Wilson. I've known the lad for a long time, because he used to play with my son Albert when they were both children. His mother lives in Redcar Road, not far from my shop and she brought him up well. He knows right from wrong and he wouldn't ever deliberately hurt anyone'"

"When Dennison mentioned the lad's name, we all saw William clench his hand as it rested on the arm of the chair. It was obvious to us all that William recognised the name, but he still wouldn't look up from his examination of the floor."

"'Oh yes, he knows who I'm talking about.' Dennison had also seen the involuntary movement and he was smiling that mirthless smile again as he looked at William."

"'It's very nice for you that you can have conversations with other drunkards in the pub, Dennison, but what has it got to do with William?' Sam said. 'Why don't you spit it out, man, and then we can all go home?'"

"Sammy's patience was obviously running out, or he had some idea where this was all leading, because this was the first time he had spoken since we had forced our way into the warehouse. I glanced across at him and his face was pale and weary, as though he did know what was going to come next."

"'Oh, I'll spit it out all right.' Dennison snarled. 'You're going to get every little detail of what happened that day, just in case our friend William here has forgotten some of it. When I've told you what happened, I'm going to kill William Drinkwater and the rest of you as well, so there'll be no-one to tell tales about what happened here. Before I leave, I'll set the warehouse on fire, so there won't be any evidence left and I'll get away with killing you all.'"

"There was silence after Dennison stopped speaking. I think we were all so taken aback at the casual way in which he talked of committing multiple murder, that no-one could think of anything to say in reply. The pig butcher was the only one who was capable of speaking at that point in time, although I honestly believe he didn't know that he had shocked us all that much. When he'd gathered his thoughts, he took up the story again."

"'So. Davy Wilson was in the Red Lion the other night and because I've known him for years, when I'd got my pint, I went and sat with the lad and asked him how it was going, over there at the Front. He was staring across the room at a man who was standing at the bar and he wouldn't take his eyes off him, even when he was answering my questions. It didn't take me long to realise that he was staring at our very own William Drinkwater and, because I have an interest in Drinkwater's wife, I asked him why he was staring at the weasel. So he told me why and that is the reason I want him dead.'"

"'When groups of men enlisted for the army when the war first started, those men tended to be kept together and served alongside men they had known all their lives.' Dennison continued. 'So my son, Albert, my only child, was in the same group of lads as Davy Wilson and dear old William Drinkwater. One early morning, before day had dawned, they were sent out into No Man's Land to set traps and barbed wire for the enemy, should they ever take it into their heads to cross over No Man's Land and attack the British trenches. It's dangerous work, out there in No Man's Land, because there are shell holes to fall into in the dark, unexploded ordinance to stumble across and set off and, worst of all, you're a sitting duck for enemy snipers.'"

" 'So, there they all were, digging holes to put wooden stakes into so that they could string barbed wire across them, when the coming of the dawn caught them a great distance from the comparative safety of their own trenches and they had to take shelter in a massive shell hole. It was possible that they were going to have to stay in it for the rest of the day and wait for darkness before they could work their way back to the English line. One of the lads had been wounded in the leg which Davy Wilson had bandaged up for him and they were all praying that he would be strong enough to move quickly on it when the time came. That day, the Hun decided that he was going to enjoy himself by staging a raid on the English front line, so, not long after they had reached the comparative safety of the crater, the guns began firing. Our English guns joined in, adding their noise and smoke to the general hell and our little band of soldiers hunkered down in their rat hole, praying that they would all survive the day and make it back to their own trenches. When it came to the bottom line, there was as good a chance that they would be killed by one of their own cannons as by a Hun cannon.'"

" 'So, they were trapped in the shell hole and all around them the war went on, guns firing and shells landing and never knowing if the next one would have your number on it. The noise and the dirt and the smells were overwhelming and there was nothing that they could do about it.'"

"I could almost hear the cacophony that Dennison was describing and I could definitely feel the fear those lads had experienced, or William's fear of what Dennison was going to do or say next was so palpable that I was picking it up from him. Whatever the cause, fear was a tangible emotion in that warehouse and I could see Peter literally vibrating with the tension."

"'There they were then,' Dennison continued, unaware of the pressures at work in the room. 'Davy and his mates, sitting in that shell crater in Flanders, waiting for the Bosche and the English to stop firing, so that they could crawl out of it and make their way back to their trenches. But the guns continued to fire, the big ones and the little ones, the cannons and the small arms, which meant that our little group of lads were all pinned down in that crater until the shelling stopped. Even when that happened, they would have to wait until it was dark, so that they could escape unseen by any snipers. The only early release would come if the fighting moved away from that frontline and, as the line hadn't moved for months, none of the lads was counting on it happening that day. My lad, my Albert, was one of that little band of soldiers and he waited with the rest of them, flinching every time a shell landed or a bullet whistled past his ear. They were all nearly deafened by the noise, Davy said, and all worrying when a shell or a bullet would arrive that had their number on it.'

"Dennison paused at that moment, whether because he was taking a breath or because he was living his son's fear, I didn't know. Before anyone else could speak, he began talking again."

"'They didn't post a look-out, because if one of them had raised his head above the level of the top of the crater, it would have been seen and become a target for a sniper. They were all hunkered down on the bottom of the hole, trying to keep as flat as possible so that they weren't used for target practise and they were all unaware that, for the first time in months, the situation was changing and the Hun had decided to mount a raid towards the Allied lines. Under cover of the smoke coming from both sets of guns, the Hun soldiers were crossing No Man's Land and one of them reached the crater where our boys were sheltering. He managed to shoot two of the lads before the others realised that he was there, but Davy was quick-witted and managed to shoot back before the Hun got any more of them. The Hun soldier keeled over into the pit and one of the lads grabbed his rifle.'"

" 'Two more of the enemy saw what had happened and they appeared over the lip of the crater, rifles at the ready, but our lads were now ready for them and Davy got the first one in the head. He was already shooting at the second one when he saw something that he would never have believed was possible. My Albert had his rifle ready and would have killed the second Hun soldier, but William Drinkwater, who was laid next to Albert at the bottom of the crater, put both his arms round Albert and rolled him over on top of himself. Albert had no idea that William Drinkwater was going to do that and so he rolled, unresisting, into Drinkwater's arms. The Hun fired his rifle and the bullet hit my son in his back and killed him instantly. The second bullet fired by the Hun went through William Drinkwater's arm and into my lad's back. Davy then managed to pull himself together and he shot the enemy soldier. Our lads lay breathless at the bottom of the shell hole and waited to see if any more of the enemy would discover their hiding place, but they didn't. The fighting moved away from the crater and Davy had time to yank Albert off Drinkwater's prone figure, to see if he could save him. But my lad was dead, killed by two bullets in the back, as though he had been trying to run away, as though he was a coward, but he wasn't. The only coward in that group was your beloved husband, who didn't care who was killed as long as it wasn't him.'"

"'The bullet in Drinkwater's arm had shattered the bone, so one of the other lads roughly bandaged it because they didn't want him to die before they could get him to a court martial. But he was lucky, was this lily-livered excuse for a soldier, and no-one believed Davy when he reported what had happened. The powers-that-be didn't want to believe that one of their soldiers was a coward so they decided that he had suffered enough when he had to have his arm amputated, so they dismissed him and he came home a hero and now he lives in luxury, when my lad's dead.'"

"Dennison stopped speaking as he immersed himself in grieving for his lost son and, even though he had just murdered my son, I could feel for him. I now knew what it was like to lose your only son, but the last thing I would have done would have been to murder somebody else's child, so my empathy only went so far. Sam, it seemed, was all out of empathy, sympathy or forgiveness that night, because he turned on William and demanded answers."

"'Is all that true? He asked. 'Did you use that lad as a shield to save yourself?' Sammy's voice was incredibly high-pitched, as though he couldn't believe the depths to which William had sunk and, for the first time that night, William reacted."

"'No I didn't!' William cried. 'He fell on top of me when the Hun soldier shot him and his body stopped the bullets that were meant for me! I'm not a coward!'"

"Dennison was on his feet immediately, yanking at the twine fastened round William's neck so strongly that the chair legs lifted with the force and William and the chair fell over sideways onto the floor. His head hit the ground with a bang that reverberated right through the building and William's whining voice stopped instantly."

"'Don't lie now, you yellow-bellied bastard!' The pig butcher screamed. 'You're going to meet your Maker in the next few minutes, at least go with a clear conscience! Davy Wilson told me exactly what you did. My lad didn't *fall* on top of you, you pulled him! Those were Davy's exact words – you wrapped your arms round my Albert and pulled him over onto you to shield you. Davy looked at you as you did it and he saw the guile and the cunning in your face. You knew exactly what you were doing. You were quick-thinking enough to use my son to save your own miserable life and now you think you can lie about it!'"

"By the time he got to the end of this speech, Dennison was breathless with rage and the rest of us were stunned by the revelations. William stayed where he was on the floor, either because the fall had stunned him or because he was frightened that if he attempted to raise himself up then the butcher would finish the job he had started. His eyes, however, were darting this way and that, as though he was looking for a means of escape. It was the most surreal moment of my life, standing in that dimly-lit warehouse, with my son dead on the floor and his murderer ready to wreak his vengeance on my husband for what my husband had done to his son. I felt as though I was in the middle of a nightmare, a nightmare that was so unreal it wasn't possible and yet I was living through it."

Nana Lymer paused in her tale and glanced across at Victoria to see how she was coping with learning these terrible things about her grandmother's earlier life. But Victoria was drinking it all in. There was no trace of revulsion or disgust on her face at what had happened. Her whole face was suffused with pity for her grandmother and, as Nana Lymer paused for breath, Victoria reached out and took hold of the tiny hand which was clenched on the counterpane.

"What a dreadful time you had, Nana." Victoria whispered. "Having your baby killed by that butcher and then learning what a miserable coward your husband was. I don't know how you could recover from that. And being threatened by him as well. He obviously didn't murder anyone else because you and Granddad Sam both lived long after that night, so how did you overpower him? Did you get to your knife and stab him? But, if you did, you would have been arrested for murder yourself. What happened?"

"I think we'll have to go into that after Mr Vine's been this afternoon. It must be nearly lunchtime by now and we need you on duty at the side door to let Mr Vine in after lunch." Nana smiled.

"Goodness! Is it that time?" Victoria screeched. "I'm supposed to be starting lunch for Mam! I'll never hear the end of it if I haven't got it done when she comes through into the kitchen from the shop. I'll be back when I bring your lunch and then I'll listen out for Mr Vine this afternoon."

"You are a good girl, Victoria." Nana Lymer said, cupping her palm round the side of Victoria's face. "Don't let your mother get you down. You are going to have a wonderful life, just you wait and see. Now, off you go because this afternoon is going to be very important."

Victoria managed to get downstairs into the kitchen and get the lunch made before her parents came through into the kitchen when they had closed the shop. Everything was going to plan so far. Her mother made no demur when Victoria said she was going back to 'revise' in Nana's bedroom straight after lunch, which meant that they would have time for some more of the story before Victoria took up her position on the first landing, ready to nip down the last few stairs and open the side door for Mr Vine when he knocked. The only problem was that Victoria now felt guilty that she was keeping a secret from her parents, although she didn't understand why Mr Vine's visit had to be so secretive. She just hoped that she wasn't going to get into trouble with her mother for not telling her what she had done when she had made the appointment for that afternoon. Each time she got to this point in her musings, her analytical brain asked why her grandmother shouldn't see her solicitor and she couldn't provide a logical answer. She was fully aware, however, that if her mother ever found out, there was going to be one hell of a row about it and she wasn't looking forward to that possible outcome.

After a quick lunch and as soon as her parents were back in the shop, Victoria shot back up the stairs to Nana's bedroom.

"It's just before 1 o'clock, Nana." She gasped out as she collapsed into her chair. "Mr Vine isn't coming until 2pm, so we've got time for some more of the story before I have to go and wait on the landing for him to come. Do you think you're up to telling me some more?"

"Of course I'm 'up to it', Victoria" Nana answered. "You don't realise how much good this is doing me. I feel as though I am getting things into perspective for the first time in years, because I've never had the opportunity to mull it over before. Granddad didn't want to discuss it after it happened and it became a subject that we all avoided, I think to my cost. It's been getting me down for the last few years and I feel so much relief now it's coming out into the open. It's been like a canker in my heart since it happened and I now feel that I am cutting it all

away. Let's get on with it!"

Chapter Twelve

"We were all standing there in silence after Dennison had told us what William had done in the shell crater." Nana Lymer began, when Victoria was settled comfortably in her chair. "I don't think any of us actually believed it at first, but William wasn't a good liar and when he denied it, his words didn't ring true for any of us so we had to accept it. But I still didn't understand why Simon had to die. His death wasn't going to bring Albert back for the pig butcher. He was only a child. He should have had a long, healthy and happy life in front of him; he shouldn't have died at his age, murdered in cold blood."

"So, I asked again the only question to which I wanted the answer."

"'Why did you kill *my* son? *He* hadn't done anything to you. If you wanted a life in exchange for the life you had lost, why didn't you just kill William? I don't think any of us would blame you for wanting William dead, but why my baby?'"

"My voice was rising as I spoke and I knew I was losing control, something I had to fight against because I needed my wits about me to finish off the pig butcher. But Dennison decided to answer me, so it gave me time to force my emotions under control again."

"The pig butcher glared at me as though I had interrupted him. His hand tightened round the end of the cord which encircled William's neck and I thought he was going to strangle him rather than answer me, but he did decide to speak again."

"' I had been looking for your husband since Davy had informed me how my boy died, then I saw him coming out of the Red Lion, with his son in tow. It was a disgrace that he could flaunt his son in front of me when he had taken away my only child, so I decided to entice him down here to the warehouses, away from any witnesses, and show your husband just what it is like to lose your son. I told him that I had just come back from my warehouse and I had seen someone trying to break into yours, so I was looking for some help to catch the burglar. He fell for it, even though he must have known that Davy would have told me the truth about how Albert died, he still was stupid enough to come with me to an out-of-the-way place like this. Or perhaps he thought he was going to be a hero again and catch the burglar himself. Whatever his reasons, he came with me like an excited child going on a summer trip with his friends. Your little boy didn't want to come with us. He kept on crying for his mummy, but your devoted husband didn't seem to care. He was so intent on catching burglars to prove to you what a clever, brave man that he was, he didn't take any notice of his child crying.'"

"The pig butcher paused for breath again and to gather his thoughts, to tell us what happened next. I couldn't believe that William could ignore Simon when he was upset, instead of

346

doing his best to comfort him, but before I could tax him with it the pig butcher spoke again."

"'I wanted to show your husband what it is like to lose a child, but even before I had touched him, I was beginning to think that Drinkwater wouldn't react as other men would do. I did it quick, so the little lad didn't suffer, because my lad didn't suffer in that crater. He was dead the minute the bullet went into his back and your boy was dead just as quickly. I broke his little neck for him, so that he wouldn't suffer any pain. But your beloved husband didn't suffer any pain, either. It didn't touch him that his son was dead. I could see in his face that he was grateful I had chosen to kill the child and not him. He thought I had used up all my anger and that he would be safe and that was the extent of the pain he was feeling. I couldn't believe that a man could watch his child die and still be trying to work out a means of escape for himself.'"

"We all stared at William as though he was the devil incarnate, but William was again staring at the floor. I couldn't believe that the man I had lived with for so long, who was the father of my child, could put his own safety above that of his son. I was so angry with William, so enraged and so furious that all I wanted to do was to hurt him as much as I could. The thought of the knife in my cold store surfaced in my mind again and I was just about to throw all caution to the winds and run to fetch it when Dennison spoke again."

"'When I realised how deep his selfishness ran, I realised that killing your boy wasn't the punishment that that bastard deserves. His punishment can only be his own death and I'm going to deal out that punishment now.'"

"There was silence after Dennison's last remark, a silence which seemed to hang in the air around us and stopped anyone moving. Sam, Peter and I just stood and stared at William, Dennison was staring at the wall, as though he could see a picture of his son hanging there and William, well William was squirming on the floor, as much as he could when his one arm was tied to the arm of the prone chair. In the silence, we all noticed another sound, like thunder in the distance on a heavy summer day. It seemed very strange to me that after the gales and the snow and the cold, we should now be treated to another aspect of nature's fury. I wondered if I could use the noise of the thunder, when it got closer, to mask any sound I might make when I attempted to retrieve the knife from the cold store. I packed the thought away into a corner of my mind and concentrated again on what the pig butcher had told us about his son's death."

"I could understand his anger that his boy had been used as a human shield to save the life of just one person, a person whose moral conduct was questionable, to say the least. I could also understand that he was incensed that this usage had been taken rather than given willingly as a sacrifice for the good of the greatest number. I could even understand that he wanted revenge on the person who had brought about the death of his son, but I couldn't understand why he had chosen to kill my baby as a means to punishing William. That he had now decided that the only way he could get revenge would be to kill the man who had killed his son, I heartily concurred with. I had no desire to save the life of my husband when he had happily watched my son die, expecting that this would save his own miserable skin. The fact that he cared more about himself than he did about his own son put him beyond any redemption. I wouldn't lift a finger to save his miserable life."

"All these thoughts travelled through my mind in less time than it takes to sneeze. What I needed to concentrate on was to get Sammy and Peter out of the warehouse and away from the pig butcher. There was no way I was going to allow either of them to pay for William's egotistical and selfish acts. What finally happened to me was of no consequence because the worst had, for me, already happened. Once I had realised that Simon was dead, I had no reason to survive, but I still had to fight for Sam and Peter. I needed to get them both out of the warehouse away from Dennison, so that they were safe. Then the pig butcher could murder William, I could kill Dennison and then lie down and die next to my son. It was crystal clear to me, so I was puzzled and concerned when Sammy spoke and I realised that he was trying to distract Dennison to give us time to save William."

"'Is it true, William?' Sam asked. 'Did you save your own miserable skin by forcing Dennison's lad to take the bullet meant for you?'"

"William raised his head from the floor and the look he gave Sam had so much hatred in it I was shocked to the core. I had known from the day William came back from the Front that he disliked Sam, but I had never realised how deep the loathing that he had for Sam was. I knew that it was based on jealousy, because Sam and I got on extremely well and William didn't like that, but the depth of his revulsion for Sam astonished me."

"'I suppose you would have flung yourself in front of everyone in that shell crater and saved all their lives by losing yours.' William almost spat at him. 'You, Mr Perfect Father, Mr Perfect Worker, Mr Perfect at everything, you would have died a hero and everybody would have loved you for ever for it. Well, I'm no hero and I'm not going to die to save anyone else's life.'"

"Sam's face was full of disgust at William's words. I think he thought more of the pig butcher at that moment than he did of William because the pig butcher had put at least one person before himself, whereas William was totally self-absorbed. It was obvious to me that Sammy was having a great deal of trouble trying to justify to himself why he should attempt to save William from Dennison. I really believe that if Peter and I hadn't existed, Sam would have walked away and let Dennison do whatever he wanted to do to William, with his blessing. Unfortunately, Sam thought that he had to try and save William for my sake and I needed to quickly disabuse him of this notion, before he got himself killed for the sake of that miserable excuse for a man who was squirming on the floor, still trying to wriggle his way out of the situation. Raising my voice so that I could be heard over the deep rumble of the thunder which seemed to be coming nearer to us, I spoke quickly to stop Sam taking any risks and trying to kill the pig butcher."

"'Go to Hell, William, where you belong.' I snarled. 'If you could stand and watch my baby die and still only think of yourself, then you don't deserve to live. I wash my hands of you. I only want to look after Simon now; I don't care what happens to you. If you don't mind, Mr Dennison, I'm going to get a blanket to wrap round my little boy before he gets cold, lying on the floor like that.'"

"I was half-way across the floor to the cold store before the pig butcher spoke."

"'Before he gets cold!' he sneered. 'You silly bitch, he's dead, he's not feeling anything now, never mind the cold! He'll never be warm again. Ask your husband. He heard his neck snap, didn't you?'"

"'He's no husband of mine.' I replied, before William had a chance to answer. I needed to get the message across to Sam, so that he didn't attempt to save William's life before I could put my plan into action. And I did have a plan. Despite everything that had happened that day, my mind was now working as sharply as it had ever done and the plan had slipped into it without me even trying to think about it. I was amazed that I was capable of thinking so clearly in such a desperate situation, but I think it was because the worst thing that could have happened to me had already happened. Compared to losing my child, everything else paled into insignificance and I could no longer feel any fear. I was determined that the pig butcher was going to pay for killing my son and that determination made me a fearless adversary."

"I could see by his face that Sam had understood what I was trying to tell him. He was no longer poised as though ready to pounce on Dennison at any time and I breathed a sigh of relief at his quick comprehension. I felt that it was going to be possible to carry out my plan and, I must admit, I relaxed somewhat at that thought. The relief I felt was rather short-lived, however, because Peter chose that moment to finally catch up with all that had happened and let out an almost animal-like cry of pain. We all froze at the sound, at the atavistic keening that emanated from his wide-open mouth which even jerked William out of his self-absorption."

"'You've killed Simon!' he wailed. 'You've killed my friend! I'm going to kill you!'"

"'NO, Peter!'"

"It was the first time that I had ever heard Sam raise his voice and it pulled me up short. Sam had grabbed Peter by both arms, struggling to keep hold of him and prevent him from launching himself at Dennison with murder in his heart. Sam was as concerned as I was that Peter shouldn't suffer for what had happened that night and was struggling to keep him away from Dennison. As I glanced around, I realised that William and the pig butcher were both staring at Peter and Sam, so no eyes were on me. The thunder, which had been growling in the background since I had first noticed it, now peeled so loudly over our heads that I thought I could almost feel the ground bucking with its power. Even above this tremendous noise, I could still hear Peter bellowing aloud his hatred and frustration. What I did at that moment was going to pass unremarked by anyone else in the warehouse."

"I knew that I had to move before Sammy's strength ran out and Peter got his freedom, so I threw myself at the cold store door and I was inside and had grabbed a piece of sacking and my butchery knife and was back in the main body of the warehouse before anyone knew I had gone. By the time Peter's screams had reduced to sobs, I was on my knees next to Simon's body, wrapping him up in the sacking, all the while keeping the knife concealed in its folds, waiting for the right moment to strike.

"'Keep the moron under control, or I swear I'll do for him like I've done for the other one.' Dennison hissed at Sam and my skin crawled at the wickedness of the man who could think of Peter in those terms."

"'Lay off him, Dennison.' Sammy growled. He was obviously as disgusted as I was at the butcher's description of Peter, but he was also as concerned as I was about what Peter might do. Peter was a smoking cannon, likely to go off at any moment and I needed to get him away from the warehouse as soon as possible."

I finished tucking the sacking around Simon's little body, my heart contracting as I touched his soft skin and brushed the cheek which would never again dimple at me as he smiled. My courage nearly failed me then. I wanted nothing more than to lie down next to him and never rise again, but I had to save Peter and Sam before I could have my heart's desire. I risked a glance at the group of four men gathered in the warehouse, noting that Dennison was on his feet, towering over William's supine body and Peter and Sam were about three feet away from the pig butcher, both facing him. The butcher turned to me at that point."

"'Finished wrapping up the baby?' he asked, sneeringly. 'Leave him there and get yourself over here with these two, where I can keep an eye on you.'"

"I acquiesced immediately, but took the butchery knife with me, holding it pointing downwards, hidden in a fold of my skirt. I made sure that I took my place to the right of Sam and Peter, with plenty of room for my right arm to be able to raise the knife to plunge it into the pig butcher's chest. The thunder rumbled over us again as I took my place, although this time it seemed quieter than before and I fleetingly wondered if the storm was passing over us, which wasn't at all what I wanted to happen. I had hoped to be able to use the cover of the thunderclaps to carry out my plan and if the storm passed us by, I would have to formulate another plan. But, before I could begin trying to produce a new strategy, William decided to try and manipulate the odds stacked against him."

"'Peter.' He gasped out, struggling to speak over the cord which was constricting his airway. 'Peter, come and help me, son, please. Get the cord off that bastard and release me. I'll pay you for it. I'll buy you anything you want, but hit that bugger and release me. Aagh!'"

"His words were cut short as Dennison yanked on the cord again, constricting his airway even further so that William gasped for breath and turned a horrible shade of purple in the lamplight. But Peter answered him as though they were having a conversation in the kitchen at the shop."

"'I won't help you, Mr Drinkwater. That man said you watched him kill Simon and you didn't do anything to stop him, so I won't do anything to stop him, either. If he wants to strangle you he can. I don't care.'"

"Dennison laughed out loud at this, his mouth wide open and the red light of madness once again visible in his eyes."

"'Did you hear that, armless? He doesn't think you are worth saving and he's right. He has enough brains to work that much out, the moron, and he's capable of speaking out. He's going to have to die, along with the rest of you. I'm not risking my neck, pretending that he's too stupid to be able to understand what's happening. But, you first, Drinkwater. I've kept you waiting long enough now, I reckon. You've had time to feel the fear of death. It's time now for you to go and meet my lad face-to-face again and explain to *him* why you were too important to die in France. Go and give him your excuses.'"

Nana Lymer paused for a moment to give herself time to recover from the overpowering feeling of despair and helplessness that engulfed her as she recalled that night. Victoria was just about to put out her hand to grasp the arm of the older woman, to show sympathy and understanding when Nana began to speak again.

"The butcher hoisted William, and the chair he was tied to, bodily off the floor, wrapped his huge red hands around his neck and squeezed with all his prodigious strength, while, at first, William's legs kicked out trying desperately to make contact with some part of the butcher's anatomy, but then they swung loose above the wooden planking. His gasping breath was cut off within seconds and his face turned an even deeper shade of puce, until his head lolled sideways and he was finally dead. When the pig butcher realised that William had breathed his last he unlocked his hands from around William's neck and let William and the chair fall to the floor. They landed with a crash that shook the wooden building, which was echoed by the thunder that suddenly seemed to be redoubling its efforts, rather than passing over."

"For a while, nobody moved. The thunder roared over our heads and we all stood and stared at William's body, supine on the floor. Even Dennison seemed taken aback by what he had done, because he too stood and stared at William. I think he was finally realising that killing those he felt were to blame for his son's death wasn't going to bring his son back and William's murder hadn't lessened the despair that gripped him. In that moment, I actually felt sorry for him because his revenge was leaving him as bitter and twisted as before and with no other road left to travel. It was an empty victory for him."

Silence fell as Nana Lymer stopped speaking, reliving the nightmare of that time. Victoria didn't want to interrupt the silence, in case Nana was only stopping to think how she was going to describe what happened next. If she spoke now she might disturb her grandmother's train of thought and she didn't want to do that. She wondered how close it was to two o'clock, when Mr Vine was coming and, as the thought crystallised in her mind, there was a knock on the side door.

"That's Mr Vine, Victoria! Run down and let him in before he goes round to the shop door. Hurry now!"

Victoria almost galloped out of the room and down the stairs to the side door, trying not to make too much noise and so warn her mother that there was a visitor at the house. She was very aware that the wall to her left, between the stairs and the shop, was only made out of plasterboard and absolutely useless at deadening any sound. Her hand slipped on the Yale lock as she tried to turn it to open the door and she grabbed frantically at it, desperate that Mr Vine shouldn't knock again. Finally, she managed to open the door and saw Mr Vine standing on the doorstep in front of her. He was accompanied by another young man, who was smiling as brightly as Mr Vine.

"Victoria. Nice to see you again!" Mr Vine said, as Victoria ushered them both through the door and upstairs to Nana Lymer's bedroom. Mr Vine wasn't perturbed about entering a lady's bedroom or having to conduct his business in that bedroom and he strode across the floor to the bed, with his hand out ready to shake hands.

"It's lovely to see you again, Mrs Lymer." He said. "May I introduce my business partner, David Lethbridge? I've brought him with me in case we need another body to witness anything. Got to keep things legal, you know."

Mrs Lymer smiled back at him.

"You were always a clever lad, Anthony and I see you haven't changed in that way, even if you have grown older since the last time we met."

Mr Vine laughed out loud at that, looking and sounding completely at his ease with Victoria's grandmother. Mr Lethbridge moved forward for his turn at the handshake, and then seated himself on the stool at Nana's dressing table. Mr Vine took the bedside chair that Victoria had vacated to answer the door, which left Victoria standing alone in the middle of the floor. She felt slightly awkward, a feeling she had never had in that room, but realised that her presence wasn't required at that time.

"I'll go and wait in my bedroom, Nana," she said. "If you need anything just shout me and I'll come and get it for you."

"Good girl." Nana said, grateful for Victoria's tact and impatient to get this interview over, before Bia found out that she had visitors. "Perhaps Mr Vine and Mr Lethbridge would like a cup of tea before we start?"

"No, Mrs Lymer," Mr Vine answered. "I would love to stay and chat about the old days, but I've got another client to see this afternoon. But now we've re-established contact I've no intention of letting you get away with not seeing me regularly again, so I'm going to call in on my free days and we can chat for an hour or so. I think you've got a definite purpose for wishing to see me today, so let's get that sorted out and your mind put at rest, shall we?"

Mrs Lymer smiled again; gratified that he could still get straight to the point when he felt it necessary. Victoria slipped out of the bedroom and crossed the landing to her own room. She left her bedroom door ajar so that she would be able to hear if Nana wanted anything and then picked up another of her set books for her English 'O' level. 'Jane Eyre' wasn't working its usual magic on her that afternoon though and, before long, she abandoned her attempts at revision and sat on her bed listening to the rumble of voices coming from Nana's room. She couldn't make out any individual words or phrases, but she could make out the difference between her Nana's speech and Mr Vine's remarks. Time passed quickly as she waited, constantly on edge in case the shop wasn't busy and her mother chose to come upstairs and find Mr Vine in Nana's room.

Another fifteen minutes passed and then Victoria distinctly heard the telephone ring downstairs. The telephone was located in the downstairs hall near the side door and its ring was often unheard in the shop if there were plenty of customers in there. Victoria wondered if she should go downstairs and answer it, but she heard the kitchen door open and her mother's voice as she answered the caller. She listened intently to see if she could work out the subject of the call, hoping it was a customer placing an order for delivery at the weekend, but as her mother's voice rose in pitch, she didn't have to strain very hard to hear.

"He's here now?" was the first part of the conversation that Victoria heard in full and a cold drip seemed to run down her spine. Whoever it was on the other end of the line could only be talking about Mr Vine, Victoria was sure and confirmation came rapidly after that.

"Right! Well thank you for letting me know about it. I'll go and sort it out straight away!"

It was with a sinking heart that Victoria heard her mother mounting the stairs, each heavy step on each tread banging out her disapproval and bad temper. She wasn't sure if she should stay in her bedroom or try to warn her grandmother that her mother was on the warpath, but any choice was taken out of her hands when her mother reached the top of the stairs. She strode straight into Nana's bedroom and Victoria rushed across the landing and halted in the doorway. Her mother had come to a stop in the middle of the room and her face was purple with temper as she glared at the two men, who both rose to their feet as she entered the room.

"I've just had Amy Butler on the 'phone, telling me that young Mr Vine is in *my* house, by appointment, discussing legal matters with my mother. I don't like finding out from comparative strangers what my own mother is doing and doing it in *my* house! I'd like to know what you think you are doing here."

Victoria's mother had her hands on her hips and her face was disfigured by the angry scowl she was wearing. Victoria held her breath, embarrassed that her mother could be so rude in front of other people, but also worried that Nana wouldn't have had time to finish what she wanted to do with Mr Vine. But it wasn't long before Victoria was under fire from her mother.

"I suppose *you* organised this, did you? How else would my mother have been able to get in touch with a solicitor, unless you helped her to do it?" Mrs Wilson was incandescent with rage, not even able to keep her mind on one subject at a time. "You'll pay for this Victoria. I'll teach you to go against my wishes."

Her mother paused to take a breath and, for the first time in her life, Victoria was able to answer her mother rationally and calmly.

"I didn't know that Nana wasn't allowed to see her own solicitor," she retorted. "You've never said that I had to keep other people away from her. But I would like to know *why* Nana isn't allowed to see her solicitor? It's a right that every person has, even if they've been arrested for an offence, and Nana hasn't been arrested, has she?"

Bia Wilson didn't have a reply for this. It was an afternoon for firsts, because this was the first time that she had ever been caught without having a put-down remark ready to use and it was the first time that another person got the last word in any discussion with her. It was at this point that Mr Vine stepped into the conversation, quietly but very firmly.

"Your Nana has never been arrested for anything in her life. She's been a pillar of society for years." Mr Vine spoke to Victoria, but then turned and addressed his next remarks to Victoria's mother.

"With-holding the right for a person to see a solicitor is an offence, Mrs Wilson, when that person has expressed a desire to be in touch with their legal representative. I'm sure you didn't intend to commit an offence, did you?"

Victoria's mother had had the rug pulled out from underneath her feet and wasn't coping well at all with it. She tried to bluster her way out of it.

"I didn't know that she wanted to see you," she snapped, "So don't be trying to get clever with me, young man."

Mr Vine wasn't going to let this matter drop.

"What is your objection to your mother seeing me?" he asked. "Why shouldn't she talk to me?"

Bia Wilson lost her temper and her capacity to disguise her reasoning went with it.

"She'll have got you here to change her will!" Bia shouted. "She doesn't want me to inherit the shop when she dies, after the years of work I've put into it, so she's going to change it to do me out of my rightful inheritance!"

Bia almost choked as the spittle in her mouth went back down her throat. In the silence which ensued, Nana Lymer's quiet calm voice was like music compared with her daughter's screeching.

"It's no business of yours whether I decide to change my will or not, but I'm sure you'll be happy to know that you haven't been 'done out of your rightful inheritance' as you put it. But, while I'm still alive, I'd like you to acknowledge the fact that this house and shop don't legally belong to you. They still are my property, so please don't come into my bedroom, shouting the odds about what is happening in *your* house. I have no wish to be vindictive, but please be aware that I could ask you to leave at any time and then the 'years of work' you have put into the shop will be nullified."

"You wouldn't dare!" Victoria's mother had managed to regain her voice. "Who would look after you if I wasn't here? Who'd put up with running up and downstairs a hundred times a day, catering to your every whim? Anyway, you're not right in the head. What about those nights when you wander the streets and you don't know who you are or where you live?"

Bia turned to Mr Vine.

"You are aware that she's going gaga, aren't you?" Bia almost spat at him. "Any change you make to her will won't be legal, you know. I can prove she's going mental, cos the police picked her up the other night when she was wandering round the town. You have a word with the sergeant, he'll tell you."

"I'm fully aware that Mrs Lymer sometimes has difficulty with her memory but I am also aware that her medical practitioner is of the opinion that her memory loss is due to stress. I have conducted all the testing I need to do today and, in my opinion, Mrs Lymer is of sound mind at this precise moment, which means I consider her perfectly capable of making whatever changes to her will that she wishes to make. May I also add that, legally, you have no right to discuss or question any aspects of her will, unless she wishes to discuss them with you. Now, Mrs Lymer, if you will just sign here where I have placed a

371

cross and then Mr Lethbridge and I can sign it and our business today will be complete."

Mr Vine presented the sheet of paper and a pen to Nana Lymer and waited until she had signed at the bottom of the page. He and Mr Lethbridge then appended their signatures to the sheet and Mr Vine placed the sheet of paper into his briefcase.

"I shall bring a copy of this for you when I call next Wednesday." Mr Vine said as he shrugged on his coat. "It's been wonderful to see you again and I look forward to being able to stay longer next week when I call and we can have a good old chin-wag about the old days. You take care of yourself and let me know if you need anything before next week."

The two men both shook Mrs Lymer's hand and then headed for the door. Victoria's mother had stepped back as they both passed her but she made no comment as they left the room. For the first time in her life, she had been bested in an argument and it was a bitter pill for her to swallow. If Victoria hadn't been the object of her mother's diatribes so often in her life, she may have found it possible to feel sympathy for her mother's stricken expression but, instead, she enjoyed passing her mother to follow the two men downstairs to let them out of the side door. When she got back to Nana Lymer's bedroom, her mother was still standing in the same place, staring at her mother as she lay in bed.

"If you don't close your mouth, Bia, a passing fly is going to get in it and that would be a bitter taste to swallow, wouldn't it?" Nana Lymer said.

"How dare you do this to me, Mam?" Bia whined. "I've waited on you hand and foot for years. Nobody else would have done it for you, none of the others in our family have bothered about you, but I've been here all the time, out of the goodness of my heart and then you want to change your will. Why? I just don't understand."

Nana Lymer looked her up and down before she answered.

"You have never done anything 'out of the goodness of your heart' in your life, Bia" Nana said. "Basically because you've never had a heart to do anything with. You've wasted a lot of years being bad-tempered and shallow and if all this makes you stop being like that then my time won't have been wasted. But I very much doubt that you are capable of learning tolerance and kindness, given that your father and I tried to teach you but you wouldn't listen to either of us. I've watched you nagging Jack until it's a wonder that he doesn't up and leave you and I've listened to you constantly deriding anything Victoria tries to do, making her feel unloved and unwanted. You don't deserve the wonderful family you have around you, but if you end up a lonely old woman, it'll be because you pushed everyone away from you. Now, if you don't mind, I'd like a cup of tea to sort my dry throat out. I've done a lot of talking today."

Chapter Thirteen

Victoria's mother had been very quiet all evening after Mr Vine had left and Nana Lymer had made her speech. Victoria hadn't dared stay in Nana's room after tea, but she was determined that she was going to get to the end of the story before the Christmas holidays were over so, the next morning, she asked if she could sit with Nana again that day.

"If you want," was her mother's terse reply. Victoria glanced across at her father when it was obvious that her mother wasn't going to expand her brusqueness, but her father only smiled and nodded his head. Victoria decided to leave her father to sort out her mother's sulk and made tea for herself and Nana and took it upstairs.

"She's not refused to let you sit with me, then." Nana smiled, when Victoria placed her tea within easy reach.

"She isn't really speaking to anyone today." Victoria replied, "So I decided I might as well make hay while the sun shines and come and listen to the rest of the story, if you want to tell me anymore."

"Of course I do, pet. You need to know all of it, to understand what happened. It's not a very edifying story, I'm afraid, but it is the truth about what happened and I'll go to my grave happier to know that the story hasn't been lost and that I've got it off my chest at last."

"Nana! Don't say that!" Victoria cried. "You aren't going to die for a long time yet. Don't think like that, please."

Nana smiled. "It happens to us all, pet, whether we like it or not and I'm not going to argue against it when my turn comes. Not unless I haven't finished telling you the story, anyway. Right. Where had I got up to?"

"William had just been strangled, Nana, and you were all standing staring at his body."

"Yes, I remember now. We all stood and stared at William, as though it was a perfectly normal thing to do, watching a man who had just been strangled. I couldn't feel any grief for him, in fact I was glad that he was dead. He hadn't deserved to live from the moment he had used young Dennison as a shield to save his own, rotten life, but the same didn't apply to Peter and Sam. They both had worthwhile lives still to be lived and I didn't want the pig butcher to shorten either of their lives, to prevent them from informing the authorities what he had done that night. I needed to act to save them both and I needed to act immediately, while Dennison was still distracted by having killed William."

"The thunder roared louder and longer than ever before and the ground beneath us definitely bucked and heaved as the thunder rolled and echoed above us. We all staggered as the warehouse floor seemed to lift as though it was trying to make us all lie prone on the floor, just like William. It gave me the opportunity to shorten the distance between myself and the pig butcher, so that I would be able to more easily slip my knife into his heart. I had thought that I would be the only person in the warehouse capable of coherent thought at that moment after William's murder and the crescendo of noise from the thunder, but I was wrong. Sammy had let go of Peter's arms when the pig butcher had started throttling William and Peter took advantage of his freedom."

"He reached Dennison before I had taken two steps towards the pig butcher and it was his deep guttural roar that alerted the butcher to the danger he was in. He spun on his heel to face Peter as Peter descended on him; hands outstretched, and grabbed him round his neck, just as the butcher had done to William. But it wasn't Peter's intention to throttle Dennison. He lifted him up by his neck and shook Dennison wildly, like a dog shakes a rabbit and we all heard Dennison's neck snap as his head flopped backwards. Even over the sound of the thunder, still rumbling high above us, we all heard the bone shatter under the strain of the force which Peter was using. The pig butcher was as strong as an ox, but even he was no match for the terrible strength, fuelled by righteous anger, which Peter had within him."

"Peter stopped shaking Dennison then and dropped his body to the floor, stepping back from where the pig butcher now lay, equal with William and Simon on the floor. I stood stock-still and the knife slipped from my nerveless fingers and clanged to rest next to the butcher's corpse. The thunder stopped suddenly and a terrible quiet descended on my warehouse, so deep a silence that we could all hear each other breathing."

"Sam was the first of us to come to his senses. He knelt down next to the butcher and checked the pulse in his neck."

"'Dead.' Sam said, although I hadn't expected any different. He then moved over to William's body and checked him for any signs of life."

"'Dead.' Once again was his conclusion and it was this second repetition of the word that brought me back to my senses."

"'We've got to get them out of here.' I said, my mind suddenly working as clearly as though I was serving a customer in the shop. 'We've got to work out a way for it to look as though all three of them died somewhere else, in some sort of accident or something, so that none of us can be blamed for their deaths. Sam, what can we do? Where can we take them?'"

"Before Sammy could answer me, Peter began to cry. I had to soothe him because we were going to need his strength if we were going to move the bodies of William and the pig butcher. I could carry Simon, but Sam and Peter were going to have to move the two men. I hunkered down next to Peter and wrapped my arms about his shaking shoulders."

"'He shouldn't have killed Simon.' Peter wailed. 'I don't care about William, because he was a selfish, cruel man, but the pig butcher shouldn't have killed Simon. Simon was my friend and he hadn't done anything to hurt the butcher, so why did he kill him? It's not fair, Bia, it's not fair at all.'"

"I know, pet.' I said. 'But he had lost his son and I think that had affected his mind. He didn't really know what he was doing.'"

"'He knew what he was doing.' Peter's pet lip came out and the tears continued to rain down his face. 'He was a wicked man and I'm glad that I killed him. I know that the Bible says that you mustn't kill people, but he was really wicked and he deserved to die. He called me a moron as well. That's not kind at all.'"

"I clutched him to me, rubbing my hands up and down his back in an effort to soothe him and the tears rained down my face as I did so. I wanted to take my time with him and explain everything in detail for him, but we didn't have the time for a luxury like that. We had to get the bodies moved before the storm passed over and we lost the cover of the bad weather. I could feel the anxiety building inside me and I turned to see what Sammy was doing, hoping that he would come and help me with Peter. He seemed lost in thought, standing next to the warehouse door, almost as though he was listening to the storm outside."

"'We've got to get them out of here.' I repeated to Sam. 'When the storm is over, any ships waiting to dock will come in and there'll be sailors and dock workers all over this area. We've got to be away from here before then or someone will see us. I'm not risking Peter being sent to jail for what he's done tonight.' I didn't say it out loud because I didn't want to startle Peter, but, if he was caught for murdering Dennison, then he would hang."

"'I don't think we're going to be able to carry out any plan.' Sam said as he walked towards Peter and me. If he thought he was reassuring me, he was on the wrong track altogether. I opened my mouth to ask him what he meant, but the thunder suddenly returned, this time with double the intensity it had had before. I waited for it to fade before I spoke again because I knew it would be impossible for Sam to hear me over the crescendo of noise which was battering our eardrums. I could see the lightening flashing through the gaps in the boards of the warehouse walls and, even at that time and after all the dreadful things that had happened that night, I could still wonder at the intensity of that storm. It was so unlike anything I had ever experienced before in my life, but the power and the force it was displaying seemed to fit with the tableau of Hell which was the inside of my warehouse."

"Peter disentangled himself from me and stood upright, so I followed his lead, although the ground was shaking so much with the storm that I was having difficulty staying on my feet. I watched Peter cross the floor to where Simon lay and crouch down next to him. He cradled Simon's head in his arms and rocked him back and forth, as though to soothe a frightened child. I could feel the hysteria rising in me as I watched him holding my dead son and I turned to Sam for his strength."

"'Sammy, we will have to move the bodies before the storm fades. Where can we take them and how are we going to get them there?' I was almost wailing at him, but he seemed to be miles away and I wasn't getting through to him. My panic level rose as I concluded that he was going to walk out and leave me. It was Peter who answered me, in a quiet calm voice as though everything was normal and I was over-reacting badly."

"'This isn't a storm.' Peter said. 'That's not thunder out there.'"

"I stared at him, wondering if his mind had been unhinged by what had happened that night and wondering what I was going to do if both of my mainstays abandoned me now. Sam snapped my attention back from Peter."

"'Peter's right.' Sam said. 'That's not the noise from a storm out there.'"

"I decided that I was surrounded by people who were in shock after the events of the evening and my panic and anxiety levels shot through the roof. What would I do without them both? Why had they both let me down when I needed them the most? But Sam was suddenly making for the warehouse door at a run. He snatched it open and ran out into the night. But it was a night the like of which I had never seen in my life before. The gap where the warehouse door stood open was filled with an intense red light and there were terrible sounds coming from every direction. Before I had chance to wonder if Sam had left me to deal with the bodies on my own, he was back, racing in through the door and crashing it closed behind him."

"He crouched down, gasping and panting for breath as though he had run miles in those few seconds he had been out of the warehouse. When he had enough breath to speak he raised his head and looked me squarely in the eye."

"'We've got to get out of here, Bia, immediately. Grab Peter and run back to the shop. Don't hang about, or none of us will make it.'"

"'But, Sam, we've got to hide the bodies before we can run away.' I said, but Sam interrupted me.

"'Peter is right, Bia.' He said. 'That's no thunder storm that we've been hearing out there tonight. I ran to the end of the little lane and I could see ships out at sea, firing their guns at us. What we all thought was thunder is the noise of the guns, both from the Hun ships and from the shore battery at Hartlepool. I just hope that our gunners have managed to hit the ships. But the shells which have landed on shore have set fire to the docks and the two streets of houses at the end of the breakwater. We need to get out of here before either a shell lands on us or before the fires spread further and reach us here. And that won't be long before it happens, not the way it's burning out there. So many of the warehouses must have had combustible materials inside them, because they're going up like tinder boxes. Come on, Bia, we've got to get out of here.'"

"I stood transfixed. I couldn't comprehend what Sam was telling me. We were being shelled by the enemy? But that only happened to soldiers on a battlefield, or perhaps sailors on a warship. We were hundreds of miles away from a battlefield and we weren't on a ship. How could the enemy be attacking us? Sam looked as though he could scream his frustration at my incompetence in understanding what he was saying. He grabbed me by the arm and shook me."

"'Bia, the Hun has got ships out at sea and they are firing at us. The docks and the warehouses are already on fire and those bangs that shook the ground were the shells exploding on the docks and on warehouses nearest to the sea. If we don't move now we will be blown to smithereens when the gunners on the ships get our range, or we'll be burnt to a crisp when the fires reach here. If we get out of here, then the Hun will settle the problem of the bodies for us. We have got to go, now!'"

"'But I can't leave Simon!' I wailed. 'And we've got to move the pig butcher and William, so that no-one will know what has happened tonight.' I couldn't leave my baby's body to be blown to smithereens by a Hun shell, not to save my own life. Wasn't that the crux of the matter, of all that had happened? Wasn't it what raised me above the level of the pig butcher and William? The fact that I put somebody else before myself? Then Peter spoke."

"'I'll bring Simon for you, Bia.' He said, lifting my baby into his arms. 'You run on with Sam and I'll bring Simon. Don't you worry about him, I'll look after him. He's a little angel now and I'll care for him.'"

"I was anxious about Peter's tone of voice, as he spoke those words, but Sam didn't give me time to question what Peter was doing. He grabbed my arm and dragged me out of the warehouse door and we started to run away towards the dock road into the town. Even in the panic to get away, I could see the numerous fires burning fiercely against the night sky and that a wind seemed to have arrived which was blowing the flames towards the town. Before we got to the end of the first block of warehouses, a shell came in from the sea and blew the warehouse opposite mine into splinters of wood and flame which floated on the newly born wind and threatened to land on other buildings, setting them alight. We were thrown to the ground by the intensity of the blast and I knocked my cheek on a boulder as we landed. I could feel the warm sticky blood dripping down my face, but I wiped my face with my sleeve and turned to see if Peter was close behind us."

"There was no sign of Peter as I looked back towards my warehouse. I wondered what he was doing that was taking him so long. Had he understood that he was supposed to be bringing Simon out of the warehouse and joining Sam and I as we escaped from the docks area? Sam grabbed my hand at that point and hauled me to my feet. He wanted me to keep on running with him, but I pulled my hand out of his and put my mouth close to his ear. If I shouted I hoped he would be able to hear me above the sound of the explosions."

"'Peter's still inside the warehouse with Simon.' I yelled into Sam's ear. 'We've got to go back and get him and Simon.' I tugged at his arm, expecting him to turn and follow me back to the warehouse, but he took hold of my hand and bent his head to my ear."

"'If we don't go now then one of those shells is going to land on us,' He shouted back at me. 'Peter will come when he can, but we can't go back for them.' He continued to tug at my sleeve, but I pulled roughly away from him and took a couple of steps towards my warehouse. I could see that the warehouse door was open and swinging in the wind from all the explosions and, as I continued towards the warehouse, I saw Peter appear in the doorway, with Simon clasped in his arms. I made to run back towards them when Sam grabbed me bodily by the waist and stopped me going any further. I turned my head to argue with him, but before I could utter a word a weird shrieking noise began. It was so loud and so eerie a noise that I stopped struggling in Sam's arms and stared at my warehouse, which seemed to be where the noise was coming from."

"The noise got louder and louder until I had to clap my hands over my ears to try and cut off the dreadful sound, while still staring at Peter and Simon, silhouetted in the doorway. Peter raised one hand at me, as though he was waving goodbye and then I saw a ball of light, which I realised was the source of the keening noise, coming from the sea. It seemed to be moving in slow motion, although I am sure that the noise it was making was because it was pushing the air in front of it out of the way and was therefore moving at tremendous speed. But to me it seemed to take an age from when I first saw it to when it slammed into that open doorway and Peter and Simon disappeared from view behind a huge wall of flame."

"I screamed, 'Nooooo!!!' as the shell exploded, although not even the angels in Heaven would have been able to hear me above the sound of the explosion, and I tried desperately to loosen Sam's grip of me so that I could run to try and save Peter and Simon. Sam wouldn't let go of me, nor would he let me move one inch nearer to the conflagration which used to be my warehouse."

"'No, Bia, NOOO!! He screamed at me. 'You can't go back into that inferno. No-one is left alive in there. We've got to run away as fast as we can, before we get hit. Run, run like the wind!'"

"And Sam half-carried and half-dragged me away from the open mouth of Hell and we didn't stop until we reached the market-place, where we had talked to the one-legged tramp what seemed like a lifetime ago."

"I couldn't run any further. Even if the whole of the dockyards had exploded in a sheet of molten metal, I couldn't have taken another step. I sank down onto the steps of the market cross and put my head in my hands. Sam sat down next to me and started chafing my hands as though to keep the blood circulating. I leant my head against his shoulder and cried the tears I had been holding back since I had found Simon dead. Sam made encouraging noises and rubbed my hands and my shoulders and my back until the paroxysm of weeping was over and I lifted my head."

"'Is it really true, Sammy?' I asked. 'Is Simon really dead? And Peter? Is he dead too? Do you think it's possible that he might have survived?'"

"Sammy shook his head. 'Nobody could have survived that explosion. Your warehouse took a direct hit and everything in it will be burnt to ashes. There's no way that Peter can still be alive after that. He deliberately stayed in the warehouse, knowing what would happen to him if he was caught and tried for murder.'"

"I caught my breath as Sam said this. 'Do you really think Peter knew what he was doing when he chose to stay in the warehouse, instead of trying to escape with us? If he had come with us, no-one would have known that he had murdered Dennison, because there won't be enough left of any of the bodies after the explosion and the fire. He wouldn't have been arrested and charged with anything.'"

"'No, he wouldn't, but he would have known that he had murdered the pig butcher and he didn't want to live with that on his conscience for the rest of his life. He took the only way out that he could see. That lad understood much more than anyone ever gave him credit for, throughout the whole of his life. His only problem was that it took him a little longer than other people to come to the same conclusion. I think he had decided he was staying in the warehouse before he killed the pig butcher. He was the only one of us who knew that the sound wasn't that of thunder and he also was the only one to make the connection between the sound and ships out at sea. He knew what he was doing when he told you that he would look after Simon.'"

"Sam fell quiet after this and, for a few moments, I just sat next to him and let the tears course silently down my cheeks. The explosion in my warehouse had finally melted the ice in my heart and all the sorrow over Simon and Peter was flowing out of me."

"'I've lost my little boy, Sam,' I said when I could finally manage to speak again. 'He was my everything, the only reason I had for living and without him I might as well be dead too. I wish I could just stop breathing right here and now.'"

"'You can't do that, lass,' Sam said. 'We've got to tell Annie the truth about what happened tonight, but no-one else need know. Annie will need you now, more than ever before and you'll have to be there for her. Having to look after Peter has been what has kept her going since her husband died and she'll be as lost as you are from now on. You are going to have to be strong for her and, hopefully, together you'll get through this and come out the other side. Of course, it means that no-one will ever know that Dennison murdered your husband and son, but it also means that Peter won't live for years with it on his conscience. They will all be listed as victims of the Bosche and only you, I and Annie will know the truth of what happened tonight.'"

"I thought about what Sammy said, but I still didn't understand why Peter hadn't escaped with us. We could all have then told the same story of what happened and nobody would have known the truth. I tried to explain how I was feeling to Sam, but he was forthright in his reply."

"'Even if nobody else knew the truth of what happened tonight, Peter would have carried the guilt around with him. Eventually, it would have eaten away at him and he would have wanted to confess to what he had done. That would have put you and I in danger and he could have gone to prison for it or even been hanged for it. He decided to take the best way out for him because he knew he couldn't have coped with a life behind bars and he wouldn't have wanted his mother to carry the stigma of being the parent of a murderer. So it's better this way. Annie has still lost her son, but the break has been clean and his death will be seen as a sacrifice. Peter knew very well what he was doing staying behind in the warehouse. He has always understood more than anyone has ever given him credit for and, in my eyes, he will always be a hero.'"

"I had to admit that Sam was right in everything that he had said and, although I had never felt less like carrying any burden in the whole of my life, I dragged myself to my feet, ready to set off for Queen Street and the shop and the task of telling Annie what had happened."

"We stuck to the smaller roads and the back alleys as we made our way back to the shop, hoping that there was less likelihood that we would be seen by curious townsfolk. Sam kept his arm around my waist, holding me up and pouring some of his strength into me as we walked along."

" 'Once we have told Annie what has happened, we'll have to go back to the docks and join the rest of the town as they wait for news on casualties,' Sam said. 'We've got to act as shocked as everyone else, because we aren't supposed to know what has happened. People know that we have been looking for Simon and William because we stopped and asked when we were searching for them, but we will say that we went back to the shop before the bombardment started.'"

"'I don't know if I can do it, Sam,' I wailed. 'I don't know if I'm strong enough to face it all, not when I've lost Simon.'"

"'You've got to do it, Bia,' he said. 'For Annie's sake, you are going to have to be strong.'"

"I listened to Sam and I could see the truth in what he said. But why was it always me who had to be strong and carry the load? Why couldn't someone else support me, look after me, carry me through the difficult times? I suddenly felt that I had been alone all my life. My marriage to William had obviously always been a sham, he had always been egotistical and self-absorbed and I had kidded myself that he loved me and I loved him."

"'I'll care for Annie for the rest of my life, but I do wish that someone would look after me, Sam. I'm not as strong as other people believe, you know. I just hide my insecurities better, that's all.'"

"'Do you think I don't know that, lass?' Sam replied. 'I've watched you for over two years now and you've always put everybody else before yourself, but I've seen the frightened girl behind the smart business-woman and I've longed to tell you to lean on me. I've never had the courage to say it before but I'm saying it now. You can lean on me whenever and wherever you want. I'll always be there for you. But now, we really are going to have to get back to the shop. It sounds as though the bombardment is over and people will be coming out of their houses to find out what has happened. Are you up to it, pet?'"

"'I am, Sammy.' I said. 'I can face this if I know that I've got you at my side.'"

"We reached the shop in Queen Street before any townsfolk plucked up the courage to venture outside and assess the damage done that night. Annie was in the kitchen with Hannah and her sisters and her face was creased with the concern she had been feeling all night. Sam sent the three girls up to Hannah's bedroom so that they wouldn't hear what William and Peter had done. Sam would give them the expurgated version later. True to his word that he would always support me it was Sam who explained to Annie what had happened at the warehouse. She took the news of Peter's death better than I had expected her to, although she shed tears over it. His death didn't knock her off her feet, as Simon's death had knocked me, and I admired her even more for her courage and fortitude."

"It didn't take Annie long to absorb all that had happened that night and she was ready with her sympathy for me over Simon's death, although she didn't waste any of it on William."

"'Yon lad was always too wrapped up in himself and how he was feeling,' was her conclusion to what William had said and done. 'It's no surprise to me that he would put himself before the bairn, although that little mite didn't deserve to die for his father's weaknesses. I can understand Dennison wanting revenge for his lad's death when he found out how it had happened, but he must have been a twisted, evil bugger to try and get that revenge by killing a child. I don't blame him for wanting William dead, but he should have concentrated on William and left the rest of the family alone.'"

"'But you've lost Peter,' I said to her, amazed that she could look at all that had happened so logically."

" 'I know that, pet,' she answered, 'And I'll grieve for him for the rest of my life, believe me, but he chose the way he was going to die. Not many folk get to make that choice, certainly little Simon didn't. I'm just glad that he didn't have to spend years in prison for what he did. And, if I'm being honest, I won't have to worry about what's going to happen to him after I've gone. He would never have been able to care for himself, not with his handicap, and I've worried all his life about how he would cope when I died. He's saved me that worry now.'"

"'I would have cared for him, Annie.' I cried, hurt that she thought I would have abandoned Peter. 'I would have looked after him for the rest of my life and loved him like my own.'"

"'I know you would have done, lass, but it wouldn't have been fair on you,' Annie answered. 'He wasn't your responsibility, even though you seem to think that you have to take on the cares of the world. No, it's better like this and I think Peter knew that, even if he couldn't have put it into words.'"

"I was ready to argue this point, but Sam interrupted before I could begin."

"'I know you want to talk about this, you two, but Bia and I need to get down to the docks. It would look suspicious if we didn't turn up at the same time as everyone else, when so many people know that we were out searching for William and Simon earlier this evening. We can't risk any out –of- the - ordinary behaviour at the moment. I can hear people out in the street and it's time we joined them. Can you manage it, Bia?'"

"I assured him that I could and would do all that was needed that night and, after hugging Annie, we left her to look after Sam's three daughters and made our way, once more, to the docks."

Nana Lymer fell silent at this point and Victoria took the opportunity to take hold of her hand and rub it gently, rather like her Granddad Sam had done that long-ago night during the First World War. The more she heard about the events of that time, the more she pitied her grandmother, wishing that she could do something to alleviate the pain she must be feeling. She wasn't sure if she should comment on what Nana had told her or if she should ask questions about the events (and she had a stack of questions rocketing through her brain) or if she should let Nana Lymer take the lead and wait for her comments. It was a few moments before she realised that Nana was watching her face, as though to gauge her reactions to what she had heard.

"Do you think we did the wrong thing, keeping the truth a secret all these years?" Nana asked when she knew she had Victoria's attention.

"No, Nana." Victoria's reply came very quickly. "I don't think you could have done anything else. Nobody would have gained anything by learning the truth and you and Granddad and Annie would all have suffered in other ways if the

403

truth had come out. The pig butcher was dead, so he paid for the murders he had committed; William was dead, so he paid for his cowardice and his shameful abandonment of his son; Peter was dead, so he wouldn't have to suffer a trial for what he had done; and Simon was dead, although, if there was any justice in this world, he should never have died. The outcome was the best for all concerned. It made the best of a bad job, as Mam would say. You don't feel guilty about it, surely, do you?"

Nana thought about this for a while and then spoke.

"No. I don't feel guilty about it. I've always felt that it seemed a neatly tied bundle, solving a lot of problems without adding more. Of course, Annie and I both lost a son, but how could we complain about that when so many other mothers lost their sons during that terrible time. And both of them died quickly, not screaming in an agony that went on for hours. You have to learn to be grateful for small mercies in this life."

Nana Lymer suddenly snuggled further down into her bed, her eyes heavy and her face pale. Victoria was immediately all concern, knowing that her Nana had spoken for far too long that day and that she had raked up memories that must have been very painful for her.

"You go to sleep, Nana," she said. "I'll go and help Mam with the tea and bring it up for you when it's ready."

"Good lass," Nana managed to whisper. "It's made me very tired today, going over that terrible night. I think we should manage to finish the story tomorrow, and then I can die content that Simon and Peter haven't been forgotten."

"Nana! You aren't going to die anytime soon. Don't be silly!" But Victoria realised her protests were falling on deaf ears. Her grandmother was fast asleep, with a slight smile on her lips and the lines of old age hardly apparent.

Chapter Fourteen

Victoria was making her breakfast the next morning when her mother slammed into the kitchen, throwing some bacon and a loaf of bread that she had brought out of the shop, onto the kitchen table. Victoria managed to infer from this that her mother wasn't in a particularly good mood, but no longer felt that she had to enquire what had upset her. She had done a lot of growing-up this Christmas holidays and there were times when it made life so much easier than it used to be. She continued to butter her toast and then decided that apricot jam was her choice for a preserve that morning. As she turned to get it out of the cupboard, she realised that her mother was still in the room, standing staring at her, with her arms folded in front of her and a face like thunder.

"Well?" her mother barked at her. "Why did she want to see her solicitor the other day, then? Tell me what she's done."

Victoria was shocked by the bald question and by the anger showing on her mother's face. It made her look quite ugly and Victoria wondered if *she* looked like that when she lost her temper. Resolving to never lose her temper to the same degree ever again, she shrugged her shoulders at her mother's questions.

"I've no idea why Nana wanted to see Mr Vine, but it's none of my business. If you want to know, why don't you go and ask Nana what she wanted to see him for?"

"Haven't you asked her?" Her mother snapped, as though she couldn't believe that Victoria could be so stupid as to miss the opportunity of grilling her grandmother. It made Victoria's blood boil that her mother could infuse so much into one statement but, whereas before Christmas she would have been apologising for her lack of intelligence, now she could rise above it.

"If Nana wanted me to know what she had discussed with Mr Vine I'm sure she would have told me. I've no intentions of giving her the third degree, just to find out what she obviously wants to keep private."

"You stupid girl," her mother snarled, all pretence at civility forgotten. "What if she's changed her will so that you don't get anything out of it? You wouldn't be so high and mighty then, would you? You will have wasted all these holidays, spending time with her. You want to think about that before you start looking down your nose at your mother."

Bia was almost screaming now, very close to losing all self-control. Victoria didn't want to stay near her, in case she did lose control, but she had one more thing that she wanted to say before she went upstairs to Nana's bedroom.

"I haven't sat with Nana these holidays just to get her to leave me something in her will. I've sat with her because I like to talk to her and to listen to the stories she can tell about what life was like when she was young. I don't know if she has any money to leave and I don't care. I love her because of who she is, not because of what she has got. Now, I'm going back to her bedroom, but I'll come down and help you make lunch, if you need me to."

Victoria walked away from her mother, knowing that it was the first time in her life that she had answered her back successfully. She was pleased that she could sound so calm, but inside she was shaking in case Bia started screaming at her again. She decided that she really didn't like conflict or confrontation, but that she wasn't going to back down and let other people benefit from her peaceful nature.

Upstairs, Nana Lymer didn't look very well at all. She was pale and her eyes seemed huge in her little face. She was resting against her pillows, as though she didn't have the strength to sit upright without them.

"Are you ok, Nana?" Victoria asked, concerned about her grandmother's frailty but when Nana Lymer spoke it was in her usual strong voice.

"Of course I'm ok. Why shouldn't I be?" she said. "I'm just a bit tired, that's all. I didn't sleep very well last night and I think it was because I hadn't finished telling you the entire story. I'm worried that I'm going to kick the bucket before we get to the end and then you'll never find out what happened."

"You aren't going to kick the bucket, as you put it!" Victoria said. "You are as strong as a horse and you're far too young to be talking about dying!"

"Death comes when it wants to, Victoria, not when it suits the person. But let's not be morbid, let's enjoy today. Did I hear raised voices downstairs? Or should I re-phrase that? Did I hear your mother having a tantrum again?"

"Yes, you did. She seems to think that I should be asking you why you wanted to see Mr Vine, instead of wasting time listening to stories."

"And what did you tell her? Presumably whatever you said, it didn't suit her and that's why she was ranting."

"I told her that if you wanted me to know, then you would have told me. I'm not going to pry into your private concerns, just to satisfy her curiosity and greed."

Nana laughed out loud. "It's lovely to know that you've finally got the measure of her, lass. I've wondered for a long time when you would turn on her. She's had it coming for years and it'll do her a power of good to be bested, for once. I'll tell you what I discussed with Mr Vine, if you want to know."

"I don't want to know, Nana." Victoria was quick to reply. "I want to know what happened in the rest of the story so, if you are feeling strong enough, shall we start? I'm going downstairs at lunchtime to help with lunch, but I'll come straight back upstairs when I've done the washing-up and we can talk again. If you're up to it, of course." Victoria added hastily.

"Of course I'm up to it. I've done nothing for months but stay in this bed, so I should have energy and to spare. But let's get on with the story. I'm not pegging it until I've told you everything!"

"Sam and I had left Annie looking after the three girls at the shop and we made our way back to the dockside area. Compared to how it had been when Sam, Peter and I had been looking for Simon and William, the place was crowded. The whole of the town was awash with humanity, huddled in small groups and talking in hushed voices as they tried to come to terms with the havoc and destruction which had been wreaked on the town by the might of the Hun forces. There was a wave of movement towards the docks, some going slowly because they didn't want to get there and hear bad news and some going quickly because they were desperate to find out what had happened to loved ones and friends and couldn't wait an extra second to find out. It was such a contrast to the silence and emptiness which we had waded through when we were conducting our search."

"As we got closer to the docks we could see that the whole of the area was ablaze, lighting up the darkness as though it were the middle of the day. It was eerie in that the fires made the night as though it were day, but if you looked away from the docks, everywhere else seemed to be so much darker and blacker by contrast. There were gaps in the skyline that used to be filled with houses and warehouses which had been bombed out of existence, but everywhere there were people running hither and thither trying to fight the fires and save the lives of people trapped in the burning and partially demolished buildings."

"It was like a scene from Hell with the red glow from the fires and the leaping flames, contrasted with the pitch dark of areas hidden from the inferno. It's difficult to describe how frightening it was to look at that tableau and to listen to the crackling flames and the noise of crashing timbers, bricks and stones as buildings fell. The heat was intense, juxtaposed with the heavy frost which lay around the town, so that those people standing and staring at the fires were being roasted from the front and were being frozen from behind."

"There was a harsh contrast between that scene of Hell's destruction and the people gathered at the dock gates, which was the closest that they could get to the centre of the fires. The crowd, mostly consisting of women and children, made no noise at all as they waited for news, hoping against hope that their friends and loved ones would be the people who were saved from the inferno. They waited in absolute silence while men could be seen silhouetted against the conflagration, desperately trying to put out the blaze and search for survivors."

"It was easy to join the crowd, melding with one of the groups as we all stood and stared at the devastation. Our presence was accepted into the fold and we didn't have to answer any questions or give reasons why we too were waiting for news. The shock emanating from the townsfolk was a palpable entity, but it moulded us all together and Sam and I were absorbed into the horror of the moment."

"I could feel the tears drying on my face in the heat from the conflagration, although I hadn't been aware that I was weeping. My sorrow was reflected in the faces of the rest of the crowd, where shiny tear tracks were obvious on so many of those faces, men and women alike, as we all waited for news. It took a very long time before any of the fire-fighters' efforts were rewarded by a reduction in the scale of the inferno but, eventually, we could all see that they were finally winning their fight against the flames. This realisation led to the first sounds that any of the crowd had made that night. Although it seemed impossible for the gathered throng to concentrate any harder than they had been doing for hours, this first sign was greeted by movement, almost as though we had all been holding our breath for that moment and we collectively released it. It made a sound like a gentle wind rippling through a field full of ripe corn and the crowd, as a whole, moved slightly closer to the dock gates."

"Not long after this, a man appeared walking towards the gathered throng, carrying a bundle wrapped in a blanket. He placed his bundle reverently on the pavement and then looked about him at the crowd. He picked out a face he recognised and headed towards it, gathering the whole family about him as they listened to his news. He could be seen shaking his head vehemently until the oldest member of the family laid his hand on the fire-fighter's arm and spoke a few words. The fire-fighter nodded once and then led the old man to the bundle as it lay on the pavement. He raised the blanket from its contents and the old man staggered as he looked at what the blanket had concealed. The fire-fighter dropped the blanket immediately and supported the old man back to where his family were waiting for him. The family gathered round and there was a lot of head-shaking, until the group split apart and the whole family turned their faces towards the town. The women were holding handkerchiefs to their faces and the men looked at the ground they were walking on as they made their way towards their home. The crowd parted willingly to let them pass and many patted backs and shoulders in commiseration as they passed, and then closed ranks again and looked towards the docks."

"The rest of us continued with our vigil, once again standing in silence as we watched the black figures of the fire-fighting teams moving amongst the broken teeth of the buildings. We were all shivering in the cold, now that the heat radiating from the fires was reducing, but nobody would give up the self-imposed vigil until we had the answers we were waiting for. This was when Sam turned to me and spoke for the first time in what seemed like hours."

"'Do you think I should go and help the rescue teams to see if I can do anything?' he asked me."

"'Please, don't leave me alone Sam,' I wailed. 'I can't stand here on my own.'"

"'There's not much you can do that they aren't already doing.' A man in the crowd said. 'Stay with the lass and keep her company. We all need our friends and family with us tonight.'"

"'He's right, Sammy,' I moaned. 'I can't stay here alone tonight. I need you with me.'" I could feel panic rising inside me at the thought that Sam might leave me. What if anyone asked me any questions? How would I answer them? I didn't know if I could hold it together if I was asked any questions. I might make the authorities suspicious if I said the wrong thing. To my great relief, Sam listened to the man and stayed with me."

"'Don't panic, Bia,' he said, soothingly. 'I'll not leave you alone. I just didn't want to look as though I wasn't prepared to help. It might make me look suspicious.'"

"'It'll look suspicious if we both put too much effort into *not* looking suspicious.' I answered, quite tartly. I was astonished when Sam managed a small smile and squeezed my hand under cover of my coat and shawl."

"'Good lass. I knew I could rely on you if I started to go overboard with my acting.'"

"I couldn't help but smile at him and the wound tension inside me unrolled itself a little so that I could breath. We carried on standing there; watching as more and more fire-fighters and policemen came out from the docks, carrying bundles in their arms which they placed, each as reverently as the last, onto the pavement. Each one then looked around for a relative and went and spoke quietly to them. Not many wanted to view the mangled remains underneath those blankets, not after watching the old man's reaction at the beginning of the rescue, so most people, once singled out, left the dockside either to go home, or if home no longer existed, to go and stay with other relatives."

"It wasn't long before the pavement underneath the docks' railings was filled with bodies, all carefully concealed in the blankets which had been brought from the cottage hospital on Harcourt Road and the crowd waiting at the dock gates was reducing in size. Those of us who were left gathered closer together, as though for warmth, but in reality what we wanted was the comfort of the presence of others in the same boat as us. The night was nearly over and the dawn light was just starting to brighten the skyline over the sea when a policeman carried out from the docks a small shape wrapped in a blanket. The policeman placed this tiny parcel down on the pavement at the end of the line of bodies and then straightened up slowly as though this latest task was more than he could bear."

"In the wash of light from the dawn sky, I recognised him as a boy I had been at school with, by the name of Evans. He was looking for a relative to match the small body he had been carrying and, when his eyes met mine and he started to walk towards me, I grabbed Sam's hand and squeezed as though my life depended on it."

"'Mrs Drinkwater?' he asked, as though we hadn't known each other nearly all our lives. 'I'm afraid it's bad news that I've got for you.'"

"That was all he needed to say. Even though I, unlike the rest of the hopeful people gathered there that night, already knew that my family were dead, it was as though his words sent a signal to my brain and shut down the use of my limbs. My legs gave way beneath me and I sank into the melted snow and the ash of the road and rested my face in my hands. Breathing was difficult, but I couldn't stop sobbing to try and take a breath properly. I could only moan Simon's name and wish that the ground would open up and swallow me whole."

"Despite my sobs, I clearly heard Ted Evans telling Sam that William had been found with Simon and that there were two more bodies in what remained of the warehouse."

"'It looks like the warehouse took a direct hit, like, 'cos nothing is recognisable in what's left of the place. There's another two bodies in there, as well as Mr Drinkwater's. I don't suppose you might know who they are?'"

"I heard Sam saying that Peter was missing from home, but he had no idea who the other body might belong to and I marvelled that he was cool enough to be able to say all this and sound believable. Perhaps I had done the right thing by collapsing, because I didn't think I could have answered those questions so well. Ted's next words made me draw in the deepest breath I had breathed in a long time."

"'The other body might belong to Butcher Dennison. He was seen earlier in the evening with Mr Drinkwater and the little boy. The butcher had heard noises coming from the Drinkwater's warehouse and thought that there may be a burglar inside. He and Mr Drinkwater went off to try and catch him, evidently, so they would all have been inside when the bombardment started. One of the regulars in the Red Lion had heard them talking about it.'"

" 'Aye, we heard that tale, so Peter went off to bring Simon home, it being such bad weather and so late.' Sam agreed. 'It must be fate that brought them all together in that place and at that time, but it's a very cruel fate.'"

"Ted Evans muttered his agreement and then turned back to the job in hand, after telling Sam to 'get that poor lass home'. We could finally leave the docks and make our way back to the shop, for the umpteenth time that night. Hands lifted me to my feet and many people patted me in condolence or hugged me and then released me to go on my way. I managed to utter some faint 'thank you's' and then we were on our way home."

"I sobbed every step of the way home. I wasn't acting for the benefit of any who may have been watching me. I wasn't pretending that the news of the deaths of my husband and son had come as a great shock to me. It was because I couldn't help it. It was almost as though I *had* only just found out about their deaths. I had realised that I would never see or hold Simon again; that he would never grow up into a man and have a family of his own and I was totally bereft because of this realisation."

"Not once on that walk home did I think about William. I had shut him out of my mind completely, because the whole damnable business was his fault. If he hadn't gone off to war to stroke his own ego; if he hadn't shielded himself behind Dennison's son so that the boy died; if Dennison hadn't found out about his cowardice and taken his revenge; if William hadn't been so stupid as to believe the pig butcher when he had said that there was a burglar in the warehouse and so took my son to his death; it all went back to William. I couldn't think about him without wanting to scream my hatred of him to the skies. IT WAS ALL WILLIAM'S FAULT! So I shut him completely out of my mind, otherwise I would have betrayed Peter and Sam. It was the only way that I could cope that night."

"So, slowly we made our way back to Queen Street, through the quiet, freezing streets, even more cold now that there was such a contrast between them and the heat of the dockside and we let ourselves in through the side door of the shop."

"Annie was sitting out a vigil next to the fire in the range. She had been crying for Peter while we had been at the dock, that much was obvious from her haggard face as she looked up as we entered. But she busied herself making hot drinks for us, brushing aside any suggestion that she should go to bed."

"'I'd not sleep,' she declared. 'There's no point in my trying to sleep because my mind is so full of what Peter did tonight. I keep remembering things that happened to him when he was a child and I've thanked God a hundred times tonight, at least, that He brought us together. I know that this is the best outcome I could have hoped for, but I will miss him for the rest of my life.'" And she put her face in her hands and wept again for the son she had lost."

"I gave her what comfort I could, but I was also thinking back over the few short years Simon and I had had together. I wasn't as Christian in my attitude as Annie was and I always came back to the same conclusion: that it had all been William's fault. His actions had affected so many lives and never once in a good way. Everything that he had done had had repercussions throughout our household and throughout our town and yet he had never once given any thought to any other person other than himself. What sort of an obituary was that for any human being? I knew that if I continued to probe into these thoughts I would send myself mad, but that first night I couldn't help poking at the nagging toothache with my tongue. Over the years since then I have managed to regain my perspective on those events, but I have still always come to the same conclusion. The whole thing was William's fault and if there is any justice in the afterlife he will still be paying for his sins."

Mrs Lymer's face had hardened as she talked about that night and Victoria realised that she was still affected by what had happened. Could any mother ever forgive the person who caused her child's death or did the parents of murdered children carry that depth of hatred with them until they too died? She took hold of Nana's hand and stroked it for her, not speaking but hoping to convey her sympathy by touch. Nana was staring into space, not aware of where she was or what Victoria was doing. It was with a great effort that she brought herself back to the present and smiled at her granddaughter.

"Would you make me a cup of tea, please?" she asked. "Telling stories makes me very thirsty, you know. It's a good thing that I wasn't employed to tell stories, I'd have drunk the river dry every day!"

"It's lunchtime." Victoria answered. "Will you have a chicken sandwich or perhaps a cheese and tomato one?"

"I'm not hungry, pet, thank you." Nana said. "I'd just like a cup of tea and then we can finish my story. We'll be done before teatime and then I'll have a good long rest."

"Ok." Victoria acquiesced, not wanting to quarrel with her grandmother, who was still looking very frail.

In the kitchen, Victoria prepared lunch for her parents and then put Nana's cup of tea and a shortbread biscuit on a tray, ready to carry them upstairs.

"Still listening to her stories, then?" Her mother growled as she took her place at the table to eat her lunch. Victoria's head was so full of the bombardment of the docks and of the deaths of

Simon and Peter that she hardly heard what her mother said. She nodded vaguely in her direction and then left the kitchen, so intent on getting back upstairs for the last part of the story that she didn't hear her mother's comment as she left the room, but was vaguely aware that her father had spoken as well.

"Leave the lass alone, Bia." Her father said. "She's caring for her grandmother and that's a good thing. There's not many her age would have the kindness and patience that she's got."

Bia merely grunted into her teacup, not bothering to waste her energy on an argument that wouldn't give her any satisfaction, but she resolved to ask her mother what she had wanted to see Mr Vine for, she was unlikely to get any information from her daughter.

In Nana Lymer's bedroom, Victoria had to help her grandmother to lift the cup to her lips. She seemed to be rapidly running out of energy and strength and Victoria wanted to call the doctor, although Nana Lymer refused her offer.

"I'll do, lass. There's nothing wrong with me that a good night's sleep won't cure. Leave doctors for folk that need them. I don't. Let me finish the story and then I'll sleep better than I've done for years."

There was nothing that Victoria could say that would make her change her mind so, in the end, she capitulated and resumed her seat next to the bed.

"Sam, Annie and I didn't go to bed that night. The girls were all snuggled in together in Hannah's room, so we left them alone, not wanting to spoil their sleep with bad news. We three spent what little of the night that remained, sitting in the kitchen next to the range and going over all that had happened. It didn't make any difference to the outcome, but we all felt the need to reiterate certain points and quiz the other two about certain events, as though talking about it would make it easier to bear. It didn't, but we each attempted it."

"Sam went off to work and Annie and I opened the shop as usual. It was an unspoken agreement between us to open the shop, but I think it was the best thing we could have done. We would eventually have to face our customers and our neighbours and it was sensible to do it as soon as possible, before any of us got cold feet. We were prepared for the curiosity that would inevitably be part of meeting any neighbour or customer, but I wasn't prepared for the kindness and empathy shown us by all who came into the shop that day and for months afterwards. Some people were uncomfortable, having to talk to two recently bereaved women, but most were very understanding and I did gain strength from knowing that so many people were genuinely feeling such sympathy for me and Annie."

"Right from that first day, it was obvious that everyone accepted the story that the pig butcher and William were looking for a burglar in the warehouse and they commiserated with me that Simon happened to be with his father that night. No-one even suggested that there might be something strange about William and Dennison being together, because I don't think it was widely known that they disliked each other. It seemed that the tale of Young Dennison's death hadn't been spread among the general population so nobody put two and two together and made five, a situation which made life a lot easier for me."

"The fact that so many people had been killed on that same night meant that the whole town was grieving because everyone was so directly connected to at least one person who had died. This meant that when I could no longer hold down my grief, no-one seemed at all surprised when I dissolved into tears while slicing ham or pouring a pint of vinegar and people tried to comfort me with hugs and their own tears when anyone found me doing it. One and all agreed that it was probably 'the best thing' for us to try and carry on by opening the shop and I must admit having to serve customers stopped me dwelling on the events of the previous night and probably stopped me from going mad."

"We had told the three girls the whitewashed tale of what had happened the night before when they all came downstairs the next morning. They weren't as closely involved as us, of course, although the deaths of Simon and Peter hit Hannah very hard. She tried to be a brave little trouper and declared that she was 'fine' when I caught her crying as she mixed the pastry for some pies, but the flour mixed with tears on her face belied her words. She forgot how to be happy and didn't sing as she went about her work and it was heart-breaking to see her so depressed and miserable. She missed Simon a great deal, because they had played together so much when she was working in the kitchen but she also missed Peter as well and I often saw her raise her head in hope if she heard a deep voice in the shop. I think their deaths reminded her of the death of her mother and she grieved twice over every day. I fervently hoped that she would find joy in her life again soon because the world had lost one of its angels while she was wrapped in sorrow."

"The next few weeks passed in a blur to me. There were countless questions asked by the authorities as they tried to piece together all that had happened that night along the riverside. We learned that Middlesbrough hadn't been the only town attacked by the Hun that night. The same group of ships had also bombarded Scarborough and Hartlepool, causing an equal amount of damage and destruction and devastation in both those towns. The loss of life in all three places had been horrendous and the attacks were pointed out as an example of the barbarism of the German nation for attacking unarmed civilians."

"We learned that the Royal Navy had launched ships to counter-attack the Hun and try and sink or capture the ships which had done so much damage to the North Eastern coast, and I believe they did have some success, although their sailors lost their lives as well as our civilians that night. Because so many people had been killed and because most people were so shocked that we could be attacked in our own homes, we didn't stand out amongst the townsfolk at having lost so many of our little family. The deaths of William, Simon, Peter and the pig butcher weren't discussed endlessly by the town gossips, because they had so much 'material' to discuss, so no-one probed too deeply into their deaths and discovered facts that we didn't want uncovering. Their deaths were only a handful amongst many, or as Sammy put it, four more trees in that dreadful forest and, as so, unremarkable."

"There was an inquest into all the deaths that had occurred that night, originally intended as separate, independent inquests for each death, but it soon became apparent that that way was unworkable, so it became a combined inquest for all the dead. It was dealt with with great sensitivity and the combined result was that all had died as the result of enemy action. Death certificates were issued and, eventually, everything settled back down to its normal wartime pattern and the town moved on, still mourning its losses, but facing them resolutely."

"I awoke every morning to the fresh realisation that Simon was dead. Sometimes I remembered immediately on waking, so that the knowledge was with me before I had chance to draw some strength into me, other times it was a while before my brain was limber enough to process the information but, whether I realised immediately or remembered after a few moments, each realisation was like learning of his death all over again. I got to the point where I tried *not* to sleep, so that I wouldn't have to wake up and go through the whole experience again, seeing him dead on the warehouse floor. My body invariably defeated me and I fell into an exhausted sleep every night."

"But I was so lucky at that time, in the people I had who surrounded me and gave me the strength to carry on with everyday life. Annie was much stronger than I in how she coped with Peter's death and she helped me live through that terrible time in the few weeks after their deaths. She often caught me sitting next to the embers of the fire late at night, trying desperately *not* to go to sleep so that I wouldn't have to wake the next morning and have the realisation of Simon's death to live through again. She would make hot drinks for us both and we would sit and talk about our boys, remembering things they had done and, eventually, smiling at our memories instead of crying over them."

"I saw on Annie's face the same sorrow that I could see in my own, on the rare occasions when I looked in a mirror. It was the same sorrow and anguish which was on the faces of all the people in our town who had lost loved ones in the bombardment or whose boys had died at the Front. It was a cruel world at that time, with so many people feeling this great sadness and that was when I lost my belief in any god. I know many people turned to the Church at that time and it helped them battle through to the end but I turned against it and after William and Simon's funerals, I didn't set foot in either church or chapel ever again."

"That time was the only time in my life when I didn't know if I could cope with what life was throwing at me basically because I didn't have control over events, I didn't make the decisions. All I could do was flounder along in the wake of this flood of horrendous happenings and try and cope as best I may. It made me feel insignificant and weak and incapable of ever being able to make a decision about my life ever again. I was constantly waiting for the next horrible event to happen and I couldn't get rid of the feeling that the Sword of Damocles was swinging noisily over my head, all day every day, and I didn't know when, or why, it would fall. Perhaps I've always been a basically weak person, I don't know, but I do know that living with the constant daily fear of disaster is extremely exhausting. If it hadn't been for Sam, encouraging me to eat when I didn't have any appetite and reading aloud to me to calm me, I do believe that I would have gone under at that time."

"All through those terrible days, Sam was at my side. He supported me both physically and emotionally, whenever I looked as though I was faltering he was there, urging me forever onwards until, eventually, with his and Annie's help, I stopped wishing I had died along with my child and I turned my face towards the future once again."

Chapter Fifteen

Nana Lymer stopped speaking and Victoria realised that she had fallen asleep, even though she was still sitting upright, propped against her pillows. She tried to slide her down so that she could rest more comfortably but her body seemed almost wedged somewhere, so this was no easy manoeuvre. As Victoria was watching her, trying to think of some way to be able to move her without waking her up, Nana's eyes opened sluggishly and she slid herself quite easily down into the bed.

"I'll finish the story tomorrow, Victoria," she whispered, before she turned over and made herself comfortable under the covers.

Victoria was more concerned than she had ever been before about the state of Nana's health. She had never seen her so frail and tired and she briefly wondered if she was coming down with some sort of bug.

"Please don't let it be that she is exhausted from reliving her experiences during the First World War." Victoria didn't think that she could cope with being the reason for her grandmother being ill. She would never forgive herself if Nana died because Victoria wanted to hear the story of her life; that would be unbearable. She resolved to keep an extra special eye on her grandmother the next day and to stop her from finishing the story if she looked at all tired.

Once again, Victoria's mother made no complaint when Victoria said she intended spending the day with Nana Lymer again. She didn't react in any way other than raising her eyes above her teacup as she drank her tea and glancing at her daughter. Victoria took this unspoken communication as leave to spend her day however she chose, so she quickly finished her toast and washed the pots which were waiting on the draining board, before making her exit from the kitchen. Her mother ignored her completely, but her father winked at her as she passed him on her way to the hall and staircase.

Nana Lymer was awake and sitting up in bed when Victoria entered her bedroom, finishing her own breakfast.

"I'll just take your pots downstairs and wash them, and then I'll be straight back up." Victoria said.

"Ok. Then I've got a story to finish telling you. We should get through the rest of it today and then it doesn't matter if I peg it tomorrow." The old lady smiled at Victoria, ignoring the frown that her words had produced on her granddaughter's forehead. Within minutes, Victoria was back in Nana Lymer's bedroom, making herself comfortable on the chair next to the bed.

"Before you ask, I'm as healthy as anyone my age can expect to be, so there's no need for you to worry about me." Nana Lymer smiled at the expression on Victoria's face. "If I wasn't well enough I would let you know, so let's just get on with the story, shall we?"

"Ok, I give in." Victoria said, raising her hands in submission.

"Good. Once I had decided that I wasn't going to try and join Simon by killing myself, I turned my face towards the future and that was when Mrs Dennison came to see me. She turned up in the shop one rainy Wednesday afternoon, shaking the raindrops from her shawl and asked Hannah if she could have a word with me. I was in the kitchen with the door open into the shop so I heard her voice as soon as she spoke. Hannah's face appeared at the open doorway and she raised her eyebrows as she tilted her head towards Mrs Dennison. I carried on making the fresh batch of ginger beer that I had started but nodded my agreement at Hannah and she went and brought Mrs Dennison into the kitchen. I watched her enter the room with some trepidation. Was she going to accuse me of murdering her husband? Could she possibly have some idea of what had happened that night? I went cold through to my bones, but then shook myself mentally over my guilty conscience and civilly asked her what I could do for her. Her answer to my question knocked me for six.

"I've come to ask for your help, Mrs Drinkwater." she said, looking me straight in the eye as she spoke. She didn't seem as meek and mild as she had been the last time I had seen her, when she was sporting the black eye the pig butcher had given her. She stood upright and looked me square in the eyes.

"I know my husband was making life difficult for you, before he was killed in the raid and I'm right sorry that he was doing that. I heard about him carrying on in your backyard and making a fool of himself in front of all your neighbours. I'll not lie to you, Mrs Drinkwater, he wasn't a pleasant man, he was often more of a pig than the animals he butchered in our shop but he was my husband and now he's dead, so I'm on my own. Our Albert was killed last year on the Somme, so I've got no-one to provide for me, but I do now own the shop. I was wondering if you could give me some advice on getting the business up and running again."

"She raised her hand to stop me before I had a chance to speak."

"'I know I don't deserve your help, seeing as how it was my husband who was threatening you in your own backyard, but you're the only woman I know who's running a business on your own and I wondered if you would help me do the same. My shop wouldn't interfere with your profits, cos we would be selling different things, so it wouldn't be detrimental to your business. Would you consider helping me? After all, my husband died trying to save your husband and son.'"

"While she had been talking, there had been so many thoughts rushing through my mind, but I nearly lost all my hard-won self-control at her last statement. Her husband hadn't died trying to save my husband and son, he'd murdered them both, but *my* husband had killed her son and then the most innocent of adults had ended the pig butcher's life. So much hatred and evil had revolved around her husband, but she was innocent of it all. Like me, she had lost her only child and realised that she didn't want to stay married to her husband, but, unlike me, she had left him when he had taken to physically abusing her. The black eye which was the last present her husband had given her had been the last in a long line of injuries he had inflicted on her, so didn't she deserve a better chance at life? She was prepared to work for it, so who was I to hold her back? I had made my decision.

"I'd be very happy to help you, Mrs Dennison." I said. "I admire people who are prepared to work hard and it's about time you had a better quality of life. Would you like to come back this evening when I've closed the shop and we can go through some of the practicalities of running a business?"

Mrs Dennison did come back that evening and we covered such subjects as suppliers, staff, stock levels and stock control. I was reassured to discover that she had learnt quite a lot about butchery from watching the pig butcher as he worked and that she had a young man who was already qualified as a butcher ready to work for her. He was one of the few young men still at home and able to work for a living because he had been born with a gammy leg. For some reason it had never grown at the same pace as his other leg and so he rolled rather than walked, but it was enough for even the army not to want him as a soldier. He became a very valued member of her team and the fact that he needed a tall stool permanently placed behind the shop counter where he could rest his leg when necessary didn't interfere with his ability to carry out his job. All her customers were prepared to wait a few minutes more than usual when he served them, especially as he was a particularly good butcher."

"I gave Mrs Dennison what help I could in re-starting her business, even to the extent of lending her some money at a very low rate of interest in order for her to re-stock the shop. Within a year of the night of the bombardment, she was running a profitable business and was able to pay me back the money I had lent her. She harboured no great ambitions, wanting to simply be able to live comfortably on what she earned and her life entered a new phase with the re-opening of the butcher's shop. She met a local pig farmer not long after the war ended and she sold her profitable business, married him and went to live very comfortably on his farm for the rest of her life. I was pleased I had helped in turning her life around and very glad that I hadn't turned her away when she came to me for help. Of the four of us who had been affected most by the night of the bombardment she was as innocent as Annie and deserved her chance for a better life."

"My businesses flourished through that time as well. After the docks area had been cleared and rebuilt by the authorities, I bought one of the new warehouses which occupied a site almost, but not quite, on the ground plan of the old one. The docks themselves were working again very quickly after the night of the bombardment both because the country needed the contribution those docks made to keeping the country going with both food and armaments and because the dockworkers needed their jobs. The railway station hadn't been affected by the shelling at all as though the Hun hadn't realised that it was there and consequently hadn't aimed their shells at it, so food and other commodities continued to be moved around the country by rail. I still had my contracts with the local farmers, so my supplies didn't dry up, which had been a constant fear of mine throughout the previous two years."

"It was late 1917 when I had purchased another shop, but this time in Eston. It was smaller than the Queen Street shop, but

447

had sufficient space to be able to carry a fairly wide range of stock and I was very lucky in that I managed to find a young man in his thirties ready and willing to work as a manager for me. He had lost an arm in the fighting at the Front and hadn't thought he would be able to work and make a decent living for himself, his wife and two small daughters ever again, but I knew he was the one for that position as soon as he entered my kitchen when he came for his interview."

"He had suffered exactly the same injuries as had William but, in every other way he was the absolute antithesis of my late husband. He cared for his wife and children incredibly deeply and always put them before himself; he was a very hard worker although he was slightly limited because of his injuries; his outlook on life was always positive and he never, ever moaned or complained about his situation. I had employed him because of his disability not in spite of it and, in some strange way; I felt I was squaring the circle with a possibly vengeful Fate over William's attitude and behaviour. I had also taken on a young boy to help David in the shop, a boy whose father had been killed at the Front and his salary kept his mother and younger brother and himself fed and housed, when an ungrateful country would have ignored them and left them to starve. I couldn't have explained my motives to the rest of the world, but they made sense to me and that was what was important."

"Sammy understood all that I was doing and his support, together with that of Annie, kept me always facing in the right direction. He recognised the need in me to put right what had gone wrong in my life and somehow make reparation for the evil done by some of those around me. Sammy supported me through it all, even keeping the secret of who actually owned the shop in Eston, because I had deliberately had the name 'Harrison' put above the shop door, reckoning, and rightly, that few people would recognise my mother's maiden name. David was quite happy to go along with my little whim and even encouraged the gossips to think that the shop possibly belonged to him, although he didn't ever say that it was so."

"Sammy and I continued with our programme of buying houses and renting them out, although we now moved away from houses near to the docks because I had a horror of another visit from enemy warships, although they never did come back during that war. We eventually put all of our properties into the hands of a large property company based in Newcastle who, for a fee, found tenants, arranged repairs and collected the rents. It ate into our profits but I reckoned it was a good move because it meant that no-one in the town had any idea of how much we owned or how much money we had."

"Sammy continued to work in the iron works as the labour shortage was so acute by that time, but he refused to do any overtime unless it was absolutely necessary. He bought some waste land next to the railway lines and set out an allotment, even going so far as to build a one bedroomed cottage on the same land. It was good use of what used to be good farm land before the railway came and the authorities looked more kindly on developments in those days than they do now. When it was all finished, Sammy went looking for the tramp we had met the night that Simon died and installed him in the cottage, with instructions to grow vegetables for me to sell in the shops. Old

Walter took to allotment gardening with a will, proving to be remarkably adept at adapting gardening tools for his own use and set out the most wonderful kitchen garden, even growing a few flowers to brighten our days. He was eternally grateful to Sam for giving him a chance in life when the rest of the world had abandoned him, but Sam refused to take any credit for what he had done; only commenting that there was a lot of good in so many people who only needed a chance in life."

"Sam was my rock all through those dreadful days after Simon's death. As he had promised that night he was always available for help and advice and supported me as I tried to get my life back together. I couldn't have got through that time without him. I admired him for his unswerving devotion to family and friends, for his deep sense of right and wrong, for his intelligence and good humour and, above all, for his determination to gather every last speck of enjoyment out of life, both for himself and for others. I wouldn't have got through 1917 if I hadn't had Sammy at my side, but he helped me through it all and I came to rely heavily on his advice and help and unfailing good humour."

"It was that good humour of Sammy's that supported me through the Inquest into the night of the bombardment. I was still very unsure about answering questions about that night and I was terrified I would let something slip and that the truth of the night's events would come out, but the Inquest was very delicately handled and I wasn't asked any difficult questions. I was only asked to confirm that I had owned the warehouse and that my husband and son had taken shelter there from the storm. The Inquest ruled that William, Peter and Simon had been killed by the German bombardment and that Dennison, the pig butcher, had been killed alongside them as he had tried to save them from the shelling and the subsequent inferno. It seemed so unfair to me that Dennison could be hailed as a hero, albeit a failed hero, when he had in reality been a double murderer and the reason for Peter's death. I wanted to set the Coroner straight, but I couldn't do that without blackening Peter's name and upsetting Annie, so I had to grit my teeth and accept the pig butcher's new status in the town. It was only the strength that Sam gave me which made it possible for me to rise above it and smile agreement when I wanted to scream out the truth."

"As that year rolled by, it got easier to cope with day-to-day living, although I continued to miss Simon with every beat of my heart. I was heartily glad to get through 1917, even though the end of the year brought snow once again to our town, reminding me of that dreadful night. The war was still going on and it was another Christmas that saw our boys on the wrong side of the English Channel, with little hope of them returning home. The casualty lists lengthened and more families lost husbands and brothers and sons and I'm sure I wasn't the only person who couldn't understand the futility of it all. Life was hard for everyone and shortages became the norm for everything; food, raw materials, clothing, transport and, above all, hope. That was when Sam got two telegrams, letting him know that both his boys, George and Bill, were lost, 'missing in action', presumed killed, at some unpronounceable place in Flanders, and all his joy in life evaporated out of him and it became my turn to care for him."

"That was when I insisted that he left his poky, little house and brought the other two of his daughters to live with Hannah, Annie and I in Queen Street. We had the attic bedrooms as well as the three on the first floor so there was plenty of room for us all and I could make sure that he remembered to eat every day. I knew that he didn't sleep very much, as I hadn't when Simon was killed and I followed him downstairs one night when I heard him moving around in the kitchen. The fire had gone out because we didn't have coal to waste and Sammy was sitting next to the dead embers, sobbing his heart out as quietly as he could. I crossed the room and wrapped my arms about his neck and cried with him as he sobbed out his sorrow at the loss of his two boys. I don't know whether I was crying for his sons or for the loss of my own, but I know that when we had both sobbed ourselves dry, the huge rock which I had been carrying about in my chest all year had reduced in size."

Nana Lymer wriggled a little to make herself more comfortable and then asked Victoria if she could make her a cup of tea. Victoria managed to get into the kitchen, brew the tea and collect some biscuits and then make her escape back upstairs without either her mother or father entering the kitchen. She could hear the usual level of noise from the shop and guessed it was busy enough to keep her mother occupied and not so busy that she was screaming for help.

As she re-entered her grandmother's bedroom, Victoria heard the unmistakeable sound of the letterbox in the side door being opened and a heavy document being pushed through it. It was an unusual occurrence because the postman generally carried their post into the shop and gave it to whoever had a hand free to receive it. Victoria placed the tea carefully onto Nana's bedside table and then ran lightly down the stairs to remove the large brown envelope which was sticking out of the letterbox. It was addressed to Mrs A Lymer so she carried it back upstairs and handed it over to Nana, noticing how tiny Nana looked in comparison to the large envelope, rather like a toddler trying to manage a pint mug.

Nana opened the envelope with difficulty and withdrew the many closely written sheets from inside it. Attached to the top, handwritten sheet was a letter which had obviously been typed and signed with Anthony Vine's rather elaborate signature.

"It's my copy of my will." Nana said when she had perused the top sheet. "Anthony's had it all legally tied up so it can't be ignored when I die. Put it in the top drawer of my dressing table, will you? There's a good girl. I can rest happy now that I know that's been done. Will you do me one more little task today, Victoria? Will you promise me that you will let Mr Vine know when I die, as quickly as you can? I want him to start carrying out my wishes as soon as he can after I've gone."

"Nana, please don't distress yourself." Victoria begged. "Please don't talk about dying like that. You are frightening me, now. It's almost as though you want to die tonight."

Nana Lymer shook her head vigorously and then helped herself to one of the biscuits that Victoria had put on the tray.

"Rubbish." She declared, twinkling her eyes at her granddaughter. "Let's finish the story now, shall we? I've nearly told you all there is to tell. What happened after this was incredibly boring, so I'm sure you won't want to hear about the rest of my life."

"That was the turning point in our relationship." Nana Lymer continued with the story. "After that night, Sam and I became more than friends. We had both tasted every nuance of the full load of human emotions and Sam losing his two boys seemed to balance out the death of Simon. There was only one road left that we could travel together and that was as proper partners in life- as husband and wife. We waited a little while until we felt it was acceptable for us both to make this commitment, when no-one could say that we had married because I was looking for a replacement for William or that Sam didn't know what he was doing so close to losing both his boys and then we made arrangements to close the shop and have the

457

quietest wedding ever in the Registry Office on Middlesbrough Road."

"All three of Sam's girls were bridesmaids for us and Sam bought them all a gold chain with a small locket as presents for wishing us both well. Annie gave me away because I didn't have any other family and Sam bought her the same gold chain, which she cherished for the rest of her life. She had been very quiet after we had told her that we were getting married and I worried that she thought I shouldn't have been looking for any happiness in this life after the loss of Simon, but, when I finally got the truth out of her it was so much simpler than that. She thought that Sam and I wouldn't want her to continue living with us after we got married, because she wasn't a family member and we had no duty to care for her. I soon disabused her of that notion and she finally accepted that we looked on her as family and that we wouldn't tolerate her moving away from us. If the truth were known, I would get a cold sweat at the thought of her moving away, because she was as important to me as my bones were."

"The three girls were all delighted that their father was going to marry me. Sarah admitted that they had been dropping hints to Sam for weeks for him to 'pop the question' but he had acted remarkably obtuse about the subject. They were even more pleased when they discovered that it was to be a spring wedding and that they were all to get new dresses for the occasion. They all made a trip to the wild meadow over behind the railway line and came back with armfuls of early spring flowers which they wove into coronets and wore atop their shining curls. I carried a bunch of wild violets which Hannah had managed to find in some hidden corner of the meadow and they released a delicate scent for the rest of the day, so beautiful that I am transported back to that wonderful day whenever I catch even a faint whiff of the perfume."

Nana Lymer didn't even pause for breath, but carried straight on to the next part of the story. It was obvious to Victoria that she fully intended getting through the rest of the story that day and nobody was going to stop her.

"In the run-up to the wedding, I had worried about the age difference between Sammy and I. He was forty seven and I was thirty three and fourteen years is a big age gap. I didn't want the town gossips spreading vitriol about me marrying an older man for his money, as the townsfolk knew that Sammy rented out houses, but no-one knew I was part-owner of those houses. They would think I only had the income from my shop and my bit of pawn brokering and might look on me as a gold digger, marrying an older man for his money. When I mentioned this to Annie she laughed my fears away."

"'Fourteen years is nothing, Bia.' She said, when I mentioned my concerns to her. 'Any lass needs a man with a bit of maturity and there's so many war widows marrying anything so long as it wears trousers to give themselves and their bairns a bit of security, that nobody is going to say anything about you. Anyway, you've only got to see the way you two smile at each other to know that you're both in love. You worry too much about everything. Take a deep breath and get out there and enjoy your wedding day without worrying what other folks may say.'"

"She was right, as Annie usually was, although I took a few deep breaths, not just the one. I didn't think that one would be sufficient. It was a wonderful day and we left the girls with Annie after the ceremony and went to Redcar on the train. The sun shone, although there was a chilly breeze coming off the sea, as there usually is at Redcar, but I was well wrapped up in my new shawl which I had crocheted for that day and so we walked along the sea front, watching the water lapping on the shore. It was so peaceful a scene that it was almost unbelievable that such death and destruction had come out of that same sea eighteen months before. We couldn't help but wonder if the cruel ships would come again during this terrible war and wreak the same amount of damage again. It was the only dark moment of that glorious day, which soon dissipated when we left the sea front and went and had afternoon tea in the tea shop on the corner opposite the clock."

"'I'd like to run a teashop.' I said to Sammy as we ate cucumber sandwiches and delicate little cakes from porcelain plates. 'I'm sure I could make a go of it. I've got plenty of recipes for scones and cakes, people love the ones I sell in the shop, so the next step is to sell them with a cup of tea in a nice place like this.'"

"'Don't you ever stop, Bia?' Sammy laughed, his face crinkling in the way I loved so much. 'It's our wedding day and here you are talking about wanting to open another shop! Business can wait until tomorrow; let's enjoy being waited-on today.'

"He was right, of course, I did concentrate too much on business, but it had become a way of life for me and when I got an idea into my head which I thought would prove profitable, I wanted to run with it. So I tucked the idea away into the back of my mind for that day at least and concentrated on being happy for the rest of that day."

"We caught the last train back from Redcar to Middlesbrough, getting off at the station and strolling up Station Road, past Turner's the photographers and Mr Vine's solicitors office, before turning into King Street, from where we could see the shop in the distance on the corner with Queen Street."

"'I wonder how many times I've walked this road since the war started.' I said. 'I remember going to see Mr Vine about starting my shop in Albion Street, when I was renting the house from him. If he hadn't given his permission for me to use the parlour for my shop, I don't know what I would have done. I certainly wouldn't have succeeded as well as I have.'"

"'He's done a lot for us.' Sammy agreed. 'We've used him for all of our property buying and I'm sure he charges us under the going rate. I think he's always had a soft spot for you, so he reduces the charges. It has its good points, being married to you, you know, cheap solicitor's fees!'"

"'I hope that isn't the only reason you married me, Mr Lymer.' I laughed."

"'No, Bia. I could think of a million reasons for marrying you and cheap solicitor's fees would still be at the bottom of the list.'"

"He swung me round by my arm and we stood in the middle of the street and kissed and cuddled like youngsters. Laughing, we turned back towards Queen Street and started walking again until Sammy put his hand on my arm and drew me to a halt."

"'That's Annie; she's out in the street. She must be looking for us.'"

I stared ahead, trying to make out Annie's figure in the sparse light, immediately worrying what could have happened that she was outside waiting for us. My heart was hammering loudly and I was breathing with difficulty, afraid that something bad had happened."

"Oh please, not today of all days.' I moaned. 'Please don't let our day be spoilt by any more disasters.'"

"I didn't know what or who I was praying to, my faith in a god having left me during the dock bombardment, but here I was, praying again. Sammy grabbed my hand and we ran down the road to meet Annie, who was trying to see if it was us in the darkness."

"'It is you.' She exclaimed, as soon as we got close enough to her for her to be able to see us. 'Thank goodness. I didn't know when you would be home.'"

"'What's happened, Annie?' Sam was as worried as I was, I could tell by his clipped tone. 'Is it one of the girls? Which one? Is she ok?'"

"The questions were tumbling out of his mouth, one after the other, not leaving Annie any time to answer any of them. She took Sam by his hand."

"'Come away in, lad. It's one of them telegram things. It came this afternoon after you'd gone off to Redcar and I didn't know when you would be back.'"

"We were inside the house by this time and the three girls turned their worried faces towards us from where they were sitting grouped round the kitchen table. The telegram was in solitary state, face up in the middle of the table."

"'It's for you, Dad.' Hannah was almost whispering with the fear of it. 'The boy took it to our old house but Mr Stevens next door sent him round here with it, knowing that we are living here now. We didn't know what to do with it.'"

"She looked up at her father, her brown eyes huge with concern and her merry face creased with worry."

"'I don't understand,' Sammy said, slowly. 'We've nobody else at the Front, not since George and William died, so why are we getting another telegram?'"

"That was the way of it during the War. We were all so used to getting the worst news in the form of a telegram that nobody remembered that they could be used for other news as well and their arrival always caused the deepest concern. Sam picked the telegram up and turned it over in his hand. Puzzlement was etched across his features as he opened it and began reading its contents. Then the hand that was holding it dropped to his side and a huge grin spread across his face."

"'It's Bill.' He gasped out. 'He's not dead! They've found him in a casualty clearing station, wounded but alive. He's on his way home! That's the perfect end to a perfect day!'"

"We all rejoiced at this news. The girls were overjoyed because they were getting their big brother back, Sam was overjoyed because he was getting one son back and Annie was happy because everyone else was happy. I was the only one with reservations. Oh I was ecstatic for Sam and the girls, but I had never met Bill. What if he didn't like me or didn't like the idea of his father getting married again? The girls were happy for me to be their step-mother, but they were still really children. Bill was twenty one and a man. He may have had a different idea altogether."

"Annie saw me hanging back from the group of Lymers who were hugging and laughing and she moved round the table until she was standing next to me."

"'What is it, Bia? Aren't you pleased that he's coming home?'"

"Of course I am, how couldn't I be? But what if he doesn't like me? What if he thinks Sam shouldn't have got married again and takes against me?'"

"'You silly girl.' Annie said in her forthright way. 'Why do you always fear the worst? He'll love you because his father does and because you are one of the kindest and nicest people he could ever hope to meet. Now, stop worrying and join in with the celebrations. I'm going to get that bottle of sherry you got me for Christmas and we'll all have a double toast – one for your wedding and one for Bill's return,'"

"So I tried to shake off the remaining doubts I had and we all had a glass of sherry, even the girls. Sam mixed theirs with some of my home-made lemonade so that it was mostly innocuous and we solemnly toasted our wedding and Bill's return from the dead."

.   "'Life is going to be better for all of us from now on.' Sam declared as he raised his glass in the toast. 'To the Lymer family and our new and better lives.'"

"'To us and our better lives.' We all chorused together.

Chapter Sixteen

Nana Lymer paused and eased her shoulders away from her pillow. She grimaced slightly as she did so and Victoria automatically leant forward and rearranged the pillows behind her, to make her more comfortable.

"I bet you would make a pretty good job of caring for me even if you had your eyes closed." Nana smiled at her granddaughter.

"Yes, I'm number one nurse now," she agreed. "But I don't mind. I quite like it when I know that I can do something for you that makes you feel better."

"I know you do, pet, but I don't want to be a burden on you and if you're looking after me then I'm stopping you from living your own life. Nobody has the right to use another person's life like that. You only get one go at this living game, so you've got to make the most of it. My story is nearly finished now and, when it is, I want you to promise me you'll stop thinking about my past life and concentrate on living your own life to its fullest extent."

Victoria promised, although at that moment, she couldn't see beyond the next few minutes, wanting only that Nana would finish the story. Mrs Lymer seemed to be able to sense this impatience wafting from her granddaughter, so she settled herself a little more comfortably and began again.

"I needn't to have worried about Bill's reaction to my marrying Sam. When he arrived home, about three weeks after our wedding, I realised he was the carbon copy of his father, always smiling and always seeing the best in life and in other people. He soon settled in with us although he was determined that he was going to recover from his wounds and go back to work. But I could tell from the moment he walked into the kitchen when he first came home that he was never going to work again. The wounds he carried, particularly to his legs and stomach, were too severe to ever allow him to return to a normal life and in my opinion he was never going to make old bones. He adapted happily, however, to becoming our amateur accountant, a task he carried out with great diligence and accuracy."

"It was about that time that we realised that the Queen Street shop and house were far too small for the family that we now had and began looking for somewhere bigger. I had had a hankering to own one of the large houses off Normanby Road for quite some time and we were both delighted when we found just such a house on our first serious house-seeking expedition. There was an immense amount of land that came with the house and Sam soon came up with a use for it. He decided he was going to open a market garden and, with the help of Charlie who was promoted from working on the allotment near the railway lines, he set to with a will and soon had the whole garden set out and producing foodstuffs. It proved to be as profitable as our other business ventures and it wasn't long before he was looking to hire more men to help. He found three good workers, all lads who had served their time on the battlefields of Flanders and France and had returned home from the war expecting to find a land that was oozing milk and honey to welcome home its saviours and found a land that had turned its back on them."

"We had a very happy life in our new house, bolstered by the arrival of our joint ventures in the shape of David, born 1919; Abia, born 1920 and baby Annabel, born 1921. Sammy said Annabel was far too posh a name for a little scrap of a lass from Middlesbrough, but gave in when I explained that her name was to be shortened to Annie, an event which made our 'big Annie' gleam with pride. 'Little Annie' was a pleasure to have around, with a nature as sunny as that of her father and her older brother, David. Abia, however, was a different kettle of fish altogether. From birth, she viewed the world around her through piercing eyes, judging all who came within her sphere and finding all wanting, apart from her father. For him, she would smile and occasionally chuckle at his antics, for the rest of the world she showed her dislike and disapprobation with narrowed eyes, a sneer on her mouth and her nose lifted into the air. By the time she was five years old even Sam could see that she was totally without any humour, had a boredom level which didn't reach the height of the skirting boards and lacked any trace of empathy or compassion. It was her presence in our lives that made me a great believer in the 'nature not nurture' school of child-rearing. She hasn't changed as she has grown older, she still acts as though nobody could ever attain her high standards of intelligence and behaviour and I still don't understand what your father sees in her. I could ignore it all if she wasn't so vindictive towards you, as though you had personally set out to make her life a misery. Never mind, you'll be able to escape when you go to college."

Victoria didn't answer these comments because her relationship with her mother was a very sensitive subject for her. She had grown up knowing that her mother didn't like her, in fact, at times, her mother actively disliked her and she had no idea why this was so. She couldn't remember ever having committed some unforgivable sin which could explain why she produced this hatred in her mother and, consequently, she was incredibly insecure and vulnerable, a state of mind she tried to hide by always being the first to make fun of herself.

Over the Christmas holidays, while she had been listening to her grandmother's tale of her life during the First World War, Victoria had matured immensely. It was almost as though learning of the terrible events which had shaped her grandmother's life had made her grow up faster and grow a carapace round her insecurities which her mother could no longer penetrate. Victoria had no idea how this had happened or even why it had happened but it had given her the confidence to ignore the vitriol which emanated from her mother and had wrapped a shield round her tiny ego so that it wasn't pierced by any spoken daggers.

"I don't know why Mam hates me so much," she almost whispered, "But I'm learning to cope with it now and she doesn't frighten me as much as she used to. That's how I could stand up to her about Mr Vine coming to visit. I think I'm growing up, Nana and its making life easier for me."

Mrs Lymer quickly scanned the pretty face of her granddaughter and hoped against hope that it was true that she was finally growing a defensive shield against her mother's spite. She knew that she wasn't long for this world and she wanted Victoria to reach adulthood without any more scars on her personality. She reached out and squeezed the slender hand resting on her eiderdown.

"Now then, where was I? Oh, that's it, we had bought the big house and Sammy turned himself into a market gardener! We had many happy years there, while the family was growing up, even though we had an economic depression to live through and then another world war. They were tough times again, but we all pulled together and we managed to keep the bulk of our business holdings, although we had to sell a few of our terraced houses when we needed the extra money to keep us going through the Depression. As in the First War, opportunities for making money were plentiful during the Second World War and we got through to 1945 without losing much in the way of savings and property."

"What we did lose during that War was Annie. She had mostly enjoyed her life after Peter died, although I knew that she missed him with every beat of her heart, but not having to worry about the costs of day-to-day living or who was going to look after Peter when she died, meant that life was easier for her than it had been for many years before she entered my life. But not even the easing of so much tension and worry could prolong her life and we lost her as the whole country was celebrating VE Day. I missed her terribly because I had grown to rely on her hard work and her unshakeable good sense and I felt as though I had lost my mother."

"Once again, Sammy and I grieved together, drawing what comfort we could from the fact that we were both equally distraught over her death and couldn't fill the space she had left in our lives and in our hearts. Less than two years after her death, we lost Bill when he succumbed to the influenza epidemic which visited our shores after the War was over. He had never got back to full fitness after the wounds he had received at the Front and I suppose he was an easy target for the disease. It was after his death that Sammy made the comment that the death of one's child was the hardest to cope with, because it seemed to go against all the laws of nature. I agreed wholeheartedly with that statement."

"One of the jobs I had to take back on after Bill's death was the accounts from our businesses. Only Sam and I and Mr Vine now knew just how much we were worth and when we sold the market garden and the big house we split the proceeds amongst Sam's girls and our three little angels who were all growing up by that time. They all thought that that was the extent of our wealth and we did nothing to disabuse any of them of that idea. We moved back into the Queen Street shop and then your Mam and Dad took over the running of it, while Sam and I enjoyed our retirement. It didn't last long enough, because I lost my Sam only a few years after we retired, but it had been a very enjoyable life we had had together, although far too short for either of us."

"You've been a long time without your Sam." Victoria sympathised, wondering if she could have carried on with her life after losing as many loved ones as Nana Lymer had lost.

"I have, haven't I?" Nana sighed. "But we had a wonderful life together and it's those memories I cling on to. I would rather have had a shorter married life with the happiness we had, than a much longer life without Sam. I cherish those years and they keep me warm and happy through the darkest days."

Victoria could have wept at the sad smile which was lighting up the creased soft face in front of her, but she thought she could understand what Nana meant. She only hoped that she could one day meet someone who could engender those same feelings of love and happiness in her, although the part of her character which she had inherited from her more prosaic mother told her not to be so slushy.

"So Mam and Dad don't own the shop and this house, then." Victoria felt she needed to get the facts straight in her mind in case of future disputes. "And neither of them know that you still actually own a shop in Eston, a teashop in Acklam and numerous houses which are rented out to other people."

"That's right. After Granddad Sam died and we'd lost Bill and Annie so many years before, I decided that none of the rest of the family should know exactly what I owned. None of Sam's three girls knew anything, even though Hannah worked in the Queen Street shop every day, neither Sam nor I had ever told her or her sisters what we were doing. She may have wondered if she ever sat down and added two and two together, but I don't believe she ever did. Of course, Mr Vine will have a very good idea of my holdings, but he's not allowed to talk about such a subject. He'd lose a lot of clients if he ever blabbed about what his clients did and didn't have."

"It can't possibly be the same Mr Vine who let you open a shop in your front parlour all those years ago. He *must* be dead by now!" Victoria tried to work out just how many years ago that Nana had opened her first shop, but her brain wouldn't catch up with her mouth. "Is it his son?"

"No, oh no." Nana answered. "This Mr Vine is *my* Mr Vine's grandson, but I'm afraid I've treated them all as though they were the same person and none of them seem to have minded about it. I've brought them plenty of business over the years so I deserve to be well-treated by them. It's my due." Nana stuck her chin out as though she expected someone to argue the case with her, but Victoria was with her right down the line. The Vines should be grateful for Nana Lymer's business and for her loyalty to the firm. After all, there were a lot more solicitors in Middlesbrough now than there had been in 1914 and Nana could easily have changed her allegiance at any time over those years. But it did sound as though they had been suitably aware of what her business had meant to them and had always been particularly helpful towards her.

Victoria decided she wouldn't creep into the Vine's office when she went to report Nana's death to them, as Nana had asked her to do. She would walk in with her head held high and she certainly wouldn't let Mr Vine's secretary treat her as though she was the dirt beneath her feet. Then she realised that she was thinking about her grandmother's death as though it was an intellectual exercise and not the source of a great deal of gloom and despair and shook herself mentally to remove the thoughts from her mind. Almost as though she could read her granddaughter's mind, Nana Lymer spoke and brought Victoria back to the present.

"You haven't forgotten that I want you to inform Mr Vine as soon as possible after I die, have you?" Nana sounded almost panic-stricken. "I did ask you to do that, didn't I?" She reached forward from her pillows and took hold of Victoria's hand, forcing Victoria to look her in the face.

"Yes, you did tell me that was what you wanted me to do and no, I haven't forgotten. I promise that it will be the first thing I do after I find out. But I don't want to think about you dying, I want to think about the happy times we have when I listen to the story of your life so please, don't mention it again. It isn't as though you're going to die any time soon. You've got years left in you yet, so stop making me miserable!" Victoria tried to laugh as she said this, hoping to sound as though the prospect of

Nana's death was far away, but she didn't feel that her protestations sounded as though they were ringing true, so she changed the subject to one which didn't give her the feeling that her stomach was falling through her body and landing on the floor of the bedroom.

While Victoria had been thinking this through, Nana Lymer had leant back against her pillows again and, as Victoria watched her, Nana's eyes fluttered and then closed, almost it seemed against her will. Victoria sat very still while she waited to see if Nana opened her eyes again to continue with the story. But Nana's breathing got heavier and it soon became obvious to Victoria that she had fallen asleep. Not wanting to disturb her, Victoria forbore from removing any pillows to let her lay flatter on the bed and decided she would go and get one of her set books and do some of the revision she should have been doing all holidays.

It took a few minutes to locate the books she wanted, but Nana was still sound asleep when she crept back into her bedroom. Victoria settled herself in her chair and began her revision. Over the next couple of hours, she constantly raised her head to see if Nana was waking up, but she didn't stir at all. Victoria was grateful for the heavy breathing coming from her Nana, because she had a terrible feeling in her chest that that breathing was going to stop. She kept telling herself not to be so silly, but any differentiation in the rhythm made her look up to check that Nana Lymer was still sleeping peacefully. She lowered her head back to her revision each time and tried to absorb the intricacies of life in Shakespeare's England, a life she was finding ever more boring as thoughts of the bombardment of the docks and Simon's death kept pushing the quaint language of Shakespeare into a different world.

Nana remained asleep for the rest of the day, causing Victoria's blood pressure to rise as she worried over the reason for it. Eventually, her mother came to find her to inform her that her tea was ready, even though she hadn't been down to collect either of their meals.

"Why has she slept for so long?" Victoria demanded to know. "She's never done this before so why is she

485

doing it today? Do you think that she's ill? Should I go and get the doctor so that he can come and have a look at her?" Panic was making her voice rise.

"Don't speak to me in that tone of voice!" Bia was back to her old self and took these comments as criticism of her care of her mother. She was not in the mood to let such insolence go unpunished. "She's just tired, everybody needs more sleep the older they get. It's just caught up with her today, that's all. You come and get your tea and we'll see how she is after that. If she has problems breathing or talking to us, *then* we'll call the doctor."

Bia ushered Victoria out of Nana's bedroom, but turned and went back in when she saw Victoria making for the stairs.

"Is this it then, Mam? Are you finally going to give in to the inevitable or will you rise, phoenix-like, from the ashes and start again?"

There was no reply from the bed so Bia turned and followed her daughter down the stairs, her mind racing with all the possibilities for change which would come if her mother gave up her battle for life. She smiled to herself as she pictured herself turning up at the Middlesbrough and District Grocers' Federation Annual Dinner wearing a fur coat, with matching shoes and handbag. Those thoughts made her spirits rise and she served their evening meal without any of her usual sniping at Victoria or acerbic comments on the activities of any of their customers. Victoria and her father were both grateful for the peaceful atmosphere so neither of them spoke during the meal, not wanting to remind Bia of her mother or the imagined laziness of their neighbours.

It was a long evening, given that Bia refused to let Victoria sit in Nana Lymer's bedroom watching her grandmother sleep. She knew that Victoria would get more and more agitated the longer that Nana remained sleeping during a part of the day when she normally didn't and Bia didn't want her daughter all worked up before the inevitable happened. Bia was convinced that her mother was entering the last phase of her life and doing it in a very peaceful way, with as little fuss as possible. Even though she rarely thought well of her daughter, she knew that Victoria had a very close relationship with her grandmother and she didn't want her seeing anything distressing for her, beyond the actual death of Nana Lymer.

With tacit agreement, the whole family decided to retire to bed at eleven o'clock, earlier than usual for them, although Victoria did go downstairs before bedtime to sit with her father in the kitchen, watching him boning a side of bacon ready for selling the next day in the shop. He glanced at her solemn face and gently tried to lift her spirits.

"If Nana Lymer is getting ready to move on, there's nothing that you can do about it, Victoria," he said. "It's very unkind to try and delay a death when the person is ready for it. She's very tired now, because she's had a long and busy life and trying to impose your personality on her to make her cling on to life is a selfish thing to do. You don't want to lose her because you love her, but it looks as though her time has come and she's not fighting against it. You've got to love her enough to give her the space to do what she's ready to do without making her feel guilty at *your* loss. That is too unfair for her."

Victoria could understand what her father was trying to say, although she didn't really want to hear it and she managed a faint smile.

"I know, Dad," she murmured, "But I don't want to lose her yet. If she could only last a few more years, so that we can spend some more time together, then I would feel all right about it. But I don't want her to die now." The last was almost a wail.

"It would never be the right time, pet, believe me. There would always be a reason for wanting to keep her close to you and it doesn't get any easier to cope with. In fact, I would think that if you could delay it, you would feel even worse when she did die. Go to bed and let's see what the morning brings. Things always look better when they're seen in daylight."

Victoria climbed the stairs slowly and couldn't resist popping her head round Nana's door on the way to her bedroom. Nana was still breathing deeply and hadn't moved since before tea. As she closed the door quietly behind her, Bia emerged from her bedroom further along the landing.

"I'll wake you if anything happens during the night." Bia said, in a very gruff voice. "Go and get yourself to bed. You look shattered."

It was the nicest that her mother had been to her for a long time and it nearly knocked Victoria's fragile equanimity for six, although she did manage to clutch it to herself for the few seconds it took her to pass into her bedroom and close the door behind her. Then she leant backwards against the door and sobbed as silently as she could so that no-one would hear her and come and investigate.

Despite her belief that she wouldn't even be able to close her eyes, Victoria did fall asleep. She hadn't got undressed in case she was needed during the night and she was incredibly dishevelled when her father put his head round her bedroom door. She had no idea whether it was still night-time, but it was dark outside.

"Can you come, chick?" He asked very gently. "Nana's taken a turn for the worse."

Victoria was out of bed and across the room in a split second.

"Do you want me to go for the doctor? Or have you rung him? Do you think an ambulance might be a better idea?"

Her father didn't answer her questions, but steered her across the landing and through Nana's bedroom door. Her mother was standing next to the bed, looking down at her parent. Victoria could see that Nana was still in exactly the same position as she had been since she had fallen asleep the previous afternoon. The only difference was that the heavy breathing and the slow rise and fall of her grandmother's chest had ceased. Tears came to her eyes and dripped, unheeded, down her cheeks as she took her place on the other side of the bed to her mother.

She made no sound but her mother answered her unspoken question.

"She never woke again, Victoria," she said quietly. "She's slipped away in her sleep, with no pain and no fuss, just as she would have wanted. She was alive the last time I checked on her at about half four this morning, but she was dead when I came back five minutes ago and it's quarter past six now."

"Do you mean she was alone when she died?" Victoria was appalled at that and her tone betrayed her. Her mother immediately dropped the façade of grieving daughter and compassionate mother.

"She died while she was asleep." Bia snapped out. "She had no idea whether she was alone or in the middle of Paddington Station, so don't be so high and mighty with me, lady. The next few days are going to be difficult enough without you having temper tantrums, criticising your own mother's actions. I didn't know she was going to die during the night. She could have lasted for weeks yet and if I spent every hour of every night watching her, I'd have been in no fit state to care for a doll, never mind a human being. Keep those remarks to yourself, particularly when the doctor comes."

Victoria could see the sense in her mother's words and was actually slightly ashamed that she'd spoken as she had. If she'd been so determined that Nana didn't die alone, she, Victoria, could have sat with her all night. The point her mother made about not knowing when she would die was perfectly valid and Victoria could see the logic in not spending all night with her grandmother. She modified her tone and then asked a question that was bothering her.

"Why is the doctor coming now? It seems a bit of a waste of time now that she's dead!"

This time it was her father who answered her. He had followed Victoria into Nana's bedroom, but had been keeping out of the way until now.

"The doctor has to come to sign the death certificate, because without that we can't organise a funeral or start putting her affairs in order." Dad answered. "Your Nana has found the best way to die and I think you should be happy for her that she's left this life without being in pain, without any fear of what faces her and without a room full of grieving relatives, all weeping and wailing and making her feel worse. She's been very lucky compared to some and I think we should *all* be grateful for that."

Victoria thought of the many ways that people who Nana had known and held dear had died and she realised that her father was speaking a very profound truth. The young men who had died on the battlefields of the Front during the First World War; Simon, having his breath and his life shaken out of him; William being tortured before he was killed; Peter, dying in an enemy bombardment trying to save those he loved from committing unforgiveable sins; they had all died in terrible ways whereas Nana Lymer had breathed her last without even knowing it in her own bed in her own bedroom and in her own house, knowing that she was surrounded by people who cared for her. Dad was right; there were a lot worse ways to go when your time came.

There was a knock on the side door downstairs and Victoria heard her mother opening it. She quickly crossed the room and bent and kissed Nana on her soft sweet cheek before she went back to her own room. She waited while the doctor did whatever it was that he had to do. She could hear his deep voice and the higher voice of her mother as he asked questions about finding Nana dead, about her health over the last few weeks and lots of other questions. Her mother answered at the required times and it was obvious to Victoria that Bia was incredibly calm and self-possessed at the situation. Perhaps she had practised this scene in her mind many times over the last few years or perhaps she genuinely didn't feel any emotion at her mother's passing and could therefore be completely serene and unruffled during a possibly stressful event. Anything was possible with Bia!

Victoria realised with a slightly guilty start that she was hungry, so she went downstairs into the kitchen and began making breakfast for all three of them, hoping that her parents would be hungry as well as she. Dad came through from the shop where he had been setting out the cooked meats and cheeses he had taken out of the shop fridge, ready for a day's work. Bia could be heard letting the doctor out of the side door, then she entered the kitchen and nodded with relief when she realised that Victoria had breakfast under control.

"What are we going to do about the shop today?" her Father asked, once they were all seated and eating. "Should we not open as a mark of respect for your mother or should we carry on as normal, apart from the day of the funeral? I don't want to upset you, Bia, but I also don't want to lose customers who would go elsewhere if we aren't open."

Victoria surprised both her parents by butting in with her own thoughts.

"Nana told me about a time when she had a death in the family, but they opened the shop, not just for the convenience of the customers but also because being busy served to take their minds off the person they had lost."

"I think that's a very sensible way of looking at the situation." Dad said. "I also believe that Nana Lymer wouldn't have wanted to waste any time that could be spent making money, by being sentimental and slushy about anyone."

"But what will the neighbours think?" Bia wanted to know. "They could be appalled at the hard-nosed disregard of my mother's death."

"Well, we tell everyone that she didn't want us to close the shop, because she didn't do it when she was in the same situation. I'm sure plenty of people remember what she was like and won't be surprised at it."

"I wonder who it was who had died but Mam opened the shop." Bia mused. "I can't remember when it happened."

Victoria knew exactly when it had happened but she chose to keep that little bit of information to herself. If Nana hadn't told her daughter about Simon's death, then Victoria wasn't going to enlighten her. That was her and Nana's secret. It did cross her mind that her mother didn't know that she'd had an older brother, but would the knowing of him make any difference to her mother now? She knew very little about her sister Annie who had died when Abia was a baby so it was understandable that she would know nothing about an older half-brother. It would seem that Victoria's mother had never heard of any of her family's history from before she was born. Her mother spoke at this point in Victoria's musings.

"Very well, we'll open the shop today and let everyone know that it was what my mother would have wanted. We will only close on the day of her funeral. Somebody is bound to complain that I only care for profit, but you can't please everybody all the time. I wonder if Joan would come and do a turn in the shop today. It would give me chance to go and get Mam's death certificate and see the vicar and the undertaker as to when we can expect to have the funeral."

"You go and sort out what you need to do and I'll ring Joan to come in." Victoria's Dad said. "Word will soon get round as to what's happened and people will understand that we may be having difficulties."

Victoria remained quiet during this exchange, not wanting to be lumbered with a session working in the shop, or having to accompany her mother to see the vicar or undertaker, but, luckily, her mother seemed to have forgotten what Victoria was capable of doing and left her out of her arrangements. Victoria knew that she had to fulfil her promise to Nana that she would contact Mr Vine to let him know that Nana Lymer had died, before anyone else could tell him. She cleared the kitchen table and washed the breakfast pots, which earned her a brief 'good girl' from her mother as she passed through the kitchen on her way to the Registrar's office, then trotted upstairs to change her wrinkled clothes.

The shop was busy when she peeped through the door from the kitchen, but she still left the house through the side door, so that her Dad wouldn't see her leave and ask where she was going. Nana had been very firm about not letting anyone know about this visit. Within minutes, she was opening the front door of Mr Vine's office on Station Road and marching up to

Miss Talbot's desk with a totally different attitude from the last time she had visited the solicitor's workplace.

Chapter Seventeen

Miss Talbot didn't raise her head from the sheet of paper she was perusing, merely asking "Yes?" as she made a note with a pencil on the page. Victoria didn't answer, but continued to stand in front of the desk, taking as much interest in the naked white sheet as Miss Talbot. The battle of wills was almost won when Miss Talbot looked up at Victoria and repeated her question.

"Yes, can I help you?"

That was much better.

"I'm sure you can." Victoria replied. "I would like to see Mr Vine as soon as is convenient, please." She wasn't going to leave room for Miss Talbot to accuse her of being rude.

"Mr Vine is with a client at the moment. Perhaps you would like to leave your name and address and Mr Vine can contact you when he is free."

This wasn't good enough for Victoria. Nana Lymer had told her to insist on seeing Mr Vine that day and Miss Talbot was no longer the insurmountable barrier that she had been before, the last time that Victoria had visited the office.

"That's fine." Victoria said. "I'll wait until he is free." And she crossed the room and sat down on a wooden chair which was beside the open fire. Miss Talbot followed her across the office and stood in front of Victoria with her arms folded across her chest and a rather superior smile on her face.

"You won't be able to see Mr Vine today, because he has clients booked in all day. I told you, leave your name and address with me and he will let you know when it is convenient for you to see him. A solicitor is a busy man, with no time to be messed about by a schoolgirl."

This last was said with a distinct smirk as Miss Talbot looked down her nose at Victoria.

"You don't need me to tell you who I am." Victoria said, very calmly, meeting Miss Talbot's smirk with a clear open face.

"I have no intentions of leaving until I have spoken to Mr Vine and, as I only need a few minutes of his time, I won't be holding up any of his other clients. And if you are intending to phone my mother again to tell her that I am here, I would suggest you wait until about five o'clock. She has got numerous appointments this afternoon and will be unavailable, probably until tea time."

Victoria was rather pleased with herself at managing to remain calm and unruffled despite Miss Talbot's open hostility towards her and once again surprised herself by being so composed and adult. She wasn't sure how much longer she would be able to sustain this attitude however and was relieved to hear Mr Vine's office door open and see Mr Vine emerge, shaking hands with an elderly gentleman as he left.

Mr Vine hadn't missed Victoria's presence in the waiting room and crossed the office quickly to speak to her.

"Do I take it that the inevitable has unfortunately occurred and you have come to appraise me of your grandmother's passing?" he asked, his face creased in concern.

"I'm afraid so." Victoria answered. "Nana Lymer died in the early hours of this morning." She couldn't help but wonder if all solicitors spoke in this rather stilted fashion or if Mr Vine thought it gave him a certain gravitas which his age didn't bestow on him.

"Peacefully, I hope?" Mr Vine asked, taking hold of one of Victoria's hands and absentmindedly patting it as he spoke. "It will have come as a great shock to you, I know, even though it has been expected for quite some time. We are never truly prepared for any death and I know how close you were to your grandmother."

Victoria could feel the salt tears beginning to gather in her eyes again, but she shook them away, determined that she wasn't going to cry like a child in front of Miss Talbot. Mr Vine realised that she needed some time and space to get herself under control again, so he turned her round and began encouraging her to pass inside his office and sit down at his desk.

"I don't need to stay." Victoria spluttered. "Nana only told me to come and let you know when she died. I don't need to take up any more of your time. I know that you have other clients to see today."

"Nonsense." Mr Vine boomed. "My next appointment isn't until 3 o'clock so I've got time for a cup of tea and a chat with one of my favourite Lymer ladies. But your name won't be Lymer, will it? Lymer is your mother's side of the family. Don't tell me, I'll have it in my brain any second. Wilson! That's it. Miss Victoria Wilson. I've actually got some information for you, Miss Wilson, now that your grandmother has died, information which only you and I need to know. We will not be discussing it when I report the terms of your grandmother's will to your parents and your aunts and uncle after the funeral. That is why Mrs Lymer wanted you to come and see me immediately after she died. She wished you to be in possession of this information so that it wouldn't come as a surprise to you at the Will Reading."

Victoria glanced across at Mr Vine where he was in the process of closing his office door. In the split second's chance that she had to see into the reception area before he closed the door, she saw Miss Talbot, with her mouth hanging open and her eyes fixed on Mr Vine. Despite what had happened that day, Victoria felt an almost over – whelming urge to laugh at the shock and desire for knowledge written across Miss Talbot's face. It seemed that Mr Vine was enjoying seeing her reaction as well, because he closed the door so slowly that quite a few really nosy expressions passed across Miss Talbot's face before she managed to bring her greed for gossip under control and resumed her usual, slightly superior, facial appearance.

Mr Vine re-opened his office door immediately and neither he nor Victoria were astonished at the close proximity to the door Miss Talbot had managed to reach in those few seconds. Victoria wondered how often Mr Vine had caught his secretary blatantly listening at his office door and was surprised that he tolerated such behaviour, unless he also enjoyed thwarting Miss Talbot's attempts to glean gossip. If she had overheard any sensitive information surely it would make a reduction in his professional rating?

"Can we have two cups of tea in here, Miss Talbot please? Miss Wilson and I have a number of important matters to discuss and I always think that tea lubricates the brain cells." Mr Vine closed the door again and sat behind his desk, putting his hands together and steepling his fingers and resting his chin on them.

"When I came to see your grandmother a couple of weeks ago, she led me to understand that she was the second wife of your grandfather, Mr Samuel Lymer, and that there had been some children of the first marriage, although a number of those children had died in childhood as well as one son who died during the First World War and one son who had died as a result of the wounds he had received during that War, a number of years after it ended. This leaves your mother, your aunt in Australia and your uncle from your grandfather's second marriage and your three aunts from his first marriage still alive. Is that right?"

Victoria crossed them off on her fingers as she thought about her mother's brother and sisters. The three aunts from her granddad Sam's first marriage seemed more real to her than her aunt and uncle from his second marriage, because she had learnt from Nana Lymer exactly what they were like when they became part of Nana's life. Her true aunt in Australia and her true uncle who lived down south somewhere were shadows compared to the other three.

"Aunt Hannah, who lives in York and Aunt Jenny, who lives in Birmingham both have children and grandchildren. Do you want a list of them, Mr Vine?" Victoria asked, not sure why she needed to know about a section of her grandmother's will before anyone else in the family, and eager to help unravel the slightly complicated family tree.

"No, thank you," he replied. "Mrs Lymer's last Will and Testament contains bequests to the six children still living of Mr Lymer's two marriages. I expect she intended any children and grandchildren to be provided for by their parents and grandparents. Do you know where the third sister of the first marriage lives?"

"Oh yes," Victoria hastened to answer. "Aunt Lizzie is a companion to an old lady who lives in Bishop Auckland and lives with her there. She has never married and has no children and I would suppose that both she and the lady she looks after will be getting on in years now. Nana has her address in her address book at home. I'll find it for you and bring it round tomorrow."

"There's no need to put yourself out, Victoria. I can get it when I come to read the Will in a couple of days' time. I just wanted a rough idea so that I would recognise the correct address when I see it. Now we've cleared that up, I just want to discuss a couple of points from the Will with you without anyone else knowing what they contain. Your grandmother was determined that no-one else should know the exact amount of possessions that she has left you."

"Left me?!?" Victoria could hardly speak; she was so taken aback by that one small sentence. "But she didn't have to leave me anything. I'm going to be a teacher; I don't need to have anything left for me!"

They paused at that point as Miss Talbot knocked on the door and then entered, carrying a tray with two cups and saucers on it and a small plate of half-coated biscuits. Mr Vine removed them all from the tray and then asked Miss Talbot if she could find the files for the next two clients who would be coming later in the day. She agreed and left, closing the office door behind her as she went, effectively stopping her own chances at information gathering.

"It will take her a good while to find those files because I removed them from the filing cabinet this morning and have them here, so she won't be able to listen at the door." Mr Vine wrapped his knuckle on the two cardboard bundles sitting in his in-tray.

" To carry on from where we left off - I'm sure you will make a wonderful teacher," Mr Vine agreed, "But Mrs Lymer was determined that you would be the greatest beneficiary of her Will, so that you would have more choices in your life than you would otherwise be able to have on just a teacher's salary. She told me that you were the only member of the family who knew that she and your grandfather had made rather a good living from owning and renting out property; from two other shops apart from the one in Queen Street and from a collection of gold, silver and jewellery built up by your grandmother from before she met your grandfather and over the years after that marriage. She also said you were the only member of the family who had shown any interest in her life before the birth of her three children. These bequests can be taken as a reward for your selfless interest in her and what she had done during her life, without expecting some sort of monetary remuneration. She also told me you had made her last few weeks on this earth a happy time for her, mainly because of the love you had shown her, so she wanted you to have the following:"

1. Ownership of the property known as Number 45 Eston Square, Eston – a general dealers store, although she recommends that you sell it as a going concern before the large supermarket chains move into the area and destroy its customer base.

2. Ownership of the property known as Number 11 Ladgate Lane, Acklam – a tea and coffee shop, serving the local area as it has done for many years. She recommended that you keep this particular business going as it is becoming more profitable with every year that passes.

3. Ownership of the portfolio of rental properties spread throughout Middlesbrough, Ormesby, Normanby and Eston. This is another part of the business that your grandmother recommends that you continue to run as it is also a profitable concern.

4. Lastly, her collection of gold and silver jewellery and her collection of cut and uncut gemstones collected over many years and kept in her security box at the bank. She has only ever worn one of these items, a gold chain and locket which contains photographs of Mr Lymer and a

little boy called Simon Drinkwater, although I have no idea as to the identity of the child."

Mr Vine paused here, presumably to give Victoria time to inform him of the child's identity, but Victoria decided she wouldn't feed his desire for knowledge. If Nana Lymer had wanted him to know then she would have told him. The fact that she hadn't told him informed Victoria that she had no wish for Simon to be discussed with Mr Vine so Victoria kept Nana's council and refused to be drawn on the subject of his identity. It would make no difference to the carrying out of the Will, given that he had died in childhood and had obviously never married or produced any children of his own. Working at the 'need to know' level, Mr Vine had no need to know who Simon Drinkwater had been and therefore, Victoria wasn't holding back any potentially useful information.

If she thought about it, there was only Aunt Hannah and Aunt Jenny left alive who, apart from Victoria, would know that Nana Lymer had ever had a little boy called Simon, or even that she had been married before she married Sam Lymer. Aunt Lizzie had been too young at the time to have any memory of the events that had happened so long ago.

After listing all of this property, Mr Vine paused, presumably to give Victoria a little time to assimilate what he had said. He was surprised that Victoria didn't seem overawed by the notion that she was now a woman of property, in fact, she was remarkably calm, but he gained a little insight into her attitude when she began questioning him.

"I won't be able to have control over any property until I'm twenty-one, will I?" she asked. "If this is to be kept from my parents, who will have that control until I come of age?"

"That's correct, Victoria," Mr Vine answered. "Your grandmother has made provision for that. In fact, I and the manager of the Yorkshire Penny Bank are your trustees until you reach the age of twenty-one. When you do, sole control passes to you and you may do with the whole legacy what you will. Mrs Lymer was confident that you are sensible and intelligent enough to be able to manage your own financial affairs now, but the law demands that at least one adult must oversee them. You need have no concerns about access to any money if you are in need of it, neither I nor Mr Young (the bank manager) will refuse any reasonable request for funds at any time."

"I won't need any money until I go to college." Victoria was adamant. I don't need to buy anything and I presume that my parents will continue to keep me as they don't know what I have been bequeathed. I do get paid when I work in the shop and I've never needed any more than that. Will you and Mr Young deal with the day to day running of the shops and the houses?"

"We will be the contacts for the lettings firm who rent out the houses you own and the two shops both have a manager in who will come to Mr Young and I if there are any problems and we should be able to sort them out. You needn't worry that any of the businesses will fail through our incompetence until you can take over. We have both had dealings like these before and have proved ourselves reasonably capable."

Victoria smiled at the thought she would even dare question what her trustees were doing. She was still trying to come to terms with what Mr Vine had just told her, but one thought had sprung to mind immediately.

"You said that other goods had been left for the six children of Granddad Sam's two marriages. Is that money? And what about the Queen Street shop? What is going to happen to that?"

Mr Vine smiled.

"You needn't worry about your parents or your aunts and uncle. Mrs Lymer sold off some of the property at the beginning of last year. That money was invested and will be shared amongst the six children equally. Part of your parents' share includes the shop on Queen Street, so they will not be destitute or homeless. All they will have to do is to continue as they are at the moment, although they will be well within their rights to sell the shop if they so wish. It is entirely up to them. Now, I will be making an appointment for your parents and the other five beneficiaries to come and listen to the Will. It states within it that Mrs Lymer has left her jewellery to you, although it puts no value on the collection. It does not mention the other two shops or the house portfolio, so it will be left entirely up to you as to how much you tell them. Rest assured, I will not let it be known how much you are worth. That's entirely your own business."

Mr Vine seemed to have come to the end of what he wanted to say and Victoria was feeling a need to be on her own, to give herself chance to assimilate the idea of being a rich woman. She would keep Nana Lymer's council and not tell anyone about her legacy, although she couldn't wait to see Nana's collection of jewellery and precious stones. She took her leave from Mr Vine feeling as though her brain had been pummelled by a boxer and that she needed some space and time to assimilate the information she had received. She was walking through reception without seeing Miss Talbot until that lady placed herself in the middle of Victoria's path to the door.

"Got what you wanted then? Has he told you about it all? Lucky little tyke aren't you?" Miss Talbot was whispering so that Mr Vine wouldn't hear but the menace and poison in her voice brought Victoria to a dead stop in front of her. In a flash of insight, she realised what was wrong with the woman.

"Envy doesn't suit you, Miss Talbot," she said. "And it's a wasted emotion because nothing comes of it."

Miss Talbot stepped closer to Victoria until she could feel her hot angry breath on her cheek. Luckily, Mr Vine chose that moment to open his office door and Miss Talbot reacted immediately.

"You'll need to be wrapped up to walk home." She said. "It's starting to snow out there." She stepped away from Victoria and seated herself at her desk; the only indication of her temper left showing was the red highlight on each cheek. Victoria repeated her farewells to Mr Vine and then left the office, shaking slightly with reaction to the raw emotion shown by Miss Talbot. She wondered how many people would be as jealous of her good fortune as Miss Talbot was, but decided that she would just have to learn to ignore it. She would have to grow a hard shell to protect herself from such envy, but she would also make sure that she didn't flaunt her wealth in front of all and sundry. That was another tip that she had learnt from Nana Lymer.

Despite this resolve, the bitter hatred emanating from Miss Talbot had unsettled Victoria and she really didn't want to have to go straight back to the shop and have to face her mother with the knowledge that she now carried. She needed to come to terms with it and she needed peace and tranquillity to be able to do that despite the fact that it had started to snow while she had been in Mr Vine's office. Pulling her woolly hat down onto her head, she turned left towards the docks as she exited Mr Vine's office, instead of turning right for home. There were very few people about as most would still be at work and those who weren't had completed their shopping and gone home before the weather turned. The snow came down more quickly as Victoria made her way to the end of Station Road and, by the time she crossed the bridge over the railway line, she was having difficulty in seeing the tracks below her.

The storm was coming in from the sea and looking at the far side of the railway line was like watching a television screen that had lost its aerial, everything was indistinct and shapeless. Only the sheds which lined the entrance to the docks were visible due to their size, but Victoria ploughed on regardless. The wind had risen and the snowflakes were now so large that they hurt as they hit her face. She screwed up her nose and tried to settle the bottom of her chin into her coat to give herself some protection, but she still kept on striding towards the docks.

When she reached the dockside, she stopped and stared out at the complete whiteout which was all that she could see. She had to imagine the wharves and the warehouses and, beyond everything, the sea which had brought the Hun ships to the coastline of this quiet part of the country. It crossed her mind that it must have been just such a stormy night as this when Nana Lymer and Sam had searched for Simon and William and she pitied them from the bottom of her heart. The tears she had been holding back all day welled up and poured down her face as she stared at the white shifting wall of snow in front of her and felt the cold eat through to her bones. She was painfully aware that her grandmother had probably stood on exactly the same spot where she was now standing and taken in the vision of the cruel sea as it crashed and boiled in front of her. Her grief washed over her again and she shuddered in the wind as the cold seemed to be eating at her bones.

Suddenly, her arm was grabbed and a man spun her round away from the edge of the dock.

"Don't do it, lass," he shouted over the noise of the wind. "It's no answer and you'll likely hurt so many other people."

Victoria slumped against him as the shock of his grabbing her made her go weak at the knees and she very nearly slipped over the side of the dock. The man held onto her and dragged her back across the railway line to one of the sheds. Away from the sound of the storm, he lowered his voice and tried again to persuade her against a suicide bid. Victoria lifted her hand to try and stem the verbal flow emanating from him, so that she could reassure him that suicide was definitely not on her agenda for that day.

"I wasn't going to jump." Victoria said. "I only wanted to know what it was like to look out to sea in the middle of a snow storm and now that I've seen what it is like I shall go home out of the cold."

She left her hero sadly shaking his head as he tried to understand the vagaries of youth and turned her face towards home, more content because she had managed to release some of the difficult emotions she had been bound by that day. As she walked, she decided to write down the whole story of her grandmother's life, before she had chance to forget any of the details and keep it to show any other member of the family who showed an interest in their ancestor in the future. Simon and Peter and even William and the pig butcher deserved to have their lives remembered although she was determined she would describe the characters of all as fairly as she could. She didn't want to pass any judgement at all on any of the characters involved in her grandmother's story. Equally, there would be no whitewashing to hide the truth.

As she struggled against the stormy weather, she felt even closer to Nana Lymer and her Granddad Sam, following where they had walked as they searched the town for Bia's little son, in weather which must have been very similar to what Victoria was experiencing that day, although it had been dark that night right back at the beginning of the century. She felt very peaceful inside, although as tired as if she had run a marathon, and wondered if it was true that people go to meet loved ones after they have died. If it was the case, she sincerely hoped that Nana was now hand-in-hand with her Sam once more and holding her son Simon, her family reunited. Hugging this thought and the secret of her inheritance close inside her, she walked through the snow towards home. It felt as though she was beginning a new life and she was excited at the prospects which had opened up in front her and all thanks to that wonderful old lady she was extremely proud to be able to call her grandmother.

The End

22549531R10291

Printed in Great Britain
by Amazon